# LETTERS
## from
# GARDNER

# LETTERS from GARDNER

## A Writer's Odyssey

### by Lou Antonelli

The Merry Blacksmith Press

2014

Letters From Gardner: A writer's Odyssey

For information, address:

The Merry Blacksmith Press
70 Lenox Ave.
West Warwick, RI 02893

merryblacksmith.com

Cover photos by Lou Antonelli

Published in the USA by The Merry Blacksmith Press

ISBN—0-69229-942-4
978-0-69229-942-5

# DEDICATION

*For Gardner—because he cares.*

# Table of Contents

# Author's Introduction

This book is hard to classify, difficult to categorize.

If you flip randomly through the pages, you're most likely to think it is a short fiction collection, specifically of science fiction and fantasy stories.

But look some more, and you might think it's a how-to book, the topic being How to Break Into Writing Science Fiction and Fantasy.

On the other hand, you'd be justified in thinking it's a memoir of a kind, of one author's efforts to break in as a published science fiction and fantasy author.

Finally, you could even be forgiven in thinking it's a history, telling the tale of the last days when science fiction and fantasy original fiction was mostly propagated in print, not pixels, in real magazines made of paper compounded from ground up trees.

You'd be right in all cases, because this book combines all those threads and tells a narrative I hope you will find interesting combined with science fiction and fantasy stories I know you will find entertaining.

I'm writing this to take advantage of an unusual conjunction of circumstances in my life; the fact I started writing science fiction and fantasy relatively late in my life, combined with the fact I was able to actually achieve my initial goal as a writer; compounded with way the technology and the economy has changed the way writers and editors interact now.

I think you will find all this fascinating, and along the way you might grin a bit in recognition or raise your eyebrows in amazement of how things have changed in terms of the process of writing and publishing in general.

In most cases where I have reproduced my early work, I have gone through the old backup floppy disks (I had to buy an external floppy drive for this project) and republished the stories in their original form, as originally submitted, to Gardner as well as other editors.

I will note where and when the stories were ultimately published, and how the story may have morphed before final publication.

In any case, this is the story, of how I became of published science fiction and fantasy author in the dim mists of time whose fossil remains include floppy disks and Windows 3.1.

And of the great editor who helped me.

−/−

# Chapter 1

# On Your Mark...

Over the years as I've lectured at literary conferences and conventions, I've often recounted that I knew at a very early age I had a fascination with the English language because I appreciated how much it opened the world to me.

Both my parents were born overseas, in Italy, and as anyone in a similar situation growing up knows, language skills are not only a key to assimilation, but also to understanding the world in general

Neither of my parents spoke English fluently, but by accident our family always lived among native English speakers, so I never spoke Italian, even at home. My lack of aptitude in Italian is so bad that, when I tried to take it as a foreign language in college, I had to rapidly transfer from the class before I flunked out.

I grew up a poor lower working class Italian Catholic kid in Massachusetts—not the most auspicious of backgrounds, but far from the worst, and not a bad place to start out in life; there's a lot of room for upward mobility.

And yes, my parents weren't very good explaining the world to me; like so many people struggling to make a living with menial jobs in a new land, they pretty much kept their heads down and their mouths shut. I was born in 1957, so just as I was beginning to wonder about the world at large, it was getting very interesting.

I was in first grade when John F. Kennedy was assassinated. I was in fourth grade when Martin Luther King Jr. and Bobby Kennedy were shot. The Vietnam War was raging.

Me: "Mom, what does it mean on the television when they say the Viet Cong are conducting guerilla warfare?"

Mom: "Who knows? Somebody is uppa to monkey tricks."

Me: (Thinking)—"Jeez, you're no help."

God was good to me in that he gave me a good and quick mind, and the hyperactivity to use it. Very early on I was fascinated by books and print publications, and I realized how useful they could be for learning about the world around me that my parents were largely oblivious to.

In grade school I was able to buy inexpensive paperbacks from the Scholastic Book Club, and I was early-on drawn in by juvenile novels by authors such as Robert Heinlein and Lester Del Rey. The first book I bought was *The Runaway Robot* by Del Rey; later I was impressed with the literary skill of Heinlein in *Time for the Stars*, and the imagination of Robert Silverberg in *The Lost Race of Mars*.

The books were inexpensive, and I began to read more and plunder the stacks in the children's room of the public library—which cost nothing at all.

Thankfully I got a good solid public school education and learned to read and write thoroughly. I realized early on that newspapers are a cheap and convenient way to read about current events.

One day when I was with my father in a liquor store, which had copies of the local weekly newspaper for sale on the counter, I nudged him and he cut loose an extra quarter to buy a copy of the local newspaper.

At the same time, my vistas were opened first-hand when I became a member of the Boy Scouts, and I began to go on camping and field trips. My English skills were quickly recognized, and much to the astonishment of the adult leaders, I wrote and submitted (without asking permission first) a perfectly acceptable story about a camping trip that was published in that local weekly newspaper in December 1969, when I was 12 years old. I still have the clipping, mounted on cardboard. It was printed on a linotype and you can still feel the slight rise of the ink on the paper. Twenty years later, before he died, I visited the paper's publisher, Stanley J. Bocko—a one-time state representative—and he still had a working linotype. He typeset my name on a piece of paper, and gave that to me as a souvenir. I still have that, too.

After serving as a patrol scribe in my Boy Scout troop and earning the journalism merit badge, I moved on while in high school to work for the local paper and I was editor of the school paper for two and a half years. I was so busy and enjoyed journalism so much that by the time I went off to college, I was replaced by a fellow who had just graduated from college.

I was always able to make money and have steady work in journalism, and although my college academic career was less than spectacular, I've always been able to make a decent living in newspapers. Over the years I remained a reader of science fiction, and during the 1980s I was a fan of *Omni* magazine and its original fiction.

My best friend in college was a native Texan and returned home upon graduation, and I visited him a number of times in the early 1980s. Finally, I decided it was time to strike out while I was still single and free to see more of the U.S., so I moved to Texas in 1985 and have lived there ever since.

My personal journalism experience culminated in owning and operating my own community weekly newspaper from 1995 to 2001. I think we had a high level of journalism, but the experience brought to the fore my other deficiencies; I have no business skills, and I can't count (which is a real problem if you're trying to keep track of money).

Despite some good years, by the turn of the century we were struggling because of my business ineptitude, and the newspaper folded Labor Day 2001. I had to go out and find a paying job.

Which I did, and a year later my wife and I were living an hour from Dallas, where I was the editor of the local weekly newspaper. It was the end of August, and just as the Labor Day weekend began, the main window air conditioning unit in the small house we rented broke down.

There was no way to get a window unit serviced over the weekend, and that left us with one small unit that was in the window next to my writing desk. That meant I was comfortable while in my office, but the house otherwise was unbearable.

My mother-in-law still lived in Dallas, and so my wife took off and spent the weekend there while I stayed behind and looked after things. My wife would come back after the air conditioning was repaired.

Because of the heat, my mobility was restricted—I pretty much had to stay in that one room, and so I occupied myself on the computer. Even in such a small town they had dial-up internet by then, and I cruised the web.

Being alone, my mind began to wander, and thinking over the fact I was 45, it occurred to me, as sort of a mid-life reverie: What had I accomplished so far in my life that were goals when I was young?

People today use the expression "bucket list", a list of what you want to do or where you want to go before you kick the bucket. That term was not in use then, but as I reviewed my bucket list, I conceded I had accomplished most of what I had wanted to do:

Work as a journalist—check. Have almost always been employed. I've collected unemployment checks twice in my life since graduating from high school in 1975.

Own and operate my own newspaper—check. Got the chance, didn't turn out like I planned. Like I said earlier, I'm a good journalist but a crappy businessman.

Marry a pretty girl—check. Met her while running the newspaper, so that was a trade-off worth making.

Raise a family—flop. We both had health problems, nothing to be done. We couldn't have kids.

Get elected to public office—check. I won an election and served on the local school board for three years. Didn't win re-election.

Get my name on a plaque on a building—check. A little goofy vanity here but when I was a kid I was always fascinated by seeing plaques on buildings, and I'd wonder who were the people whose names were on the buildings. While on that school board, we passed a bond issue, so my name is on the dedication plaques of the schools that were built with that bond money.

Write science fiction stories—?

Over all those years I had continued to read SF books and especially short stories; I loved *Omni* magazine in the 1980s. And I had tried my hand at writing, both books and short stories.

The problem was, working as a journalist and newspaper editor for so many years, I knew how to judge someone's writing skills, and I also could step back evaluate my own writing. I knew I was good, but certainly not good enough to compete on a national level with all the other expert writers in the genre.

So the first attempts went in the drawer. Since I became a writer I've heard the term "trunk stories". It's very apt.

But wait. This was 2002. After so many years of pounding away at the keyboard and getting a solid feel for the English language in my bones, maybe my skills were up to the test. Maybe I should try again.

So I got on-line and began to do research—something I obviously couldn't do years earlier when you had to use hard copies of publications like *Writers Digest* and such.

I found a web site, *Speculative Visions*, which allowed people to post their stories for people to read, review and critique.

By this time, it was the evening. I decided since I had the time and the curiosity, I'd hunker down and write something quick, something for other people to read. I stayed up until 4 a.m. and wrote a story by the seat of my pants, and then posted it on *Speculative Visions*.

This is it:

# Insight

The nondescript building was shoehorned between a freeway and a shopping mall. The bland title on the polished concrete wall, barely visible behind the carelessly trimmed low-maintenance shrubbery—

"Institute for Astro-Physical Research"—would not indicate to the casual observer that it was an organization dealing with extra-terrestrial contact.

Dr. Joseph Maubin had come to the Institute after taking a pension from a government position. It was a means to indulge his more theoretical speculations while enjoying a vital semi-retirement.

The first thing he noticed this day as he wheeled his Buick Regal station wagon into the parking lot, as he had done every working day for the past five years, was the police car.

He enjoyed the more relaxed atmosphere in the private institute, but still, "No Smoking" was the rule, and so he was already putting his pipe away when he saw the police car in front of the main entrance. He almost dropped the pipe, but managed to stow it quickly with one hand and put the car in park with the other.

He walked with a firm stride through the sliding glass double doors.

His administrative assistant, Marybeth Fournier, was standing immediately inside the small reception area, arms crossed, holding both elbows. "Dr. Rayburn is missing," she said. "His wife called early this morning and left a message saying he never came home last night. I found the lights on and everything on his desk when I came in."

Dr. Maubin quickly moved down the hallway and stood in the doorway of his colleague's office, where a police detective waited.

Marybeth came and stood alongside Dr. Maubin, who could see the thin dark-haired young woman was anxious.

He was a bit self-conscious, but he put his hand on her shoulder.

"Dr. Joseph Maubin?" The plain clothes detective turned towards him. "If you would please, sir," and he beckoned him inside.

"I'm working on a missing persons report," the detective said matter-of-factly. "Ms. Fournier here has already answered many questions and been very helpful."

The trio stood in the cramped open space of the cluttered office. "She says the desk and the office looks normal and nothing is out of place," continued the detective. "I also wanted your opinion." The detective pulled a small slim notepad from his shirt pocket where his badge was clipped.

Dr. Maubin looked over the room, which was dotted with the same piles of organized clutter he had seen there for the last five years. The desk looked as if its occupant had left for a moment. A briefcase was open on the corner, the chair was slightly pushed back, a half-full cup of coffee sat to one side. Only a quarter-size patch of congealing creamer floating in the center showed it was cold and untouched for hours.

He noticed a yellow pad with scribblings he knew as Dr. Rayburn's unintelligible handwriting sitting next to a printed report with formulas he did not recognize. Both were at an angle on the desk which made it appear someone had been hunched over and leaning forward as they read them.

Dr. Maubin walked around the desk so he could read the notepad. The detective saw this and commented, "I looked at that pad, too, but I could only make out a couple of words and they don't mean anything to me."

"Jeff has horrible handwriting," said Dr. Maubin. "I can't read it, either, but it's probably very theoretical." He looked up at the detective. "We work with high level mathematics and physics here."

The detective pointed and wagged a pen. "It says, 'nitrogen ignited' at the bottom of the page. That's all I can make out. What does that mean?" He drew back the pen to scribble in his little narrow pad.

"I don't know. I'm sure it means something in context. Dr. Rayburn was working on some classical theoretical fission calculations—atomic chain reactions."

"I thought this institute is involved in extraterrestrial research?"

"We are, but Dr. Rayburn is pursuing an investigational line about fission, phasing and wave interference. It is related to why the incidence of reports of extra-terrestrial contact skyrocketed after we set off the first atomic bombs."

"OK," said the detective as he quickly closed his notepad and that line of discussion. Holding the notepad against the palm of his right hand with three fingers, he pointed with his forefinger and thumb towards the doorway. "Can we go to your office and get some background information?"

After a half hour the interview was at an end and the detective left briskly after Marybeth walked him to the door. She returned to find Dr. Maubin alone in his office, sitting thoughtfully behind his desk.

He looked up. "How's everyone taking this?"

"Well, we're all very worried. You know, his blood pressure and all. Maybe he had a stroke and wandered away." She trailed off. "We don't know what to think."

"I don't know either, especially since his car is still in the parking lot. It bothers me, too." He knitted his brow and reached down to a bottom drawer in his desk. He took out a pipe he had hidden there and caught Marybeth's attention. She gave an understanding nod and turned to close the door.

After a few puffs, he said, rather apologetically, "I don't think anyone will mind today."

Marybeth had sat down on the couch across from his desk. "Why was... I mean is... Dr. Rayburn working calculations on atomic fission?"

"Jeff is one of those guys who can look at a problem from an original angle, turn a puzzle around to find the solution. His idea was that, instead of us worrying about attempting to establish contact with extraterrestrials, maybe all those reports of UFOs and aliens indicate they are trying to contact us. It's been commented on so many times that these sightings skyrocketed after we set off the first atom bomb. Over the years many people have speculated whether this was a 'signal' that caught their attention. Jeff also asked whether it presented a problem."

Marybeth looked at him curiously. "Do you have an idea where he was going with that?"

"Jeff said at one time he wondered whether, if space travel involves phasing or some type of time-space warp, the atmospheric nuclear tests produced a disturbance or interference that, practically speaking, interfered with their coming out of phase or warp. He said perhaps setting off the first bomb was like setting a giant bonfire in the night. It catches your attention on the horizon, but when you get closer, you decide it is too hot or dangerous to get out and take a closer look.

Marybeth sat up straight on the edge of the couch as she thought about the analogy. "Isn't this a little far afield from what the Institute usually investigates?"

"Well, old astro-physicist dogs like me like to look from here on out to there," he said with an appropriate waving hand gesture. "The Institute's mission is to investigate and validate, if possible, extra-terrestrial contact. Jeff was looking at the problem from the other side, the small end of the telescope, as it were. What if extraterrestrials have attempted to make contact, and we've unintentionally thrown up a barrier?"

Dr. Maubin gave a resigned shrug. "I certainly didn't mind the investigation. It was more that, I trusted Jeff."

He looked absently out the window. "I noticed the run time on the report on his desk. It finished at 9:45 last night, so it probably was what he was reading before he disappeared or left."

"You still haven't thought of what 'nitrogen ignited" means, have you?"

"My background is in gravitational physics. I really don't understand the formulas in that report. If you feel up to it right now, please make a copy and get a courier to bring it to Dr. Habbard at the university. I'll write a cover letter."

The report left by noon and Dr. Maubin spent the next few hours on the phone with friends and colleagues. Dr. Habbard had called right after lunch, Marybeth reported, and promised he would give the report a quick read. Dr. Maubin kept the television on the cabinet in the corner of the office turned on, with the sound off, tuned to an all-news channel. Every so often he would look over. The usual scenes, he thought at one point. Global Warming. Child abductions. Terrorism. Suicide bombers. Biological threats.

"It's a sad world," he thought with rare and honest insight. "It's like a bad dream. If Jeff is gone, I'm sure he's in a better place now."

After hours of making and taking calls, he felt better in one way—but worse in another. The routine continued at the Institute, but he felt a kind of cold gray steel doubt nagging at his core. He wondered whether it was simply worry, or was there something else?

Marybeth always touched base with him before leaving for the day. "Dr. Habbard will probably have something for us bright and early tomorrow," she commented. "You know how prompt he is."

"Fast, also!" A slightly-accented voice greeted them from outside as an older man with an appropriately unstylish Teutonic haircut walked through the doorway behind Marybeth.

"Max, you didn't have to come all the way over here yourself, and so quickly," said Dr. Maubin.

"I wanted to see how my old friends are doing."

"We are all hoping for the best, but it's worrying us sick," said Marybeth.

"Still no word?"

"Not a 'word, character or syllable'," said Dr. Maubin with a sigh, echoing a phrase they both knew from having been in the same lodge together. "We can only hope for the best."

It was unconvincing and they all knew it. Dr. Maubin looked down and Dr. Habbard looked sadly at Marybeth before breaking the uncomfortable silence.

"Although Jefferson was a visionary and pioneer, his science was not always nearly as sound as it needed to be," he said as he slipped his copy of the report onto Dr. Maubin's desk top. "It's mathematically accurate, but the formulas are all wrong. This doesn't even qualify as wild speculation. I'm sorry."

"Well, Max, we don't know if it was only a pipe dream. What is it about? Could you give an old space hound a quick and dirty explanation?"

Dr. Habbard explained, with alternating tinges of irritation at the subject and apologies for criticizing an absent colleague. "It would have been better if Jeff had stuck to astro-physics, although I do understand he had some background in nuclear physics."

Dr. Maubin interjected, "You know his physics background goes back over 50 years, to when we were considering nuclear propulsion for the first space projects."

"I quite understand, but that still doesn't mean he could be considered competent in that field today. He may have even read some of the equations he used in this report when they were first published. That doesn't mean he should have used them the way he did."

"So what is the matter, Max?" Dr. Maubin knew his colleague usually got to the point.

"It's the matter of whether, if you successfully instigate an uncontrolled chain reaction in a predictably fissionable material, would it spread to more stable elements? The infinitesimally small possibility, which is what these formulas egregiously extrapolate, was obviously disproved at Alamogordo. I wanted to return the report to you myself. I didn't even want this to be found in my waste basket."

Marybeth could tell Dr. Habbard was uncomfortable at letting his irritation show, and so she jumped in and thanked him for his time. Dr. Maubin looked stunned but managed to mumble some thanks as he hastily sat down.

"I hope our next get-together will be in more relaxed circumstances" Dr. Habbard said clumsily as he left.

Marybeth looked down at Dr. Maubin and saw the look on his face. "Are you OK?"

He looked at the silent television, at her, and then the report. "It's a bad dream," he said quietly, as if to himself.

"What's a bad dream?"

He looked up at her, and continued, still somewhat vacantly. "Jeff earlier this year spent weeks gathering the latest and most up-to-date research on nuclear weights and electron resonances. It was that information he used for his latest formulas. He could look at a problem from a different angle to figure it out. He questioned whether the reason the extraterrestrials cannot contact us is because they are phased in their space travel. Being as thorough and open-minded as he was, he also thought to ask—are we the ones who are phased?"

Marybeth slowly brought her hand to her mouth. He continued. "He intuited, with the timing of Alamogordo, a possible answer. He ran his own formulas, with the weights and resonances data he collected."

He looked at the silent flickering images on the muted television screen across the room. "The nitrogen in the atmosphere ignited. It happened so quickly and unexpectedly, we didn't notice. We've just been carrying on like normal ever since."

Marybeth asked in a tremulous voice, "If we blew ourselves into another dimension, how could we land on the moon?"

Dr. Maubin looked down at his desk, picked up his pipe, and with great deliberation, stoked it and puffed. "I've always enjoyed a good smoke," he thought to himself. "I'm going to miss this thing."

He looked the pretty young lady in the face.

"We're not phased. We're dead. We blew ourselves up. The glimpse we have been catching of extraterrestrials, like ghosts in the night, are just that. They're floating through the smoke and dust that remains of our planet. We are the ghosts."

They looked into each other's eyes and together had the same insight.

A few seconds later, Dr. Habbard walked through the door, remorseful at his previous tone and the curt manner in which he had taken his leave. He looked around the room, and saw no one, although a pipe sat on the desk top, a thick curl of smoke rising upwards.

He turned around and looked down the hall. "I guess they've both left for home. Strange," he thought, "I didn't hear anything or see anyone pass me."

He picked up the copy of the report from the desk. "Maybe I shouldn't have been so judgmental," he thought. "I'll read this again and see if there is anything I missed." He set the pipe in its ashtray and left.

After hours of reading that evening, he felt he almost—almost—he had a glimmer into what Dr. Rayburn was getting at. Perhaps a short conversation with Dr. Maubin might bring some insight.

The first thing he noticed the next morning as he pulled into the Institute parking lot was the police car in front of the main entrance.

\* \* \*

It was 2,000 words, as I noted, written between 8 p.m. and 4 a.m. I know some people might cringe at tossing off a story so quickly with no fore-thought, but being a journalist, I'm used to writing fast and dirty. I was mainly curious at what people would think of the story.

Since I was up until the wee hours of the morning I didn't get up that day until noon, and by the time I logged onto the web site, a number of people had read and commented on the story.

All the feedback was positive; people said they enjoyed the story, and that I wrote dialogue especially well. That struck a chord and made sense, since as a journalist I interview people all the time. That got the wheels turning upstairs, and I began to think of whether I actually might be able to become a published science fiction author.

The editor who published my first story ("Silvern" in June 2003), Jayme Blashke, commented right off the bat when I first submitted to him, "You seem to have skipped the novice stage of writing."

There's an old trusim in fiction writing, "You need to write a million words before you're any good." It's a crude, but practical yardstick—if you want to rise in the world of fiction writing, you really need to write, re-write and write again until you get the English language in your bones at the atomic level.

I realized that in my case, I *had* written my million words—but they were in newspapers. My crappy early stories were newspaper stories. And indeed, over the past ten years as I have written science fiction and fantasy, no editor has ever told me a story was poorly or sloppily written.

The basics of good, straight writing are the same for both fiction and non-fiction:

Don't beat around the bush. Get straight to the heart of the matter. Forget about long and elaborate set-ups. The reader has to make a quick decision whether what you have written is worth their time to stop and read.

Newspapers have the advantage of using headlines. If you story title can't be that hook, make it the first line in your story.

In only his fourth story, Robert Heinlein starts "Blowups Happen" with the line:

*"Put down that wrench!"*

Which is a great example of hooking the reader and getting right into the action at the same time.

Practically speaking, having a quick and clean start with a well-written hook will get your story read in the first place by an editor.

Then don't bog down your story with unnecessary explanations ("info dumps") or clumsy expository dialogue ("As you know, Bob..."). Don't go in for purple prose and convoluted sentences. The emotion your reader should have is pleasure, excitement, wonder or joy—not irritation at trying to follow your plot, parse your sentences or get past the dead places.

Don't try to show off how clever you are; until and unless you are a top notch writer, don't expect your editors or readers to endure your self-indulgence.

Let the story move the action along, don't narrate it (or as it is commonly put, "Show, don't tell.") This is often done by classic photographs (such as the flag raising on Iwo Jima), but let's face it, your reader is following your story along in their mind's eye. Help them enter the story by allowing them to "see" it for themselves.

Don't get bogged down by specificity. In addition to stifling your reader's imagination, you bog down the narrative. Give your readers some credit for intelligence, they're a self-selected lot.

Don't overlook basic advice. Don't make characters' names so strange they are a distraction. Use simple basic English; if you have a choice between the basic Germanic root word and the word that came from Norman French—and hence Latin—use the Germanic root. If your character had a heart attack, say so, instead of a cardiac infarction. It's clearer and shorter to ask "How much is that doggy in the window?" as opposed to "Can I query what is the remuneration required for the acquisition of the canine in the casement?"

When you submit, make sure you've not overlooked the practical aspects of writing, such as proper formatting of your manuscript (or at least formatting it to meet the standards of your market). Proofread carefully. No editor shoves aside a story for one mistake, but they will when typos proliferate. It shows that you're careless—so why should the editor care?

One big difference between journalism and fiction writing is that, as a journalist you know your stories are going to be published—one way or another, whether rewritten, revised, or completely made over. Selling genre stories is completely speculative (although that's not why it is called speculative fiction!).

The major venues get hundreds of stories each week, and up to a thousand or more each month. And they make cold and hard-hearted business decisions based on whether what they buy—and what you have to offer—will keep people paying for their publication or logging onto their web sites.

As part of this process, you are in competition with people who have been at it for years and are seasoned pros, with great experience and lengthy track records. When my first story was published in *Asimov's Sci-*

*ence Fiction* in 2005, it shared the issue with a story by Fred Pohl, whose first story was published in 1937.

Even if your story is very good, there are a number of reasons it still may not be bought:

Not original enough.

Doesn't fit the tone of the publication or a particular theme.

There's a glut on the market of that particular kind of story.

It accidentally seems to be too much like another story.

The magazine just ran out of space or space for your length of story.

And so forth, any on for any combination of the above.

Rejection, although its hurts, is not personal, and constantly writing and submitting will only help you hone and improve your prose. Horror writer Joe Lansdale says the imagination is like a muscle, you need to keep exercising it. Stephen King's first short story was rejected 60 times before he sold it, to a magazine that paid him with two free copies. Years later, in his own book of writing advice, he said "The nail in my wall would no longer support the weight of the rejection slips impaled upon it. I replaced the nail with a spike and kept on writing."

I had learned the basic of simple, understandable English writing after decades of working at newspapers.

I had been a reader for many years, since I was a kid—as I mentioned earlier—but now I had to research from scratch how to write genre stories and then submit them properly for publication.

Thankfully, one big change from the days when I started reading SF was the internet, and while the search engines may have changed—Google wasn't as prominent as it is today, and I was just as likely to search the web using Lycos, Webcrawler, or AltaVista—they were still sophisticated enough to get me the information I needed.

I quickly saw that Gardner Dozois, the editor of *Asimov's Science Fiction* since 1985, had—up to that date—won the Hugo Award for Best Professional Editor 13 times! The Hugo Awards are a set of awards given annually for the best science fiction or fantasy works. The awards are given each year at the annual World Science Fiction Convention.

I realized this Dozois dude was the most prestigious science fiction editor, and so I decided he would be my first target in trying to break into the field. Aim high!

I mailed him a copy of "Insight" in early September 2002 (remember, back then electronic submissions were very uncommon). On November

22, I got the standard printed long form rejection, which I reprint here for the record:

"Thank you very much for letting us see the enclosed submission. Unfortunately, it does not suit the needs of the magazine at this time.

"Your submission has been read by an editor, but the press of time and manuscripts (about 850 per month) does not permit personal replies or criticism. For your general information, though, most stories are rejected because they lack a new idea or theme. A great many of the ideas that may seem innovative to an SF newcomer are in fact overfamiliar to readers more experienced in the field. The odds greatly favor this being the cause of this rejection.

"Another common cause (all too common, we're afraid) of rejection is the obvious lack of basic English compositional skills on the part of the author. By this we mean that the writer has misspelled or misused everyday words, and/or mispunctuated same. Stories are rejected on this basis because a writer must be familiar with the tools of his or her trade, just as an electrician or carpenter must.

"Finally, your story may have been rejected, not because it lacked a new idea, or was misspelled or mispunctuated, or because the writing was not "professional" enough, but simply because it failed to rise above the other 849 seen that month."

It was signed, "Gardner Dozois, editor."

That rejection was actually a blessing in disguise. One thing I didn't know at the time I sent it off—but learned not much later—is that, once a story is published on-line, it is not considered "original" anymore. By being posting it where the public could see it, it would not be considered an original story.

I chalked that discovery up to the learning curve, thanked my lucky stars Dozois didn't accept it, and forgot about it while it remained posted on Speculative Visions for a few years, until it occurred to me to ask the web site to take it down. I then submitted it to smaller markets.

One thing you quickly learn when you submit to markets is that any personal response to your submission is good, even when it is a rejection. Aspiring authors have no idea how many stories are deposited in a magazine's "to read" pile (the traditional term for these unsolicited submissions is "slush" and the stack of stories to be read is the dreaded "slush pile".)

By the time I had "Insight" taken down from the *Speculative Visions* web site and started submitted it, I already had a number of publications under my belt. The *Speculative Visions* web site had a 2,000 word limit, but I filled out the story somewhat and added almost 500 words.

Despite the increase in words, the story actually simplified on the first rewrite (which is what you read here—the story as originally posted is gone). One important point I learned during my course of self-study is the danger of overpopulation, or as the author James Patrick Kelly put it:--

"In the attempt to recreate the sweep and richness of life, some writers keep cramming characters into a story until it resembles the Marx Brothers' stateroom in *A Night at the Opera*. The people you want readers to care about will be lost in a mob scene, so keep the cast to a minimum. Name as few characters as you can, describe even fewer. If you can combine two characters into one, you probably ought to. "

Or put otherwise by other authors, "You must murder your darlings."

I saw right off the bat there was a completely unneeded character at the Institute, and I rolled his character into that of Dr. Habbard. Since he was only in the on-line version of the story, you did not meet him, and he is (justifiably) lost to history.

I think his name was Donald.

One magazine I submitted the revised version of "Insight" to was *Ideomancer*, which has been an on-line venue since 1999. Even in 2003, you could see the proliferation of on-line publications, and *Ideomancer* also exhibited another trait of the internet age, the crumbling of geographic boundaries; it's based in Canada.

Editor Lori Ann White said in her rejection (dated March 9, 2004): "It has an old-fashioned feel to it that in some ways I liked, and the idea that the atmosphere really *did* go up at Alamogordo and we just didn't notice is fun, but the character interactions were a bit stilted—the discussion with Habbard was not very believable, for example—and there were some problems with the mechanics of the story, such as shifts in viewpoint between Maubin and Marybeth.

"Thanks again, though, and I hope to see more from you."

In this rejection, White put her finger on a couple of themes that have been repeated to me over the years about my fiction—that it is old-fashioned, and that it is fun. That last line is also crucial; I quickly learned as I hit the slush pile trail that editors are never superficially polite, and if they say something like "I hope to see more from you" they really mean it. With the volume of submission they are inundated with, they don't encourage the obviously untalented.

My reply to White was: "I wrote it in August 2002, and it really has never been revised. Before I sent 'Insight' to you, I was wondering whether it was time to give it an overhaul. I see from your comments that's probably a good idea. It had already crossed my mind to dump the Habbard character, and I agree, the back and forth between Dr. Maubin and Mary-Beth is clumsy. That's probably just due to my inexperience at the time."

I rewrote the story—Professor Habbard disappeared entirely (meaning the character count dropped by two from the original version of the story) and I inserted actual headlines in the scenes where Dr. Maubin is watching television, among other things—and White allowed me to resubmit it, but it still didn't make the grade.

The revised version was finally published in a small British print magazine called *Twisted Tongue* in May 2007.

By that time, I had over 30 stories published. But that's where it all began.

# Chapter 2

## Ready…

Since, with its public posting I assumed I had precluded myself from submitting and selling "Insight", I started right away on a new story.

As a result of my research of science fiction markets, I learned the largest original fiction magazine in the U.S. was (and still is) *Analog Science Fiction*. Founded in 1930 with the name *Astounding Tales*, it had been edited by Stanley Schmidt since 1978. I thought it would be a good place to start.

In plotting my next story, I wanted to play to my strengths. Since I knew I write dialogue well, I wanted characters with a relationship that could produce snappy dialogue. I thought some version of a "buddy story" might serve the trick.

To make the dialogue "pop" even more, I wrote it in the first person, something that would serve me well in the future.

I also learned it helps when you write what you know about, so I decided the story would be set in the East Texas town where I lived at the time, Malakoff. In the story that followed, Sebastopol is a stand-in for Malakoff, and everything about Sebastopol applies to Malakoff.

"Silence is Golden" was mailed off to Schmidt on September 13, 2002. Here it is:

# Silence Is Golden

"**H**ow much experience do you have with radiological clean-ups?" I wasn't expecting an easy time of it—my boss' body language told me the moment he walked in the door I was facing an especially nasty assignment.

"None" I snapped. "We're not supposed to do that, remember?"

"Well, I'm afraid we may have some type of radiological contamination at Stonewall Brick."

"What makes you think I can help?"

"Because I know you're sharp and smart and you like a challenge. This may be one."

Mike Amato was a pro, and dedicated. He got into the industrial hazardous waste clean-up business in the late '70s, right after Three Mile Island, when it took a lot of guts to work with companies instead of picketing them.

I was the in-house chemist; a wise guy barely a year out of UT-Austin who knew how to brew beer at home and neutralize solvents for Industro-Kleen. Our company's mission was to get the EPA's teeth out of the butts of Dallas-area business owners who hadn't been too careful about what they spilled, sprayed or dumped on or around their employees.

Despite my attitude, Mike remained polite and that made me stop and think a second. "Umm, Stonewall Brick? I thought that was a normal particulate job? Where do you get radiation?"

Mike nodded his head. "Close the door."

There was no one in the lab room anyway, so I knew what he wanted to say was important. He continued after we both sat down.

"Stonewall called us on their own. The EPA hasn't been involved. But it's a wise move, because they have a handful of pretty serious cases.

I must admit I was getting interested, despite the fact my laboratory specialty is volatiles and solvents. Because some energy-gobbling cement plants use recycled solvents to fuel their kilns, I knew a little about the construction material industry.

"There has never been any proven instance of radioactive contamination being found in solvents used as fuel," I said. "And besides, I know Stonewall doesn't use recycled fuel."

"Which is why I am all the more interested in the fact that three workers who have been recently hospitalized all have come down with cancer."

"OK, now you have my attention. Are they particulate-related respiratory carcinomas?" I felt learned.

Mike leaned forward. "One lung—and one skin and one bone."

My mind began to race around for answers—one of which came to me very quickly. "This isn't operational. It's environmental."

Mike propped one foot on the front of desk and rocked back slightly in his chair. "I thought you were the guy to ask."

I didn't want to seem eager, so I cast my best dubious look back at him. Mike looked conciliatory. "This has to be done on the hush, you understand. We've just started our evaluation, and for all anyone knows, we're looking at the normal range of particulates."

"Mike, old buddy, old chum, old pal—You do know how much trouble we can get into now, don't we?"

"Listen, John, I can say in all honesty I don't know if there is any radiological contamination. I'm running on a hunch. But after all the years I have spent in this clean-up business, I think my instincts are good."

"Didn't you work on that cesium contamination in Brazil, in the early '80s?"

"It was in Rio de Janiero. Scavengers from the favelas broke apart an imaging machine they found in a closed-up medical clinic. Broke open the tube and spilled it all over themselves. Some of them got it on their hands... and in their mouths." He grimaced.

"That must have been ugly."

He waved a few loose fingers in front of his lower jaw. "This guy... his lip..."

"OK, OK, let's not talk about it."

"While I was down there, there was this fellow—just a kid—who had held the tube after it had broken open. He had burns on his wrist and lower arm. The plant manager at Stonewall emailed me a photo of the fellow who has skin cancer. He asked me if I recognized the burns on his fingertips. He says the company doctor says he thought they looked like dry ice burns."

"Cree-rist, you think they look like...?"

Mike shook his head slightly and slowly. "John, they look like the same kind of contact radiation burns I saw on that kid in Rio."

"Do you think the plant manager has any idea of what's going on?"

"The sampling crew there says he is acting very edgy. I want to go there myself, and you're the only person on staff other than me who knows anything about radiation."

"Well, I did study some of the chemistry in college. I'm hardly an expert."

"I remember how you went around for two days shaking your head after that criticality accident in Japan."

"Well, my grandma would have more sense that to put 50 gallons of radioactive slurry into one mixing vat! I couldn't believe that!"

Mike looked impatient. "I really don't know if I am on the right track, but I wish you'd come with me."

"Is there a motel in this burg?"

"No, but I guess if we need to, we can overnight amidst the bright lights of Tyler."

I took my jacket off the hook and plunked on my cap.

"Let's get going."


It's 100 miles from Dallas to the little cross roads in East Texas where the Stonewall brick plant sits. That gave us plenty of time to talk.

Mike explained that he'd already checked, as slyly as he could, on whether there was any record or indication of illegal dumping at the site. The brick plant and quarry had been there 60 years, built right after World War II when the home building boom in Dallas demanded ever-increasing brick production. Nearby gas wells provided the fuel to fire the high quality clay found adjacent to an intrusive quartz "dike" formation which rose to the surface in this location—hence the name Stonewall.

The operation is stable, continuous and conservative, he said. The company is the largest employer in the community.

"I don't think this is your standard case of CYA," Mike said as we sped out of the searing city. "I think they really are worried they've struck something dangerous. The illnesses started after they opened up a new section of the clay pit."

I was jotting down some ideas and notes on a pad on my knee as we crossed into Kaufman County. "Have you thought about some biological contaminant, something that may have been uncovered in the clay, dried out and blown around?"

"Yes, and no, that clay is sterile."

I must have looked surprised, because Mike looked over.

"Yep, I thought that was strange, too, like the dog that didn't bark in the Sherlock Holmes story."

"Silver Blaze."

"What?" Mike turned his head again.

"The Mystery of Silver Blaze. Holmes knew the horse-napping was an inside job because the watchdog didn't bark. Sterile, huh?"

"Yep. Couldn't even raise a culture."

"How did you get a sample back to Dallas so quick? And where did you keep a culture? Like you know biology."

"Please, don't underestimate me. It was a hunch, but I was right."

I was scratching the back of my head. "Dammit, I understand the clay being sterile after it leaves the kiln—but before?"

"Makes you think of radiation sterilization, doesn't it?"

"Yes, but that's impossible, you won't even find that in uranium deposits—I think."

"We may be in over our heads," Mike said as he stared straight ahead down the highway,

I hunched back in the seat. "What's that Hondo Crouch said— 'Onwards through the fog'."

Mike smiled as we crossed into Henderson County.


It was obvious when we came to Sebastopol, the small town with the big name that was the plant's home, because almost all the houses and buildings we passed were of the same red brick. The Stonewall plant wasn't very hard to find. A towering brick chimney loomed like a rocket.

The plant manager, Rudy Gerfertig, knew we were coming to join the project thanks to an extended phone call from Mike along the way. He knew Mike was the overall project director, and he was told I was an environmental engineer.

The headquarters looked out of place, dwarfed by towers, conveyor belts and looming piles of clay and sand.

Gerfertig was a small man with blond hair; Mike loomed over him as he shook his hand and introduced me.

"It's good to meet you, too, Mr. Koster. I'm glad things are moving along." He seemed almost too polite, perhaps self-conscious. "Do you prefer John or Jack?"

"Call me John; I prefer John. Something about the way 'Jack Koster' trips off the tongue invites trouble."

Gerfertig gave a little laugh while Mike rolled his eyes. I nudged him as we walked down the hallway to the back door, "Hey, I really don't like being called Jack."

We hopped into Gerfertig's Ford 350 diesel and drove the mile or so to the clay pit. Two or three trucks were scattered around as bulldozers and backhoes scraped and hoisted the red clay.

Gerfertig pointed to the area farthest from us, right up against and below a low, long cliff. "That's the dike, the stonewall," he said. "After all these years, we finally started digging right up against it, and that's the place where we had the problems.

"Last week, when we had the men taken to the hospital, I stopped operations there," Gerfertig explained. "Nobody's been back since."

"Has our team been there yet?" I asked Mike.

"They are still in the plant, they haven't worked their way out here," he said. "We're fixin' to leapfrog them."

Gerfertig did seem genuinely unhappy. "Even though there are only three sick men, that's three too many. I hope you understand. We've never had an illness cluster in the history of the company, now three men in one day."

"It's obvious you care about your employees," I said. "You're probably like a big family here."

Mike saw how I was looking over the landscape and asked Gerfertig if we could drive towards the dike/cliff. After a while, as I walked around the area, I noticed a spot where the clay seemed to be darker and denser, almost crumbly. I waved towards Mike and the manager and they walked over.

I poked at the spot with a branch which had fallen from the nearby cliff. "Anything different about this spot right here?" I asked Gerfertig. I was poking with a stick and grasping at straws at the same time.

I have no idea what I expected him to say—"Well, that's where we found the petrified buffalo crap," maybe. He took a gulp and after a little hesitation, said, "I guess that's caused by the mercury."

Mike did a double take and then looked at him very hard. It was obvious this was a revelation. "Goddam, you've got mercury contamination in this pit?"

Gerfertig looked nervous and confused at the same time. "I've tried to figure it out myself. I don't understand it at all."

Mike was getting hostile and his body language showed it. "How complicated can mercury contamination be? It's easy to test for!"

Gerfertig looked helpless. "It looks like liquid mercury. We've found in inside some of clay lumps, in untouched strata."

Now, even the little geology I knew made me jump on that statement. "That's ridiculous. Mercury doesn't occur free in nature. Even I know that. And this isn't its ore. That's called cinnabar. It can't be mercury. Did you test it?"

The manager looked like we wouldn't believe him. And we didn't. "We tried to collect a sample. By the time we carried it to our testing lab, it had evaporated."

Mike and I both looked at him trying to figure out if he was crazy or lying, but he only looked sick. I finally had a clear thought. "When you say 'we', do you mean 'you', or do you mean some other people?"

Mike jumped in harshly. "Let me guess. The three sick guys either handled the sample or were there when you hit some of this stuff."

The manager nodded. "Actually, there were four sick men. The fourth guy wasn't too sick and he took off and headed back to Mexico."

"Let's get back to your office and lab. Now." Mike barked.

It was a very tense ride back to the main building. The manager steered and looked straight ahead like he was afraid. Mike was seething. I knew I was breathing hard, and my mind was racing.

When we got back to the manager's office, Mike slammed his door. "Well, since we are playing truth or dare, or some damn thing like it, I guess I'll let you know Mr. Koster here is not an environmental engineer. He's a chemist, specializing in nuclear chemistry."

I didn't react to the lie, but in the most professional tone I could muster, I asked Gerfertig "Have you seen any evidence of radiation contamination or contact?"

I thought, and Mike later told me he thought the same thing, that the manager was reaching to scratch his head. Instead his hand came up with a tuft of hair as a tear rolled down his cheek and he began to shake.

"Oh, God," was all I could say.


Mike drove the Ford 350 to Gerfertig's home, which was in the piney woods nearby on company property. He was a widower and so there was no one home. It was obvious, after he got himself together, that he was scared, not only for himself but for the employees, to whom he felt a genuine responsibility. It was dread mixed with uncertainty.

Mike explained that the cancers in the three hospitalized men made him suspect a radiological contamination, and he thought we were the men to look into it, because of his experience and my "problem solving skills".

Gerfertig told how, after they had progressed into the new section, they found a strange lump in the clay, maybe a little larger than a basketball. He wasn't in the pit that day, but he was told how the backhoe operator cracked open the lump and how the 'mercury' ran out along the ground. During the past month, they found six of these balls. Everyone assumed they contained mercury, although one or two veteran workers seemed to recall, as I knew, that you don't dig up pure mercury. Gerfertig instructed the workers not to mix the clay from the lumps into the regular stockpile, but put it aside for testing. The workers, made up of equal parts of poor whites and Mexicans, saw this as a gesture of concern.

One thing which was reported back to him was that some men said when they tore open a lump they swore they heard an almost electrical crackling sound; others said they smelled ozone. The mercury had quickly seeped into the ground, and lumps changed color, going from a darker to lighter red, almost immediately after opening.

There were no obvious health problems up until a week ago, he said, although some of the men complained of palpitations and the sweats. But none of the men had touched or gotten very close to any of the lumps.

However, a few weeks ago, one dozer operator let his blade hit a lump and rest on it. He jumped from his seat and jumped off the machine because he swore he felt an electric shock.

Gerfertig said he gave the men in the pit instructions to call him when they uncovered the next one of these clay lumps. When they did, two men waited with an ore bucket while two other men were with the dozer, one in the seat and the other hanging on the side. Gerfertig watched as the dozer blade pressed down upon the clay lump and it sundered like an old rubber ball.

One man scooped up the silvery liquid with a ladle while the second held the bucket and closed the lid. Gerfertig said he was unhappy when he noticed at the last minute the man with the ladle left his gloves hanging on his belt. It was obvious the liquid was putting out fumes and the men hurried back to the lab in a rattletrap pickup only used in the pit.

The man running the dozer said he did feel a slight shock when the blade made contact. The second man on the dozer, who got a whiff of the fumes as they quickly rose upward, immediately complained that his chest hurt.

Gerfertig opened the bucket inside the company lab himself, but it was already empty. That was two weeks ago, he noted. Two days after, three men were in the hospital. He called Industro-Kleen the next day.

He told us the man diagnosed with skin cancer had handled the ladle, the man with bone cancer closed the bucket. The man on the dozer who caught a whiff of the fumes had lung cancer. It was the dozer operator who made the sign of the cross in the changing room and went back to Mexico.

Gerfertig said he began feeling nauseous a week ago and his hair began to loosen in the past few days. I knew enough from my hazardous training to check the pale inside of his wrist for petechiae, the small subcutaneous hemorrhaging that comes from severe radiation exposure. Whatever radiation he had received wasn't enough to cause that—a positive sign.

He was a slight, fair-haired man, which made him seem even more nervous when he spoke. "You can imagine how worried I am, both for myself, but also for my employees. I don't think I can even go to the hospital. I thought of radiation sickness, too, but I don't know what caused it, and can you imagine what the government will think?"

"What do the employees think?" asked Mike.

"I told them I had called you in to check out what the stuff was, and we've steered totally clear of the area ever since. Since it was only a handful of people who ever worked the new area, there are hardly any people who know what we're talking about. And the people who were there a week ago when we got up close, well, three are in the hospital and the other guy took off. I 'm still here, for now, I guess."

He trailed off.

After a thoughtful pause, he continued. "I've tried to buck up, because people know I was there and I didn't want to look sick. But I probably need to go see a doctor."

"I know what accidental radiological contamination can do to somebody," Mike shot out. "Right now, we are all in big trouble, especially with the government. I thought at first we might be dealing with uncovering illegal waste dumping. Medical radioactive waste or something like that. This is serious. Do you have any ideas?

He was looking at me, and I took a stab at a stalling tactic. "Why don't you two keep talking and compare notes," I said, "while I hit the computer for a while."

While they talked in the kitchen, I was on a computer in Gerfertig's den, doing the most frenzied searches of my life. I thought this might be a way to both calm my nerves and use my age and energy to the best advantage.

It was like I was on speed as my fingers flashed over the keyboard and I kept doing searches and following links. The words and combinations zipped by: Mercury, silver, radioactive, clay, quartz, Texas, geology, dikes, on and on for five hours.

I met those guys in Japan again who poured 50 lbs. of radioactive slurry in that one vat, and people I never met before, like Louis Slotin, the atomic scientist at Los Alamos who accidentally dropped one half of an atomic bomb core atop the other half in 1946 and had a criticality go off in his face. He lived another nine days.

And I met the first people who talked about atoms and molecules. These philosophers and alchemists helped me ask the right questions so I could come up with a theory. By 9 p.m., any theory would do. We all knew instinctively that something would have to change by tomorrow.

I walked back to the kitchen and asked Gerfertig, "The dike—is it quartz?"

"Why. Yes, mostly, it's a type of metamorphic quartz. It's an extrusion of the bedrock formation that runs through this part of Texas, this is the only place it gets close to the surface."

"Do you find geodes in this area?"

"Over the years, people have dug up some real nice ones. There's a shop in Sebastopol where they slice them up and polish them."

"I assume some these geodes have been hollow"?

"Yes, most are."

I sat down at the table. "I have a hunch. Here's what we know."

I counted off on my fingers. "One, the substance is silvery and liquid. Two, it is highly volatile. Three, it is apparently highly radioactive. Four, it is naturally occurring. Five, it is self-contained."

"So far, so good, those are the facts," said Mike. "But I have no idea how these all tie together."

"Well, if you do a search for 'silvery' and 'liquid' and 'radioactive', you find an interesting piece of nuclear physics. Uranium is the heaviest naturally-occurring radioactive substance, but that's because the heavier elements have decayed over billions of years. Of course, some of those trans-uranium elements are still quite stable. I think the half-life of plutonium is ten thousand years."

"God, you don't think we found plutonium!" Gerfertig gasped.

"No, plutonium is a dark blue metal. Still, as radioactive as this stuff seems to be, it must be a

transuranium element, and indeed, if you match up predicted characteristics based on the periodic table, you do find an element which would be a silvery liquid at room temperature.

It's element 126. There is a predicted island of stability for that element because it would have a complete electron shell."

"An element that high in the periodic table would have a ridiculously short half-life," said Mike. "It would have decayed ten seconds after the big bang."

"Wow, your physics is shaky," I said. "Hear me out. There's good evidence that the very heavy elements and metals are produced in the cores of stars as a result of fusion processes and shot across the galaxy by novas. It's quite possible that many transuranium elements were present when the earth first formed."

"Present at the creation, yes, but these elements have all decayed, and so would have Element 126 by now."

"True, but let's suppose that, being a liquid, it globbed up as the primordial earth cooled, and as the magma cooled into quartz, the radioactive resonance of the element made the quartz crystalize."

"I see where you're heading, but this stuff popped out of clay balls, not geodes."

"Do you realize what crystalline quartz would look like after being bombarded internally by intense low-frequency radiation for four billion years?"

Gerfertig had been listening intently and jumped in at this point. "The dike is a very old formation, one of the oldest in the world. It's part of the stable bedrock that makes Texas so impervious to earthquakes."

I forged ahead. "OK, so my theory is that this element collected up against a quartz formation while much of the surface of the earth was still cooling, and it has been preserved here because of the extremely stable geologic conditions."

"That may be all well and good, but as Mr. Amato said, the Element 126 would have still decayed," Gerfertig said.

"I don't know, and from what I've read, I don't think anyone knows the effects of high levels of radioactivity inside crystal structures. But I know how another kind of energy can be isolated and preserved. It's called a thermos."

Mike asked, in his most reasonable tone, "then why are we the first people in the history of the whole human race to ever find this Element 126?"

"Well, I'm glad you asked. We aren't. It's been around for thousands of years." Mike made a dismissive sound.

I looked evenly at Mike. "It jumped out at me while doing the search. Ancient alchemists claimed they had a formula to turn lead into gold. And the main ingredient, from what has come down to us, was mercury. Maybe they made the same mistake we just made, and thought it was mercury. What if it was this Element 126, which looks so much like mercury. If you could stabilize it, it is so radioactive that, with a little prodding by adding a small amount of energy, a low frequency wave of radiation could easily pop an electron shell lose."

I let it sink in. "If you read the accounts of the alchemists working to turn lead into gold, they mention the pungent smell of what we know today is ozone. They used primitive stills and distillation apparatuses to agitate the 'mercury' and it pulsed out an intense low-frequency wave of radiation."

"Who knows, whether it was in Atlantis or Egypt or Rome, someone found one of these decayed geodes and released the element? It might be considered the start of atomic science, the transmutation of lead into gold. And descriptions of some of the alchemists from the middle ages indicate they might have been exposed to radiation. Remember, they also claimed to have found the Elixir of Life. Small doses of radiation in the right range would help kill off the germs they were laden with because of poor hygiene."

"Radiation sterilization," said Mike.

"Right. But after a while, no one could find more of this magic liquid, at least in the civilized world, after it had all been searched out. They only had mercury left to use."

"The element is too volatile, once exposed, to do anything with it," said Mike. Even if someone had found it, they couldn't have done anything with it."

I turned to Gerfertig. "What was the temperature on the days you found these balls?"

"It was during July and August. It was probably 95 to 100 degrees any of those days."

"In a more temperate climate, who knows?" I said to Mike.

"Cripes, I almost think you've solved the secret of the ages!" he blurted. "This could be one of the greatest scientific discoveries of the ages."

"Not unless we find another of these things."

Gerfertig spoke up. "I know where there's one sitting at the base of the cliff. I haven't been eager to poke at it."

"Let's get real," said Mike. "We are tickling the dragon's tail. We can't handle something as potentially dangerous as this."

Gerfertig interrupted. "Mr. Amato, have you ever heard the saying about owing the bank money? If you owe the bank a thousand dollars, it's your problem. If you owe them a million dollars..."

"...it's their problem. So what has this got to do with us?"

"Oh, I know exactly what he means." And I did. "If this was a case of illegal radiological waste dumping, it would be a problem for Stonewall Bricks and Industro-Kleen. But we're dealing with the discovery of a previously unknown source of a radioactive element"

I turned to Gerfertig and said in mock formal fashion, "I would suggest, as the head of this 'mining operation', you contact the Dept. of Energy immediately."

"I have a 24-hour emergency number," he said. "I think it's time to use it."

The people from the government were there before midnight.


The people of Sebastopol at first despised Industro-Kleen for its report identifying a rare but toxic mold found in the clay, but the scads of government buy-out dollars made the end of the era much more bearable.

Stonewall Brick was bought out by an previously unheard German company, EHSS (Einhundertsechundswansig) GmBh., supposedly for strategic business reasons.

Mike and I were both offered generous positions with the dummy outfit that bought Stonewall and Industro-Kleen—based on our abiding by the very precise terms of an agreement.

Mike signed off and took a very nice retirement with the family in Alaska. So much for the Texas summer.

I had qualms for a little while, but I didn't see much alternative. There was no way, with the terrorism abroad in the world, I would let it get out that a new naturally occurring radioactive element had been discovered—especially a liquid one. Yep, I could have just seen Saddam Hussein with a lead-lined thermos of that juice.

The most satisfying thing, for me, was how Gerfertig and the other men got the medical care they needed, thoroughly and discretely. Strangely enough, the fellow with lung cancer succumbed nevertheless, but it was learned his two-pack a day habit was the real culprit.

Careful tests conducted in private facilities at an undisclosed location showed my theory to be correct. A thin lead religious medal which belonged to a scientist was transmuted into gold. I was the most popular chemist certain physicists ever knew. Element 126 was unofficially dubbed 'Kosteranium'—although the expenditures made by the government covertly to collect the element, and to also explore geographic formations across the world where it was also thought it could be found, led to the unflattering 'Kost-too-muchium'".

As it was, the geology under Sebastopol is unique, and mining continues very quietly at the clay pit. Rudy Gerfertig still lives there; the townspeople assume he is just a caretaker for the shuttered property.

I found myself at age 23 with a guaranteed lifelong salary and some very lucrative investments, and plenty of time to work on my formula for the perfect beer.

The government treated us all quite well, when they realized we were reasonable guys and the discovery was an easily concealed accident. I don't feel guilty at all for taking the government's 'gold', because the money is my payment for having to suppress the gloat of knowing I am the guy who solved the great riddle of history—How to make gold out of lead.

Actually, I like to flatter myself because I think I went the alchemists and philosophers one better, because I was able to make 'gold' out of thin air. Silence is golden. I think that's a heck of a transmutation.

*   *   *

It's obvious I'm leaning on dialogue to develop character in this story, and I certainly developed the characters better than I did in "Insight".

Also, stuff from the authors' real life often insinuate themselves into a story. There's always been a joke that a hard-boiled detective in a crime novel lights up a cigarette every time the author does behind his typewriter, and so forth.

I didn't see it until later, but John Koster's frantic internet search probably reflects all the internet searching I was doing at the time as I tried to find my way in the genre.

Schmidt returned the story a month later with a printed form rejection, but he added a personal, practical note at the bottom. It shows my inexperience, but I mailed him a manuscript printed on fancy cream-colored stock paper. He said it's always best to stick to plain white 20 lbs. stock. I've subsequently learned editors hate any deviation from standard manuscript format. But I still had a lot of learning to do.

"Silence is Golden" publication history has a happy ending. I know the story made it past the first readers or screeners or Schmidt wouldn't have had it to write a note back. So I knew it had potential. But at a second glance, a serious flaw jumped out at me.

The story is told in the first person, but it's also clearly implied Koster has to sign some kind of confidentiality agreement. So who's he talking to?

This stumped me for months, and then in 2003 I thought of funny framing device. The version of the story as ultimately published has a different beginning and ending, which I reprint here:

New Beginning:

"Padre Island is pretty this time of year, don't you think? Now that the college kids have gone back home. We pretty much have this stretch of beach to ourselves. Would you like a beer? I didn't think so. You must be a local. Do you live nearby? Don't look at me like that with those pretty brown eyes. Hey, would you like to hear something really crazy. I'm filthy rich, and I can't really tell anyone why. Well, maybe I can tell a pretty girl like you. Sit down, you want to hear an interesting story? OK, here goes."

New Ending:

"Anyhow, that's the story. Whenever anyone asks me where I got my money, I tell them I inherited it from my Uncle Norm. Of course, I guess I technically broke my agreement with the government, by telling you. But you won't tell anyone, will you, now? That's a good girl. Anyhow, I think I've gotten enough sun. I think it's time for me to take off. Oh, yes, look what we have here. Want the stick? Sure. Fetch!"

That fixed that problem. It also marks the first appearance in my fiction in the kind of perfectly logical but still surprising ending that was made popular in short fiction at the turn of the 20<sup>th</sup> Century by O. Henry and later became a fixture on Rod Serling's *Twilight Zone*.

There were a number of other changes made in rewrite. That reference to "Uncle Norm" in the conclusion refers to a little piece of funny business I inserted during the opening scene, the beginning which was changed to this:

"A year ago I was a wise guy barely a year out of UT-Austin who knew how to brew beer at home and neutralize solvents for Industro-Kleen in Dallas. I was an in-house chemist. Our company's mission was to get the EPA's teeth out of the butts of Dallas-area business owners who hadn't been too careful about what they spilled, sprayed or dumped on or around their employees.

One day my boss appeared in my doorway. "How much experience do you have with NORM?"

"Who is Norm? Is there some asshole here I haven't met yet?"

"That kinda answers my question," he said. "NORM is Naturally Occurring Radioactive Material."

"None" I snapped."

In the process of researching the subject, I learned that NORM is the Environmental Protection Agency's term for radioactive elements found in the environment. This is not as uncommon as you would think, but the levels are very low and there really are no federal regulations. Years later I heard a story from SF author Jay Lake about when he and some friends were touring a national park in the American Southwest, when a park ranger pointed out a boulder made of pitchblende—which is uranium ore—and warned them not to fall asleep on it.

Just sitting on it was the equivalent of getting a chest x-ray, Lake said he was told. Ironically, because of its location being a national park, the boulder could not be removed.

Other little changes were made to the revised version of the story to smooth it out. I decided just swapping the name of one Russian city for another was clumsy, so I renamed the locale Pineville—much more in keeping with its location in the Piney Woods of East Texas.

By the time I made these revisions, which I felt were definite improvements, I had begun getting feedback from Gardner Dozois at *Asimov's* on my subsequent submissions (which is the core of this book and coming up), and I had my first publication, with the ezine Revolution SF, in June 2003.

My first story at *Revolution SF* was so well received that I started looking around immediately for another to send editor Jayme Blaschke. One hard and fast rule in publishing is, no matter how splendid the revisions are, you never resubmit a rejected story to the same market. So as much as I would have liked to, I didn't send it to Gardner; I sent it to Jayme instead.

He snapped it up and it was published August 18, 2003.

Remember the happy ending I mentioned earlier? Dozois has edited since 1984 an annual anthology called *The Year's Best Science Fiction*, currently published by St. Martin's Press (he still does this, despite having left *Asimov's* in 2004). Each year he reads through new and original fiction as it comes out.

When he gets ready to compile his annual anthology—he has stated—any story he recalls just by reading the title again is considered memorable enough to earn an honorable mention. Although the anthology itself usually features the two dozen best stories of the year, the honorable mentions list is also considered a good indicator of quality fiction.

In the summer of 2004, when the Year's Best came out, I was startled to see "Silence is Golden" was recognized with an honorable mention. It was a great morale booster, and the first of a total of eleven I've accumulated since then.

And by then, Gardner and I had corresponded much more, a lot more—as you will read in the next chapter.

# Chapter 3

## Set...

Although I had been a science fiction reader for decades, I knew nothing about the way magazines are run and how stories are selected. As I mentioned in the previous chapter, I hit the internet—hard—to catch up on my research.

It didn't take long to realize the formative role Gardner Dozois played in the genre. Helpfully, the *Asimov's Science Fiction* web site had a discussion board where people met and discussed a slew of topics, and Dozois participated and interacted with the readers, fans and authors. I thought this would be a good place to gather information I needed to

I was still unsure of whether this science fiction writing would pan out for me, and in case it didn't—and I wanted to pretend it never happened—I didn't use my real name. I participated on the discussion board using the ID "Texarcana"—a play on the name of the largest city in the area where I lived, Texarkana.

The next story I wrote wasn't the next story I sent to Dozois. "Body by Fisher" went to *Analog*, *Fantasy & Science Fiction*, and long-gone small publication called *Palace of Reason* before Gardner saw it.

The next story I wrote after that was "S.P.P.A.M." and it went to Gardner in January 2003. At this point, I was moving *Asimov's* towards the top of my submissions priorities.

"S.P.P.A.M." is a case of a story that starts, like a pearl in an oyster, with a little grain. In this case, the Maguffin was what "S.P.P.A.M." would stand for. It may be hard for younger people to believe, but back in 2003 the problem of unsolicited advertising messages on the web was just busting out, people were very vexed by it all; I know, today we have just come to accept it.

The term "spam" was on everyone's lips and fingertips, and nobody knew where it came from. I thought if I could come up with a clever abbreviation I could generate a story around it.

Writers have learned through experience that if you get an idea or a burst of inspiration, write or record it immediately. I had been racking my brain to come up with a clever member to explain the secret meaning of "spam" (nobody really knows where it originated, anyway) when I thought of making it an acronym.

My burst of inspiration came while I was at the wheel of the car as my wife and I were driving to Dallas. As so often happens, the creativity came out while my mind was relaxed and distracted. I asked my wife to grab a pen and scrap of paper to write down my "Maguffin".

After I wrote the story and mailed it to Gardner, it took four months for him to send it back—a positive sign itself. Rejections are swift; the longer a story is held the more consideration it is getting.

I also noticed when I looked at the pre-printed rejection slip, it was the short version—another positive sign—which read:

"Thank you very much for letting us see your work. I'm afraid, however, that it's not quite what we're looking for right now. I do appreciate your thinking of *Asimov's*, and I hope you will let us see more from you.

"I hope you will excuse this form letter. The volume of work has unfortunately made it impossible for me to respond to each submission individually, much as I'd like to be able to.

"Sincerely,

"Gardner Dozois Editor"

I knew that when an editor drops something like "I hope you will let us see more from you" he means it; no editor wants to encourage submissions from someone he's not likely to ever buy a story from.

Then my eyes darted to the bottom of the sheet, where there was some handwritten scribbling. I read:

"Tex—

"I enjoyed this. The core idea is one I've seen before, but it's professionally and enjoyably crafted, certainly better than 99% of the stuff in the slush pile. So keep trying, I think you've got the ability to succeed. This one will probably sell somewhere, for that matter.

"Gardner"

Well, I nearly fainted. This was the third story I ever wrote, and I got a personal note from the top editor in the business.

Then I realized that he addressed the note to "Tex". I had never linked my submissions to the *Asimov's* Discussion Board ID. But he knew I was "Texarcana".

Gardner Dozois knew who I was!

One author whose advice on the discussion board had been very helpful to me was James Van Pelt. I sent him an email the next day:

"Dear Jim (AKA the sci fi guru of Grand Junction): You've always been very helpful and kind to me on the *Asimov's* discussion board, and I wanted to pass along a private note about a rejection I got in the mail yesterday from *Asimov's*. Gardner Dozois sent me a "short form" and then wrote the following…"

He replied:

"Lou, That is a great note! I got one of those before he bought one from me, so keep knocking on his door."

Other authors told me the same thing. When I met Michael Swanwick at the PhilCon Convention in Philadelphia in December of that year, he agreed that Gardner would not waste time writing notes to authors unless he felt he would eventually buy something from them.

"S.P.P.A.M." marked the beginning of the process that is at the heart of this book, the communication and feedback I received from Gardner as I broke into writing science fiction. The note at the bottom of that form rejection was the first Letter from Gardner.

After a few more rejections in 2003, I decided to submit "S.P.P.A.M." to the long-running webzine Bewildering Stories, which published it in December 2003. It was my third story published that year, the first outside of Revolution Science Fiction—which earlier in the year published "Silvern" and "Silence is Golden". I felt it made it look like my publication career started off well in 2003.

(I had a fourth story, called "Comes the JuJu Man", accepted by an ezine called *Gateway Science Fiction* in 2003, but I was never able to confirm that it was actually published, and the web site evaporated; not an unknown happening among the smaller venues run as labors of love by science fiction fans.")

I didn't make any substantial changes from the version Gardner saw to what *Bewildering Stories* published. Here it is:

# S.P.P.A.M.

The email message just fit on the screen without scrolling. Murphy looked long and hard, as it presented a number of problems for him. Interpreting the shoddy spelling was not one of them, in light of his experience with the Texas educational system. But the date was all wrong, both in the message and the header. It was exactly two years in the future.

His confusion over the date was quickly overcome in his mind by the much more difficult puzzle presented by the text of the message. A high schooler claimed have read, and was asking questions about, a book he had not written yet for a class project.

Steve Murphy's one bedroom apartment was a small cracker box hidden in a warren of asphalt and nondescript two-story apartment buildings nestled in an urban planning afterthought—in this particular case, the wedge of land between Coit Rd. and the LBJ Freeway in North Dallas.

This landscape shimmered in the 105 degree late afternoon heat as Murphy had dragged himself to the door and slipped the key in the lock as he swapped the security guard's jacket to the other arm.

He deftly slipped the thermostat lever sideways in one smooth move as he slouched into the apartment; he couldn't afford to keep the a/c turned very low while he was at work.

He dropped down in the couch he had bought at the Salvation Army furniture store and stared at the impressionistic pattern of cracks decorating the opposite wall as a result of the slow and gentle heaving of the ground due to the Texas heat combined with the usual slapdash construction of fast-buck Dallas contractors.

"What a dump," he thought. "And I can barely afford it."

He had made so little as a first year English teacher in the Dallas school district he had to work a summer job, watching the parking lot of a Winn-Dixie on Ross Ave. in a neighborhood so rough people knifed each other in the parking lot to steal each other's bottle returns.

He took the day shift—brutal because of the heat, but he honestly doubted he could have survived the night shift.

After a few minutes of catching his breath and sucking in the cool air, Murphy gained enough strength to shamble to the fridge and dispose of some two-day old atomic chicken wings from the Wing Stop around the corner.

As his strength returned to his body and intelligence revived in his mind, he remembered why he had no plans for tonight.

"I need to write," he thought.

Like so many English majors who sauntered out of the University of Texas, Murphy wanted to write, and indeed, his highest grades and most praiseworthy recognition had come because of his creative writing—"a well-written combination of realism and imagination" was how one paper was described in a writing workshop he attended recently.

But he hadn't made a penny yet from his writing; instead he spent the first year out of college baby-sitting a bunch of drug-addicted teenagers at Sunrise High School for whom English was a foreign language—indeed, any form of communication which didn't include penetration by a bullet, knife or phallus was foreign to them.

Murphy would come home—then as now—drained, but after some minutes of recovery, he would regain his strength and confidence and work on an outline of the novel he contemplated writing.

Now, after ten months of outlines, research and chapter synopses, he was just about there. "I need to rock off center and start writing," he said, this time out loud as if to convince himself. "I can't go on like this forever."

He looked at the clock. "I can get a good six hours of writing in before midnight," he thought. He sat down and stared at the blank monitor, and then nudged the mouse.

The screen glowed, and he agonized whether to check his email. "It's probably the usual collection of spam," he thought. "I need to stop procrastinating."

But he weakened and logged on and received an authoritative admonition that he had mail. He clicked his spam filter software. Thirty-six of 42 messages were definitely spam, and he deleted them without reading. Six were questionable, ranked in order of probability. They were still mostly bogus, but tied in to his personal interests.

"Re: Big refund due you!"

"Manhood enlargement: $39.95"

"Huge Profits with Internet auctions"

"For your splendiferous enjoyment—Katmandu Temple Kiff!"

"View photos of singles in your area"

"Mr. Steven F.X. Murphy: I just finished reading your new novel and love it!"

He was ready to click on "Delete All" when he realized what the last one said. The first thing that caught his attention were the initials.

He blinked and squinted and rubbed his forehead a couple of times, back and forth, like he was trying to reboot his brain.

Who does he know now, who knows his middle initials?

In keeping with family tradition, and acknowledging an old family debt to the Jesuits—who had given his great-grandfather the education he needed to set the Murphys towards comfortable middle-class status in Baltimore—he was dubbed "Francis Xavier".

In places such as Boston, Baltimore or New York, "F.X." is not an uncommon set of middle initials. Growing up in suburban Dallas, it was a killer.

By the time he was in middle school, half the kids thought he was retarded because of his nickname, "Special".

Special F.X, get it? Ha-ha.

He managed to lose the initials in high school, and hadn't used or thought of them in eight years. So who sent him this last email?

He deleted the others and then opened the last one. He didn't recognize the address—(Server Protocol/Precog Authorized Mailer)—and the subject line made no sense.

The message was in the form of a letter, strangely formal.

"July 14, 2006"

"Mr. Steven F.X. Murphy

"Dallas, Tj.

"Dr. Mr. Murphy,

"I have juste finised reading your new novel, "In Giddy Anticipation of a Glorious Defeat". I agree with what moste of the critics have said, its fun and extremly well writen. I enjoyed it immensly. I am doing a report for my high school english class on "The Contemporary American Novel" and I wondered whether you would be so kind as to answer a few questions for me.

"Did you get the ideas for moste of the story from real live events, or is it mostly from your imagination? Did you actually know people who were like Chu Chu, Marina, Toby, and Judge Strange? Is one of the characters really you?

"I was wondering whether the beste place to get ideas for such an entertainin story is from real live or your mind?

"Thank you in advanse for your help. I am 14 years old and very eagre to have your advise.

"Annetje Vandemerwe-Mantanzima"

"Giddy Anticipation of a Glorious Defeat" seemed to be an amalgamation of some probable titles he had jotted down for the story which as yet only existed in outline form. The story he was ready to start tonight, before he checked his messages.

How could the girl—he thought it was a girl's name—ask specific questions about a book he hadn't written yet? And why would the message come just tonight, when he felt he was really about ready to rock off that writer's block he was hung up on and get rolling?

He did have an idea, though, and so he hit reply and began to write:

"Dear Annetje:

"Thanks for the very nice message, but I am a little perplexed. You say you read my novel, but I find that hard to believe. I am just beginning to write it now. Perhaps you used the wrong words. I noticed from your message that English may not be your first language.

"Maybe we met someplace and I discussed my story idea with you, perhaps in a pub or club. I am certainly happy you like my characters and ideas. I'm sorry I don't remember you; perhaps if you could jog my memory, maybe I will remember you.

"If you like to help critique my story as it comes along, I would welcome the help. In general, though, I am confused by your message.

"Sincerely,

"Steven F.X. Murphy"

Murphy did not recall blabbing about the plot or characters to anyone, but there was the possibility that some night, while he grabbed a few beers in a local pub, he might have discussed the story to someone he was trying to impress after liquor loosened his tongue.

He knew he certainly never discussed it in a writers' workshop, fearful of plagiarism. He thought he had a good story idea—and apparently, so did Annetje. The question was, how did she know about it?

He hit "send". Everything reset to normal, although there was no confirmation message. "I wonder whether it went through?" he thought.

He turned on the Instant Messaging and went back to the kitchen to brew some coffee and cook—or at least microwave—some fresh food. It was time to get serious, and he wanted to stay up late and finally get a start on his story. Darkness was coming around and over the little urban man-made nowhere where he lived.

He was a few pages into the first chapter story when the Instant Messaging went off. The same strange address appeared, "Server Protocol/Precog Authorized Mailer". It was the reply from Annie, as she styled herself this time.

"Mr. Murphy,

"I'm sorry my Amglish is so poor, but the truth is I really dont speak your lanjuaj. I will tell you what you want to know, but you really muste please promis not to tell anybody. This message is fries only. Do we have a deel?

"Annie"

Murphy was taken aback at how much more the language (lanjuaj?) had deteriorated, and it took him a few seconds to realize the silly-sounding "fries only" must be a pidgin contraction of "for your eyes only". This message might be from Malaysia or Indonesia or someplace like that, he thought. He began to wonder whether he was being dragged into some drug or sex sting.

Against his proverbial better judgment, he decided to play along. "First, some strong coffee, I need to stay alert on this one."

After he sat down again, he clicked reply and jabbed off a short message:

"Annie:

"I promise to keep your secret, but you better be honest, up front and clean about this. I am not into tricks, drugs, sex or scams. I am a poor struggling writer. I have a little talent, less time and no money at all, so please don't waste what I have of these."

He quickly hit the send button. This time his screen blinked briefly, but there was still no confirmation message. He went back to writing and tried to put the exchange of messages out of his mind.

It was hours later, almost midnight, and he was thinking of knocking off. He had managed to write up at least a draft of the first chapter of the novel. He was in his boxers and brushing his teeth when he heard the instant messaging go off.

When he looked, he saw two messages together, which wasn't supposed to happen. One was a spam that said "See a hot 18-year old girl have sex with her horse" ("God almighty, I need stay away from porn sites") and the other was from Annie.

"Dear Mr. Muprhy,

"I took some time to run my message through some babel software, so it would be more intelligible. I was trying to write in early 21st century English as best I could. I am happy that you agreed to keep my secret. I could get in a lot of trouble over this, but my father is an important man and I am a juvie, anyhow. I will take my chances. I was already in trouble when I sent you the first message.

"Part of what I told you is true. I am 14 and I am in what you would call high school. I am making a report for my class in "21st Century Amglish Literature". I attend the Reef Preparatory School in the city that was called Joburg in your time. My country is called Azania. I think it was still called South Africa when you are.

"Reef is very competitive, and I would like a good grade. My father works for the supranational agency that polices time travel. He is the head of the branch that coordinates operatives in the past. He doesn't know, but I have seen him working at home in his office.

"The messaging system they use to communicate with operatives in the past has a parallel time-line with a 200-year difference, and you don't have to use any special settings if you send a message this way. I remember how angry my father was a few years ago when one of his staffers sent a message warning a half dozen people not to be in New York on September 11, 2001, especially after the death toll dropped almost by 2,000 between the historic record and the archives in the stasis control server. Daddy sent the man to work on Callisto.

"When our teacher, Mrs. Iddo, gave us the assignment on 21st Century Am Lit, I did some searching and found a story in archives which described how you wrote "Glorious Defeat". You said you began and ended on July 14. I was able to figure out how to use the Precog Protocol Server, and as father is an authorized mailer, all I needed was the password, which I correctly guessed was the name of our family's pet [galgosh] Error Message babel translation failure.

"Because I was excited, I got confused, I guess. Since it is 2204, and today July 14, I knew I could get on my father's system and send you a message without using any settings because of the parallel time line. I forgot to notice that the story said you began writing on July 14, 2004, and ended on July 14, 2005. The book was published in 2006. I guess I had a brain fart or something like that.

"You were the greatest writer of early 21st Century American English. I am happy you read my message and did not think it was what you call spam—junk mail. I know the word from a story my father once told some friends, when he didn't know I overheard.

"The nickname for these messages come from the abbreviation of the system, the same system I am using, 'Server Protocol/precog Authorized Mailer'. In the 20th century, when operatives could begin to send messages through normal, for those times, computer systems, one man working in the past slipped up one day and said he was logging on to check his 'spam'.

"When some 20th century person asked him what spam was, he made up story about it meaning email nobody wants. I think he made up some really long and silly story about its origin, having something to do with a 2D video skit by a 20th century vaudeville group, the Rocky Python Flying Horror Show, I think it was called.

"I would be very grateful if you kept my secret, and also if you gave me some of the insight I asked for you when I was pretending to be an American school girl.

"Annie"

Murphy stared at the message and didn't move a muscle for a half hour. Then he stirred himself and sat up very straight. He hit "reply".

"Dear Annie:

"Although your story seems fantastic, it makes sense in light of the mistakes in your first message. Since you have been nice enough to tell me something about my future, I will answer your questions.

"Chu Chu, Marina, Toby are characters based on different aspects of my own personality. Toby is most closely modeled on myself, but there are times I have done things or acted like all three of them. One of the best pieces of advice I ever got in a writing class was that you should write what you know. I know myself, and so I created characters by expanding aspects of my own personality.

"Judge Strange is modeled on a real Justice of the Peace I know. I won't tell you his real name, though: That would unfair. As far as the plot, that is where I got real creative and I made most of that up, although the scene in Judge Strange's court is based on a real story I heard from a friend.

"I hope this is helpful. Perhaps I never discussed these aspects of my story publicly because I gave you my word to keep a secret. I am worried more about you. Won't your teacher wonder where you got your research? What will you tell her? I hope you won't get in a lot of trouble.

"Good luck.

"Steve"

Murphy really thought hard before he hit "send". He wanted to know so much more, but what could he ask, and what was fair of him to ask? This evening was if he had called Robert Louis Stevenson on the telephone and asked him about his plotting and characterization for "Dr. Jekyl and Mr. Hyde". What would Stevenson have asked him back, and what could he tell him?

Murphy felt he somewhat unfairly wanted Annie to email him back, but he didn't want to push, press or prod. He would scare her off. He clicked send, and then saved the message to a folder. "This is a keeper," he thought, feeling alternately happy, smug and nervous.

It was early in the morning, and he certainly couldn't sleep, so made more coffee and began to work on the next chapter. He was halfway through it and it was almost 3 a.m. when the Instant Messaging went off. He jumped with a start, and clicked. It was from Annie.

"Steve I may be in troublem, but you maybe too. Don't try to reply anymor. I think {transfer interrupted by remote server}.

He jumped up and lunged for his uniform pants, putting them on with one hand while punching buttons on the computer with the other. "How could I be so •••• stupid," he thought. "There must be a server here routing these messages!"

He was at the door in 30 seconds opening it with one hand while tucking a dirty shirt in his pants with another. He stopped with his hand down the front of his pants as he popped the door open wide to see a half dozen men in suits lined up like bowling pins on the landing in front of his door.

The man in front raised his eyebrows and gestured for him to step forward as the other five men flowed into his apartment.

"Ummm, let me guess, you're from a government agency I've never heard of, right?"

The man nodded.

"And I didn't get any email messages tonight, right?"

The man nodded again.

"Annnndd… if I never open my mouth and be a good boy," he suggested hopefully, "I won't have any problems?"

"What's done is done, Mr. Murphy," said the suit with a slight accent. "What happens next is up to you."

"Nothing happened tonight," he said brightly. "I have no reason to complain, do I? I mean, I can still write, can't I?"

"We're not going to change history any more than is unavoidable." The suit put his hand on Murphy's shoulder in a gesture both reassuring and menacing. "You're an intelligent young man, and you've received a remarkable gift. Accept it quietly and go on with your life."

"I have no complaints. I'm not going to look a gift horse up the tail."

Murphy could tell from the sounds from inside they were searching his apartment and hauling off his computer equipment.

"I didn't initiate the contact, you know."

"Still, Mr. Murphy, do you respond to all your spam email?"

"What would you have done, if you were in my shoes?"

"We'll just double check your computer."

The phalanx of suits were hauling off his computers, peripherals and disks in crates. When he saw his CPU go by, he realized the backup disk with his outline and draft chapters was still in the drive. He groaned.

The head man noticed and flagged down the man with the box, and popped out the disk. It was orange and Murphy has written "Glorious Defeat" with a marker on it only a few hours ago.

The man handed it to him as the others streamed away. "History says you started July 14, and so you have."

"Thanks. I hope Annie isn't in too much trouble."

The man smiled. "You might be able to hear her posterior being flogged some 200 years away."

Murphy brightened. "Tell her I said hi."

The man wagged his head in a gesture of "maybe" as he turned around and left.

Murphy returned to the shambles of his apartment and sat down in the chair where his computer used to be. He tossed the disk down and stared at the empty desktop.

After a while he felt he needed to do something, so he dressed a little more neatly and walked outside into the early morning air. It was probably only 80 degrees, a nice cool morning for summer time in Dallas.

He looked around from the second floor railing and saw the sign for a Waffle House two blocks away. He stuck his hands in his pockets and strolled over to where truck drivers, insomniacs and early risers congregated in a glass and plastic smoke-filled shoebox of a building.

He sat down at the counter and the waitress handed him a plastic laminated menu.

"That's OK, I know what I want," he said. "Two scrambled eggs with salsa and Texas Toast."

"Any meat?"

Murphy usually didn't get meat with his breakfast, to save money. But he thought about it.

"What the heck, I got some good news tonight. I'll splurge."

And in a moment he had a flash of insight. "I'm a lucky bastard. The man was right, I really have received a gift."

He looked around at the other people in the diner. "You never know what the future will hold for you, what will even happen the next day. Here I am, dirty and exhausted—but I know something none of these other people can know, or ever probably hope to know.

"I know I'm going to be a success."

He didn't realize he said the last thought aloud. "I'm happy for your good news, dude," the waitress snapped, "but what kind of meat do you want?"

"What kind of meat ya' got," he said, trying to regain his composure.

"We got breakfast links, bacon, ham or Canadian bacon, spam..."

He interrupted. "You have spam?"

"Sure, would you like a slice of grilled spam with your eggs?"

He looked at her far more incredulously than the suggestion warranted. After a few seconds she gave him a questioning look.

He snapped out of it and began nodding broadly. "Yes, I love spam."

She scribbled in her pad and turned away. Murphy felt a kind of stupid giddiness coming over him. He turned towards the biker to his left and said enthusiastically "I love spam! I really do!"

The man ignored him as just another early morning kook. Murphy swiveled around towards the delivery man to his right and started to laugh.

"I really, really, no ●●●●, love spam!"

He cracked up completely and burst out laughing out loud. The biker, the delivery man, the waitress, everyone in the diner ignored him.

He began to sing.

"I'm a happy man, I am, I am.

"Hot ●●●●, hot ●●●●, 'cuz I like spam."

And for one of the last times in his life, the world ignored Steven F.X. Murphy.

★   ★   ★

If not a twist ending, an ironic one.

There is a strange epilogue to this story. I named the protagonist after one of the most aspiring authors who haunted the *Asimov's* Discussion Board at the time. Steve Murphy and I would have a strange connection in relation to Gardner almost a year later. I don't want to give the twist away yet, you have to keep reading along in this book.

The *Asimov's* Discussion Board died a number of years ago, the victim of changing times and obnoxious posters who drove other people away—that's why I eventually stopped visiting it. This is unfortunately not an uncommon fate, the Gresham's Law of the Internet: Bad People Drive Away Good People.

But there are still people I know and talk to regularly, like Steve Murphy, who I met there, and the name "The Old *Asimov's* Gang" gets tossed around occasionally.

"S.P.P.A.M." was the first story I ever wrote that was reprinted. It was included in the first *Bewildering Stories* anthology published in 2006. I also included it in my second reprint collection, *Texas & Other Planets*, published in 2010 by Merry Blacksmith Press.

It was the last time Gardner sent me a form letter; every time I sent him a story after that, he sent me personal feedback with each rejection, until he bought a "Rocket for the Republic" a year later.

# Chapter 4

## Go!

From the time Gardner returned "S.P.P.A.M." until I sold him that first story—from April 2003 until March 2004—it was only eleven months. It seemed like a lot longer to me because it was so intense.

It was a very productive time for me. Each time I sent Gardner a story he would return it, with his analysis and comments. Ultimately, 13 stories went through this process until I sold him "A Rocket for the Republic". So all told—counting "S.P.P.A.M."—he read 15 stories of mine in a year.

There are probably some of you reading this who will say, "Wow, for how long had you stockpiled stories?" The answer is, no time at all. With my day job as a journalist, I tend to write fast. In fact, if I take too long and dawdle over a story, I usually begin to mess it up. My personal writing pattern follows the adage, "Write like crap, edit brilliantly."

All these stories I sent to Gardner were written since I began in late 2002. If that seems hard to believe, remember that each day I write a story from scratch that is published in the newspaper the following morning. There are days I have written a story at 9 a.m. in the morning that was printed and on the streets by noon. This isn't a common thing for most people.

As a result, I usually write good printable copy the first try; on the job, editing usually means tweaks and proofreading. In my fiction writing, that means my first draft is usually good; the editing is what gets it up to professional standards.

In retrospect, another reason I wrote so much in that time was because I *was* getting that feedback from Gardner. I quickly saw why he was voted the Hugo Award for Best Editor so many times—he was so appreciated by authors. You just can't put a price tag on that interaction. In a way, he was a throwback to the days of *Galaxy*'s Horace Gold and *Astounding*'s John

Campbell who would take the time—and had the time—to write long replies to submissions.

The genre and the world have changed. Editors are impersonal today and only regularly interact with established authors. Aspiring authors usually only get form letters—if that. Some magazine guidelines state, "You will only hear from us if you are accepted. You can assume if you don't hear from us in four months, you can submit the story elsewhere" or some similar cold-blooded boilerplate.

It must be extraordinarily difficult today to break in as an author—unless you're ridiculously talented. Which I'm not. On the other hand, it is easier to break in and make a reputation as a writer of short fiction—as opposed to novels—because it takes less time to create the product.

The next story I sent to Gardner was called "Body by Fisher". It was written before "S.P.P.A.M" but reached him later after going through a few other slush piles.

This story was cobbled together from a joke and a conceit. The joke was when I saw a nephew of my wife who had gotten some hardware stuck on his face—studs, pins and that kind of crap. Afterwards, I commented to my wife, "I'd love to get a big horseshoe magnet and see the look on his face when I pull all that stuff out."

The conceit was the car I was driving at the time, a 1986 Oldsmobile Delta'88. In 2001 my car broke down, and I was very broke at the time, so I went to an auto impound action in Dallas and bought an abandoned car for $175.

I supposed that because it had been stolen it would run, and it did, and after a few fixups I drove it until 2005. If you know anything about the model, you know a good name for it is "Oldsmotank".

One thing that ran across my mind was that, because of its age, it might be impervious to EMP damage.

Also, because of its age, it was one of the last GM cars whose body was a product of the separate Fisher Body company, and it bore the famous logo on the door frame. It was the first car I ever owned that had that, and I was impressed with the connection to history.

The car, the electronics, EMP attacks, implants. and all, swirled together and one day began to pour out. This was the result:

# Body By Fisher

I was ready to log on to a competitor's web site when I heard a sizzling sound and the screen went blank. An acrid smell hit my nose. I looked up and saw the calendar hologram on the wall just as it blinked out. It read March 18. I looked quickly at my watch. It was an analog style and had stopped at 3:18.

Then I began to hear the screams and moans.

I had been staring at the screen wondering whether to check my email or log on to see what the competition was up to. I could see the Sports Department out my office window; the newest writer, Dave Chaney, had the nethermost desk and sat with his back to me. He was a 23-year old kid, fresh out of UT-Austin, and I could see him occasionally rub his right ear self-consciously. I knew he recently got an audio implant.

I liked having my office in the back of the building. As Editor-in-Chief, I didn't like a lot of traffic or distractions. The Cedarburg Sentinel was founded decades earlier as a print newspaper, but changed to the internet around the turn of the century. One of the old hard copies framed in the office, from one of the last years of print publication, carried an account of the local memorial service after the attack on the World Trade Center that kicked off Cold War II.

I could see through my window as Chaney jumped up from his seat the moment "The Accident", as we later came to call it, happened. I called his name as I ran out. He turned and looked at me with an expression of intense pain, and went down like the Baghdad Tower. I saw blood splatter as his head hit the floor. I knelt down and raised his head. He was still breathing. I turned his head and saw it looked like someone had shot his right ear off.

I stood up. Those of us who were uninjured looked around at each other. It took only a few seconds for us to realize what had happened. "Great luck, Davey," I thought bitterly as I looked down at him, "How would you know this would happen because you wanted to listen to games while you work?"

All the screens in the office were blank and wisps of smoke floated in the air. Some people were moaning and others were getting up and going over to the hurt ones. A few were motionless, slumped in their seats or over their desks. A quick mental inventory indicated to those of us who were unhurt we all lacked any type of microchip implant technology, so we knew what had happened. A powerful electro-magnetic pulse had raced through the office, and that meant an atomic bomb had gone off somewhere nearby. I walked to the open part of the office. "Folks, let's take care of our people," as evenly as I could in that situation. "The government—or what's left of it—will have to worry about the war."

Tom Townzen, my worthy webmaster and second in command, was already at my side. "You would have thought there'd be some warning," he said. "Maybe some silos in West Texas or the Panhandle have been smoked. We would have seen or heard it if it had been in Dallas."

"I watched on television in high school when they blew up the World Trade Center," I snapped. "No one saw that coming, either."

"I know. I'm a little older than you," he replied. "I fought in that war."

"Let's not compare gray hairs," I said. "Let's help some people."

It was obvious that some people were gone—anyone with a brain chip implant or deep neural device. These were either older people with electronic prosthetics or younger people who had the most up-to-date "wiring". Our head Accounts Receivable Clerk was an elderly woman who had an Alzheimer's neurointerface implant, and she was face down in the keyboard. Our front desk receptionist had been implanted with artificial silicon retinas a few years back to restore the vision she lost to glaucoma. You could see from the splatter pattern under her head that her eyes had exploded.

It was eerie how quiet it was while our makeshift triage was going on; that's what so many people recall right after The Accident—the silence. Near-total silence inside except for hushed conversations and moans. There was also no noise from the outside, although we were at the corner of a busy intersection. All traffic had stopped as cars lost power and control.

It became obvious after a few minutes our most problematic employee was Jaypeg Tuggle, the telephone receptionist. Jaypeg was a sweet country girl and was named, she claimed, because her daddy had looked over her after she was born and claimed "she's as pretty as a picture." She had no implants or jacks but the multi-line telephone hanging on her ear blasted the side of her head when the EMP hit. The whole side of her head was bleeding and burned.

Other employees had set Jaypeg on the floor. They cleaned and quickly patched her up as best they could, but she was obviously deep in shock and her breathing was shallow. Tom and I crouched down.

"I don't know, Joe, she looks pretty bad," he said. "I think we need to get her to the hospital."

"What are we going to do, carry her?" I snapped. My nerves were already beginning to fray.

"Do you have any better ideas?" Tom asked reasonably.

"Maybe someone has a car that will start," I shot back.

Rena Eury, our head graphic artist, was patching up a reporter who had a blown cell phone implant in his jaw. She looked up and over at me.

"Mr. Chambers, do you still have that Oldsmobile in the warehouse?"

I looked at Tom. "Shit, I forgot about the car!"

"Will that thing crank?"

"I'm sure going to find out."

I ran out the back of the building. The warehouse that housed the old press, vending machines and the other detritus of the industry which had accumulated over fifty years was 100 feet behind the main building.

As I rolled up the door, it came into view; it would have been hard not to see it—a big heavy Reagan Era gas guzzler, an Oldsmobile Delta 88 Royale Brougham. GM stopped making Oldsmobiles years ago, but this car was old even then. Its original color was "bronze" but after so many years in the Texas sun it was now closer to a yellowish brown. It was about the size of Rhode Island; my friends in college called it the "Oldsmotank".

I had to squeeze past some junked vending machines to get to the car. I opened the door; it still smelled of 20 years of coffee and cigarettes.

I looked down at the door frame. There was a little rectangular plate with logo of an old English-style coach and the "Body by Fisher" motto. My grandfather said cars with these bodies were the best production models ever made.

It's funny the things you think of in a crisis. I've never had any electronic implants of any kid, but I had a lip stud in high school. I did it because of peer pressure. My grandfather really disliked it; he said there was something intrinsically wrong with sticking pins and needles into your body like that. I got rid of my stud just a few months before he passed away, while I was a freshman in college.

I inherited the car when he died.

I adjusted the rear view mirror and looked at the wrinkles around my eyes and the gray streaks in my hair. "Damn, I'm too old already to go through a war."

I looked around at the dingy and dirty interior. My grandfather had bought the car new, drove it daily and cared for it lovingly until he passed away; I always felt guilty I didn't keep it up. I hadn't taken care of it and it was a mess now. No headliner, and the air conditioner and half the dashboard didn't work. The transmission was on its last legs. "I'm sorry I let you down with the car, gramps," I thought.

The starter ground maybe five times or six times and then the engine coughed into action. I gave it the gas and closed the door as gusts of dirty exhaust swirled around the car. "This thing is indestructible," I thought.

The engine was still in good working order; I shoved the balky transmission into gear and slowly made my way around the back of the warehouse,

I drove up the side street and pulled up in front. I mashed the steering wheel where a 21st century car would have the airbag and the horn blared. Tom seemed surprised as he looked out the front door. A minute later he and Rena came out carrying Jaypeg. They laid her carefully in the back seat, and Rena sat on the edge of the seat beside her, while Tom slid in the front.

He looked at me. "No electronics. We're in business."

It took us 30 minutes to make what would have been a ten minute drive in normal circumstances to the hospital, because of the stalled cars and injured people in the roadway. I pulled up to the emergency entrance and honked long and loud. As we got out of the car, three people in scrubs came running out.

"Where the hell did you come from?" a young lady called out in a quavering voice.

I called back, "This woman needs help."

"God, can we borrow your car?" asked the young man behind her.

"There must be hundreds of people who need help and nobody can get here," said the second man behind him.

"Does anybody know what happened?" I asked.

"It's the end of the friggin' world," snapped the young female intern bitterly. She was already tending to Jaypeg. "We've been nuked. What else do you want to know?"

Rena was standing next to her, and she laid a hand on her shoulder. The two other orderlies put Jaypeg on an old-fashioned wheeled gurney.

"It's been an hour since the EMP," I said. "Has anybody heard anything?"

"We have civil defense links, but from what we've heard, they don't know much," said one of the orderlies.

"Because Washington is gone?"

"No, that's the screwy part. Washington is fine, but they don't know what's happened themselves."

Tom looked at me and raised an eyebrow "Shit, somebody had a nuclear accident."

One of the men tucking Jaypeg in looked up. "Maybe Comanche Peak blew up?"

"I thought nuclear power plants melted down, not blew up," the intern said harshly. I shook my head. They brought Jaypeg inside, and Tom and I followed.

People were walking in steadily. The dead and dying lined the halls. One little blond girl lay still on the floor with her head on a towel. You could see a burned and bloody cochlear implant next to her body.

In a minute Tom and I heard a murmur directed towards the emergency room entrance. A battered old green pickup truck with round fenders and running boards screeched to a shuddering halt—another jalopy with no electronics. The orderlies and a country-looking type carried two boys from the back.

A few minutes later while we stood in the waiting room, a doctor turned to Tom and I and the red-headed man in overalls who had come in with the pickup

"We really need to get out and start bringing the injured in. Could we borrow your vehicles?

"My transmission is almost dead, but I'll drive around for you, if you give me some supplies to take back to my office," I said.

"I'm staying here with my kids," said the good old boy, "but y'all welcome to use it. You cain't do it no harm."

Tom looked at me and then at the doctor. "I'll drive it."

The old boy pitched him the keys. "Good luck, boss."

I turned to the doctor. "We don't have any family nearby. I'm sure we can't get a hold of anyone right now, so we might as well help."

"Thanks, we appreciate it." In maybe two minutes a half dozen people, carrying all sorts of supplies and equipment, were in the pickup and my car, and we headed out. I dropped Rena and the supplies at the office, and we began what proved to be almost three full days on the streets.

We ferried people to the hospital most of that first night. It was dark soon, and the headlights of our two vehicles rolled like comets down the darkened streets. People would flag us down waving flashlights. We would load as many people as we could into both vehicles—we even had people lying and riding in the trunk of my car—and drive them back to the hospital.

People with subcutaneous or peripheral chips and implants—neural jacks, info chips and the like—were maimed and suffering all over the city; people with brain implants and any type of serious neurointerface technology didn't need our help. After a few hours we became accustomed to seeing bodies on lawns and sidewalks covered in blankets and sheets.

At least people understood what had happened. Dogs with smart tags or ID chips implanted under the skin in their necks wandered around maimed, either whimpering or growling. Tom found an old handgun in the glove box of the pickup, and a box of rounds under the seat. He dispatched at least a dozen dogs that night. After each time, he'd get back in the pickup, run a hand through his silver hair and grab the steering wheel tighter.

A scattering of satellite cellphones that because of design or location hadn't been scrambled provided the only link to the outside world in those first hours. If anyone had a working phone, they waved it as well as their flashlight when they saw us. Nobody really knew what happened just yet, but it wasn't a war. The handful of calls that went through said people on the East and West Coasts were fine—but the heartland of the country was silent and dark.

By maybe 4 a.m. we had ferried the most seriously injured to the hospital and we were driving around acting as a combination taxi and town crier service while the staff at the hospital were patching people up as best they could. Just as the first signs of dawn began to creep over the horizon Tom and I saw headlights coming down the highway from Dallas. They blinked and we blinked back. It was a convoy of Hummers. The lead vehicle veered off as the others came to a halt. We met on the median between the service road and the highway. "It's a terrible disaster, but the country will recover," said the National Guard Captain from Colorado. "They had a nuclear accident at the Pantex plutonium reprocessing facility outside Amarillo. A small blast, by strategic standards, but a normal EMP. We just flew in. The Utah and Nevada National Guard will here soon, and the regulars are all moving in. The president has put the whole central U.S. under martial law."

He asked the way to our emergency services headquarters. Because our police and fire departments were in different directions, Tom led some of the guardsmen to the fire station, while I showed others the way to the police. At the station, they were still working on the generator and Chief Hamrick was doing the best he could by flashlights and scented candles. The corporal sent with me by the captain presented him with a fixed palmer with the presidential order putting the central states under martial law. He read it with visible relief creeping over his face. "Well, at least someone's in charge and we're already dealing with it," said the Iraqi War veteran. "What's the estimated death toll?"

I hadn't even thought of that. "Possibly as high ten percent of the people from Minnesota to Mexico, between the Rockies and the Smokies," said the corporal. "It may be days before we really know."

The chief wiped the sweat from his forehead. "Are we in any danger—you know, because of our vulnerability?"

The young corporal shuffled a little bit. "I really don't know, sir, but from what I understand, our strategic defenses are essentially intact. Our silos and command systems are shielded, you know."

"Besides, other countries are having to deal with their part of this disaster," the corporal continued. "Most of the web-based AIs just got a lobotomy this afternoon, when one third of the American internet capacity went poof."

"A lot of people are suffering tonight," the Chief said bitterly.

I began to feel uncomfortable and stepped outside. I heard an unfamiliar voice call out, "Stop! Let me see your hands!"

My first reaction was that someone meant me, but then I saw a policeman down the block and a man beyond him, stepping through the broken front door of a store with an armload of cigarette cartons.

The looter just ignored the officer and started to lope down the block. The officer took off in a full run and when he was within 20 feet, the looter turned. Startled by how close the officer was, he dropped the cartons. He was holding a gun the whole time, and he took a quick shot at the officer. The bullet zipped through the branches of the tree next to me.

The officer tugged at the trigger of his pistol, but nothing happened. The looter sneered and took dead aim. I thought he had pulled the trigger, but then I realized the gunshot came from back of me. The officer turned and I heard Tom's voice from behind me:

"So much for a smart gun."

Tom had used the gun he had found in the pickup. The three of us went over to where the looter was sprawled amidst the cartons on the sidewalk.

"Damn, you're a good shot," I said. Tom had got him right in the middle of the chest. "Where'd you learn to shoot like that?"

"Baghdad" He bent over and picked up a cigarette which had fallen out of a crushed carton. "Smoke?"

The officer expressed his gratitude to Tom, and said he would go back to the station get an older gun out of his locker. Tom and I walked back to where we were both parked. I reported the conversation in the station, and also the chief's last comment, as I blew the smoke from about half a cigarette out in one blast.

"His wife has—had—an upload pacemaker."

I could see from the look on his face the picture in his mind. "Oh, crap."

"Yeah," I said. "This little fiasco is going to slow down implant technology, don't you think?"

Tom set his mouth. "Let's get back to work."


Sure as the Captain's word, within a couple of hours National Guard troops fanned into the suburbs and country from Dallas and Fort Worth, and the regulars were there by noon. We heard the whole story told many different ways.

"Friggin' old Soviet rusty-ass warhead," spat out one guardsman from Nevada. "They said it had a manual trigger—can you believe that, a manual trigger. The folks taking it apart probably had never seen that before."

"They say people in Amarillo saw the flash, but it really wasn't much of a blast," said an Army Captain from Upstate New York. "Air survey shows only one compound destroyed. No other bunkers were in danger of detonation—thank God."

Tom and I were on the road three full days—my Oldsmobile and the pickup were the only two private vehicles on the road for most of that time. We caught snippets of sleep here and there. As we grabbed some coffee at a Red Cross canteen on the second day, we finally got the straight story from a satellite television running off a generator. The Soviet Era warhead had been partially disassembled, but the old-fashioned design apparently included a large conventional charge which could be used to set off the payload manually—some type of sapper/suicide combo.

Apparently the people dismantling the warhead, used to looking for standard First Cold War nuclear configurations, didn't recognize the conventional explosive and accidentally set it off. Then the payload, although it was partially disassembled, detonated. All electronics between the Rockies and Appalachians were destroyed or badly damaged by the EMP. The monitoring and recording feeds produced a clear record of what happened.

Because the Sentinel office was near the main intersection in Cedarburg, we kept checking back during those three days we were on the road continuously. Rena stayed at the office for most of the time we were on the road, running a makeshift clinic for the less seriously injured with the supplies we had brought back, so they wouldn't clutter the hospital. She left with Dave Chaney on the third day after his ear scabbed up enough for him to head home.

After that, the office was empty except for the bodies.

By that third day, Tom and I were pretty gamey and punchy, but we knew we could in good conscience be able to knock off soon. The most seriously injured had been flown off in all directions to hospitals in other parts of the country. People were pouring into the whole Central United States from all over the world. Food distribution centers, cell phone booths and portable shower stations helped make people more comfortable while power was being restored and equipment hauled in. It was ironic but touching to see boxes of supplies and old computers labeled "Gift of Ghana" or "From the People of Azania" arriving on the big rigs. By the end of the third afternoon, the emergency services coordinator took one look at us, and then at the guardsmen and volunteers coming off a nearby bus. "You guys can go home," he said with a crooked smile. "We don't want to add your names to our list of casualties."

I went home and slept soundly for 30 hours.


It took us a while to get back on our feet. One of our competitors, the Cedarburg Chronicle, was able to get its old press up and running and actually printed a newspaper while all the other internet papers replaced and repaired their equipment. We all pooled our news. We reopened the Sentinel office two weeks after The Accident. We lost five employees—Mrs. Franzen in Accounts Receivable, Mrs. Bartlett at the front desk, and three junior employees, all under 25 who had neural implants. We had a short prayer service when we opened at 9 a.m. the first day back. We had a dozen employees who were not ready to return when we reopened. Jaypeg Tuggle didn't return for a month after that. When she came back she still had an enormous star-shaped scar on the side of her head. Some of the staff members said she should keep it that way. "It's better than a purple heart," said Tom.

But she had the work done over a few extended lunch breaks at one of the many temporary plastic surgery clinics that opened in the wake of The Accident. Dave Chaney went around for a few weeks with the remains of an ear that looked like it had been chewed on by a hungry Rottweiler. After a while, he was able to get into a clinic and they grafted on a respectable-looking cloned ear—although, as someone joked in the office, it wasn't hairy like his "real" ear.

We had to play a lot of catch-up after we re-opened, and I was occupied for months. I missed the local economic boom in plastic surgery and cloning clinics as well as computer reselling, and of course I wish I owned stock in companies that ran chip extraction kiosks in the other parts of the country.

After he returned to work, I ran into Dave Chaney in the employee lounge and stopped him.

"Do you remember, right after The Accident, when I ran out of my office?"

"Just barely," said David. "I was blacking out just as you were coming out.

"The look on your face was terrible."

David shuddered. "I guess it was the pain and the shock. Until I blacked out, for a few seconds there, I felt like my brain was boiling."

"And you only had a simple audio implant."

"Oh, God, it felt like somebody had plopped my brain into a pot of boiling water." He looked thoughtful. "Have you ever been to Maine?"

I cocked my head back. "No. What's Maine got to do with anything?"

"My grandmother lived in Maine. When I was a kid we used to visit her. I was always amazed to see how she would plop a live lobster into a pot of boiling water. My brain felt like that lobster must have felt."

I thought of something that hadn't crossed my mind in many years, and I gave a self-conscious little laugh. He looked at me funny.

"Sorry, I just remembered a short story I read in English class in high school."

"Was it in a book?"

"Yes, we still were using books then. You reminded me of it when you mentioned lobsters. Someday, when you've got some time on your hands, I'll tell you about it." But I never got around to it.


The old boy reclaimed his pickup at the hospital a week after The Accident and no one's ever seen him since. The Oldsmobile went back to my home. When I take it out for a drive or maintenance, I see people point as it goes by. It's a local legend. I did bite the bullet and spend the money to have it restored a year after The Accident. It's been a fixture now for years every Memorial Day in the city's parade. I also drive it to the local high school whenever they ask me to talk about The Accident. It's been 20 years since it happened and it's already history for them.

Tom retired a few years ago, and I'll be retiring soon myself. The last time I put the car away, after the most recent parade, I thought "I'm as old now as my grandfather was when he bought this car". I looked down at plate again. "Body by Fisher" I thought. "Well, they don't make them like they used to." Then I laughed to myself. "I'm even thinking like him now, too."

As I closed the garage door, I thought of my grandfather wagging his finger at my lip stud so many years ago. "I guess the old fellow might have been right about a few things after all."

* * *

"Body by Fisher" went out to Gardner on March 24, 2003. It arrived back on June 24—exactly three months later. This is what he wrote:

"Thanks for letting me see "Body by Fisher." I continue to be impressed by your progress. There's a lot of good stuff here, and, in fact, it's a very good description of a disaster in progress, and an interesting and little-used one at that.

"The problem is, it's not really a story—or not enough of one anyway. Here your journalistic instincts are working against you. In spite of all the running around taking people to the hospital that he does, the narrator is basically passive, an uninvolved observer. What's happening doesn't mean anything to him, emotionally, he doesn't have any emotional stake in the outcome, going through this experience doesn't change him in any particular way, for either good or ill.

"He's just watching what's happening, interestedly reporting the details, like a good journalist. But to involve readers in a story you have to put them into the story—which means that you have to put yourself into the story through your character in an emotionally vested way. If what's happening doesn't mean much to the main character, it's not going to mean much to the reader, either.

"Readers want to know not only, What happens next? but Why should I care what happens next? What are the stakes, what is there at risk to be lost? If the main character doesn't feel any of that edge, the reader won't either.

"So I'm going to pass on this one, but you're making good progress, and I think you're going to make it one of these days."

There's a lot of good stuff in those preceding 257 words (which is an enormous amount of feedback from an editor). Gardner was, and is, right—although my journalism background is a plus as far as the technical aspects of writing the English language, it's a hindrance because of my instinct to be objective.

The middle three paragraphs of his response are some of the best advice you can get if you want to write speculative fiction.

I took some time and heeded his advice and did a major rewrite to the story. To make the protagonist more sympathetic, in the final version I have him help minister to the wounded receptionist, Jaypeg (boy, have I caught chuckles over the years because of that name) and marry her later. That also made him have that personal stake in the action that Gardner said was needed.

To make the story easier to follow, I changed the point of view, from having the narrator recalling the story to himself, to his telling the story to his daughter, the product of his marriage to Jaypeg. The introduction of the daughter fulfilled one of the crucial things readers want in a character—to see how they were changed by the experience. Despite how horrible the accident was, the protagonist wouldn't have found his love and his family without growing through it.

Ultimately, the story was published in 2007 in the souvenir book published in conjunction with the Dallas science fiction convention Fencon. It's common for conventions to ask guest authors to contribute stories to a book which is a bonus to convention registrants. This was the first time I was asked to do that, so I gave them "Body by Fisher". The story was tweaked a number of places, but here is the final ending that shows the essential change:

\* \* \*

When I take it out for a drive or maintenance, I see people point as it goes by. After 20 years it's a local legend. I did bite the bullet and spend the money to have it restored a year after The Accident. It's been a fixture now for years every Memorial Day in the city's parade.

"When I drive it in the parade, Jaypeg usually comes along and waves. Our teenage daughter Tif is much too cool to ride along any more.

The other day I was putting the Oldsmobile into the garage, and I heard Tif behind me.

"Hey, dad, how yer doin?'"

I knew she was up to something, so I turned around.

It looked like she had a little antenna alongside her head straight up from her right ear.

"What the hell is that?"

"Latest thing, dad. New tech, you know. Great for downloads."

"I know your mother hasn't seen that, or I would have heard it. She'll smack you silly, you know."

"Actually, mom says she's OK with it."

"Ah! I don't believe that!"

"She said she knows the new shielding technology is safe. She's not as old a fart as you, you know. Besides," she said fixing me with those big blue eyes, "isn't that how y'all met?"

I stuck my hand out and waved her towards me. She came over and I put my arm around her shoulder.

"You wanna hear a story. Have I ever really told you what it was like?"

She looked up at me as we walked towards the house. "Tell me about it."

"I always ate breakfast at Whataburger. I was single back then. Your mom smiled at me when I came in the office that morning..."

*   *   *

The rewrite made the protagonist more involved in the story, and as the ending shows, the events surrounding "The Accident" really ended up meaning a lot to him.

One final note. It's been said that you have to hook the editor (or slush pile reader) at the very beginning of your story to make them turn the first page and keep reading.

One of the virtues from when "Body" was printed in the FenCon book was that it had a nice layout, a double-page spread with art—a depiction of the "Oldsmotank".

The very beginning of the story was included in the layout of that spread:

"I was ready to log on to a competitor's web site when I heard a sizzling sound and the screen went blank.  An acrid smell hit my nose.  I looked up and saw the calendar hologram on the wall just as it blinked out.  It read March 18. I looked quickly at my watch. It was an analog style and had stopped at 3:18.

"Then I began to hear the screams and moans."

Something made me pull out the original manuscript of the story, and I saw those seven sentences were what was on the cover page, as the story began beneath my identifying information and byline.

So I guess I achieved my goal of hooking the reader.

# Chapter 5

## Letting the Cat
## Out of the Bag

With the positive feedback I'd been getting I decided I'd try a more ambitious and wide-ranging story, so the next thing I sent Gardner, in March 2003, was "The Rocket-Powered Cat".

The story arises from my desire to explore what would it be like if a journalist could see the future—if he or she was a "precog".

I fall back upon my journalism background again in this story, although at its heart is a little observation I once heard about the differences between how boys and girls first fall in love.

It was my first major mis-fire.

First, the story is badly dated by a reference right off the bat to a specific incident that no one remembers any more, a documentary done by British journalist Martin Bashir that was shown in the United States in February 2003 (Bashir is most recently known in 2013 for a filthy insult on the air in the U.S. directed towards Sarah Palin).

Secondly… well, here's the story, and we'll get the Gardner's criticism and the rewrite later.

# The Rocket-Powered Cat

I was at the age when you first begin to notice the outside world—for me, it was about the third grade—when that infamous Michael Jackson interview was broadcast. I remember staring at the old-fashioned flat 2-D screen and somehow being appalled at how he was opening up and making a complete jackass of himself in front of millions.

Of course, I wouldn't have verbalized it that way then. But it was my reaction, and I wasn't following my parents' lead—they were out someplace that night. I was alone and the room was dark except for the television. Do you remember how those old screens could light up a room?

I also clearly remember having one of those deja vus precogs get when we see or encounter something that prefigures a significant event in our future. Of course, at the time I had no idea what that feeling meant, just as I had no idea I would later be identified as a precog after the government's Project Cassandra went public while I was in high school.

I didn't enjoy the 'honor' and I guess because I didn't want to feel like a freak, I didn't accept the government's offer of a scholarship and a job. I went to college and earned a journalism degree, and was hired right out of the chute as a reporter for the News of the Nation.

Most employees there looked at me sideways because of my being identified as a precog. Some said I must be borderline, otherwise I'd have that government job. Truth is, I was identified as "low functioning". There's a difference between ability and motivation. I guess I am a bit of a slouch, otherwise why would I have taken a journalism degree to a tabloid like News of the Nation?

In the St. Petersburg area, the concentration of national tabloid offices has been dubbed "Anthrax Alley" ever since the terrorist attack two decades earlier at the start of the Iraqi War. All the tabloid newspaper headquarters are boxy and windowless. Making your way through the warren of halls and cubicles at the News of the Nation, you expected to bump into a wedge of cheese any moment. The Editor-in-Chief's office was not a place I would normally pass by, so he called for me.

"How would you like to interview J.R. Powell?"

He was cracking his neck and looking away.

"Like he needs any more publicity?"

Dansko fixed his gaze on me. "He's hard to ignore, you know."

"Any intern can interview a publicity hound like him."

John Dansko was a journalism veteran. He started in the business when newspapers were still ink and paper, and he took the job at the News of the Nation so he could gather a little nest egg for his retirement. Despite the long hours and sedentary lifestyle, he still had a formidably stocky build.

"Yes, he's been overexposed. We need a new angle. That's why I think you should interview him."

He lowered his voice and wagged his bushy brows. "Maybe you can use your special powers!"

For a second I thought he was serious. "Screw you!" I laughed.

"Honestly, Zvi, I think you have the sensitivity—and honestly, who knows whether it's related to your other abilities—to snoop and sniff out a fresh angle on this story."

He sucked on a nicotine stick and looked thoughtful. "It would be a real coup if you could find out, at the risk of using a cliché, the secret of his success."

"He's never been shy about explaining that. He says 'the secret's in the software.'"

"Well, maybe you can find out whether that's true, or whether it's something else. I doubt Powell's Pardners software has some kind of magic code or super-AI. Maybe he just happens to have the very best software combined with a really savvy organization. Not to mention some good old-fashioned PR smarts."

"Well, you have to admit, the cruise ships are popular," I interjected.

Dansko could tell I was setting on the hook and he began to reel me in.

"What we—you—could contribute to the big picture is to find out how much of this is the software system—really, despite what Powell claims—and how much of this is just old fashioned bullshit and razzle-dazzle."

"In other words," he said as he put his arms around my narrow shoulders, "this is one of those special times when what we are looking for and real journalism happens to coincide."

He continued with his best New York olive oil salesman pitch. "You have a very unusual distinction among the members of the staff of this publication which might very well come in handy. A journalism degree."

"OK," I thought, "so Powell is fair game for an expose."

"Sounds good," I said.

Dansko smiled and rubbed his hands. "Take a couple of days and do some serious research, and then we'll fly you to Dallas. Don't forget to take your umbrella."

I nonchalantly gave him the traditional journalism salute as I left.

With the Powell Pardners' jingle running through my head, I spent a couple of days downloading and reading everything I could find on the dating service. I needed to do some serious research if I was going to get any special insight into Powell and his system.

Matchmaking goes back thousands of years. Only a century ago the most reliable of operations would be an umbrella-carrying shadkan strolling down the block on the Lower East Side. We had one in my family.

Just a generation ago computer databases and video archives tried to improve on that record, with little success. I remembered the hilarious "Lowered Expectations" parodies on Mad TV when I was young.

Then John Roberts Powell did a cannonball into the nationwide pool of singles. Some of his 'system' was obvious enough. It was clear from the requirement that you allow complete access to your consumer records that some kind of intelligent database was assembled by the software he was using.

If Powell's claim that 'the secret's in the software' was true, this software must be using extraordinarily sophisticated automated data discovery and analysis, and pulling out specific patterns and trends which were used to match up people in a way that only Powell understands.

I kept reading through files on the flight to Dallas. As we crossed the Louisiana border, the captain pointed out a reservoir that gleamed like blue metal below us. Lake Columbia was completed after the shuttle disaster and named because it lay in the path of the debris field that had stretched from Dallas across East Texas .

The shuttle disaster was at almost the same time as that Michael Jackson interview. I had a major deja vu then also. Remembering it, I shuddered.

DFW Airport was shrouded in a steady drizzle, and it spritzed the whole way into Dallas. You could see along the highway the new growth forest rising up as a result of the increasing rainfall out of what had been prairie before.

Dallas' economy was picking up as businesses fled Houston, fearful of what the rising Gulf of Mexico might do. But Powell was not a refugee; in fact he was a Dallas native, and had been in the travel and vacation business for years before hitting the jackpot with Powell's Pardners. That's where he had experience with cruise ships.

The cruise ships were great places for people being matched by the dating service to get to know each other without outside distractions. But Powell's Pardners had almost a 100% success rate, 99.37% to be exact. No theory advanced by anyone so far could account for that.

The North Dallas Radisson showed all the signs of the battle against the mold and mildew the city was fighting. These Texas buildings had not been designed for humid weather, and the signs of the struggle were everywhere.

I saw as we pulled up, a relatively new two-story structure that was obviously an expansion to the HVAC system shoehorned between the side of the hotel and the parking lot. Most large structures in Dallas had found it necessary to double or treble the size of their air conditioning systems to try to suck the moisture out of the air.

Inside, boxes of filters lay on a pallet in a corner of the lobby, which reeked of ammonia and soap. I'm sure the staff fought furiously to keep the mildew at bay.

More than a few of the magazines in the lobby store had stories about Powell and/or Powell's Pardners. I assumed they were displayed prominently as Dallas was obviously proud of its native son.

"How to Find Your Pardner"

"Matchmaker of the Millennium"

"This J.R. from Dallas Does Good"

And so forth.

I knew from my most recent stay in Dallas to ask for a smoking room when asked for my accommodation preferences. I hoped the smoke would overpower the mildew. The room was clammy and typical now of the Texas Tropics. I put the portable dehumidifier on the desk as I opened my laptop and popped up a few holopages.

J.R. Powell was 60 and basking in this success which had come to him so late in his life. He was careful to remain the front man and personification of the business, and it took some intensive googling to come up with the names of a few people I felt might be key contributors to his success.

There was a software company that went by the name Silverado that had an exclusive contract with Powell's Pardners. It obviously played a pivotal if undisclosed role in the development of its software system; there was no indication in any record that Powell himself knew the difference between an intelligent database and a chicken fried steak.

I also spread on my bed all the video sheets and printouts put out by Powell's Pardners itself. The interview checklist, which Dansko got somewhere, covered those kinds of personal questions that have been standard for years. Nothing enlightening here, just a way of making sure you didn't match up cat people with dog people or Mozart fans with Deadheads.

I even had a copy of the contract, a printout copied from an animated gif sheet only given to people after an interview. How Dansko got that, I wouldn't guess.

The contract demanded a complete release of a person's consumer database for their use and analysis; Of course, it promised the strictest confidentiality.

For almost 30 years now, actual and virtual commerce sites have been directly downloading their log files to data warehouses. The fact Powell's Pardners did not take any clients under 25 would lead anyone to suppose mining this data was crucial to the success of its software.

I did a meta-search on the individuals who made up Silverado Software and I began to pore over their backgrounds, published papers and curriculum vitae. The usual languages and software used in data mining went by: Intelligent database management systems, link analysis tools, automatic discovery——the work tools of so many cyber sweatshops.

The biographies and papers pretty much reflected the same types of expertise, and then I caught something out of the corner of my eye. One of the developers, a twentyish fellow named John Armstrong, also had a few papers published on game theory.

"Now we're getting somewhere," I muttered to myself. A software developer who works on software for a dating service who also knows something about game theory.

"What's your game, John Powell?" I thought as I scratched my chin and began to doze off.

Before the cab arrived the next morning, I googled more on John Armstrong and found he had a much more extensive background in game theory than first appeared. I instinctively knew this was the clue, the hook, I needed for the interview. But I would be flying by the seat of my pants because I couldn't realistically contact Armstrong first.

Not only did I not have the time, but I'm sure if I contacted Armstrong before meeting with Powell, he'd tell Powell. I knew I probably would have one shot at Powell. When he realized I wasn't doing a puff piece, the interview would probably go downhill rapidly.

I don't mind burning a bridge or two if it serves my purpose, but I can't afford to take them out before I cross them.

The Pardners corporate office was only a few miles from the Radisson and you could see from some residual outside signage it once was Powell's travel service office. It had been seriously upgraded, and had the cute and hokey Powell's Pardners western motif promotional poster sheets on its walls.

Other than a bandanna neckerchief, the lead receptionist was dressed professionally.

"Mr. Powell is expecting you, Mr. Yakir."

Powell's office was a walnut-paneled den full of western prints, shadow boxes and small bronzes. His bright shirt and florid face made him stand out like a light bulb.

"I am honored to be interviewed by a reporter from the largest newspaper in the nation," he said, as he squeezed my hand into putty.

"Bullshit," I thought, "and I don't need precog powers to know this guy is schnockered."

He introduced his personal assistant, Catherine, a thin blonde girl who looked like a first year college intern.

He had the genial affability of someone who spends his waking hours liquored up, and was actually very personable during the first half hour as he went over his personal and business background and how he founded Powell's Pardners.

"I needed a gimmick, as it were, to perk up my cruise bookings," he said, swirling around 'orange squeezings' in a juice glass. Some oranges.

"I thought of tightly bundling cruise bookings with a dating service, and I found when I used the right software and put the right people together on a first class fun cruise, happiness happened."

"I never knew Texas produced so much cheese," I thought. "I'm gonna blow."

Powell looked at his glass wistfully and I realized he was probably holding back on imbibing. I had a thought.

"By the way, can I have something to drink? I'm getting a little dry."

"What would you like?"

"Well, what you're having looks tasty."

Powell's eyes lit up. "I'll pour you one."

I pretty much avoided any pointed questions while I had a couple of drinks; as I supposed, Powell tripled my pace. I could see Catherine fidgeting.

I wanted to tighten the noose gently. "I know you can't, and really shouldn't, discuss the specifics of the software you use to organize and sift through your database."

I began to sip my third drink. "Like you say, 'the secret's in the software.'"

Powell beamed a stupid self-satisfied grin of recognition.

"It's obvious that your software has top notch database analysis tools. Maybe you'd like to talk—only in generalities, of course—about your game theory components of the software, where the genius of your system lies."

I stressed the pronouns to play to his vanity. His eyes lit up in recognition at the mention of "game theory". I could see Catherine making a move to get his attention, but he waved her off as he stood up rapidly. For a second I thought I was in trouble.

He began to pace, clutching his glass, and he talked very deliberately.

"Are you married, Mr. Yakir?"

"No sir. "

"I'm not married, now. I've been married three times so far. You know what, Mr. Yakir? None of these women were what I would have called the great loves of my life."

He turned to face me. "The problem was, the women—the girls, I was young once—that I loved the most in my life didn't want me when I wanted them."

He looked down into the glass like he expected to see something. "Then the years go by, and you run into an old flame, and you find they married some jerk who's ten times the loser you'd ever be on your worst day. Why?"

I shook my head, and realized I was feeling the liquor, too. Catherine had shrunk back in her seat and wasn't even pointing her recorder at Powell.

Powell spread wide his arms. "I found the answer, with the help of a sharp software developer named Jack Armstrong. I'm sure you never heard of him, he's actually pretty quiet. Not like me."

"Sorry, the name doesn't ring a bell."

"Like I said a while back, I thought to merge my cruise bookings with a dating service when business began to sag a few years ago. I got a good lead on an outfit called Silverado Software in Plano."

I widened my eyes and looked as interested as I could.

"Rather than adapt some off-the-shelf software they already had, Jack suggested he could really whip up something special for me."

Now I really was interested and I perched on the edge of the chair. I looked out the corner of my eye to make sure my recorder was running, and I almost slipped off the front of the seat. Powell pretended to jump and I saw his realization I was tipsy relaxed him.

"One night we met at Bennihanagan's, and got real social. Come to find out Jack had a unique idea. He had been working, on his own for his own personal use, on some real sophisticated software using, hmm…

intelligent automated analysis, he called it. He said he thought we could use it for the dating service."

"If you got people to sign off on accessing their personal databases?"

"That's it. You're a sharp kid. Jack said it was a matter of sociobioloical, uhh, sociobillical..."

"Sociobiology?"

"Anyhow, I asked Jack how he planned to make it work. He said it was all the way you played the game theory."

Somehow I had a mental image of an older embittered man boozing it up in a bar with a younger bitter man.

"He said when he was in college, of course his major was computer science, but his minor was in sociobiology."

"That's an interesting combination."

"Yes, and he never forgot a particular study he worked on for the Sociobiology Department. It was on how seriously people regard romances based on their ordinal rank."

"You mean, first love versus second love and so forth?"

"Right. Their survey showed that men and women play the dating game totally differently."

I saw out of the corner of my eye that Catherine was flat up against the back of her chair.

"You see, if you dug deep and got honest answers, John said, you found boys and girls first loves are totally different. We men are dopes. Our first love, our first crush, is the most serious. That's why it's called puppy love. We're as devoted as dopey dogs. And you know it's true."

I gave as noncommittal a nod as I could.

"Women, girls, are the opposite. Their first romance is the least serious. A flirtation, a trifle. They don't take it seriously."

Powell grabbed a white china marker that was behind a collectible plate sitting on the credenza behind his desk.

"This is what we worked out on a napkin."

He strode to a wall and made two big stars, one high and one low. He pointed to the lower star. "Here is the girl's seriousness and expectations for her first romance. And this," he said pointing to the higher star, "is the boy's."

He turned and faced me. "Now this line," and he scraped a descending line on the wall, "is the boy's seriousness and expectations as he gets rejected in each successive love affair."

He scraped an ascending line from the lower star. "The girl, on the other hand, gets more serious and expects more of a relationship each time."

Where the lines crossed, he drew a neat circle. "At some point, the man will marry the next woman who'll have him, because he doesn't care anymore. And there's a point where the woman will marry the next guy who comes around the corner because she's desperate."

He pointed triumphantly at the circle and crossed lines. "Here, where the man's apathy crosses the woman's desperation, we find true romance." His drunken words dripped of sarcasm.

Catherine had a mounted brook trout look. I must have gone completely blank, because Powell didn't seem to register a reaction from me. He looked at me and raised his eyebrows. I had to say something.

"You're telling me you worked on this together, then? I guess you want Jack to get some recognition?"

He brightened a bit. "Oh heck, there's no reason Jack should be hiding his candle under a basket. We came up with the system together. I worked up the questionnaires, and he came up with the software. He's just a lot more shy than I am."

"You think he's shy now," I thought.

I put my chin in my hands and nodded. "OK, I understand where you are coming from, but you're telling me that Armstrong came up with an analysis tool subtle enough to go through a data mine and see a pattern that tells when a person is ready for a serious relationship?"

Powell snorted. "Not only can his software run through and analyze past relationships, but it checks to see if you're telling the truth. Dinner, movies, flowers and gifts might verify a relationship. If a guy says he broke up with a gal in March 2017, and the program sees a spike in his liquor consumption that month, that's a sign he's telling the truth. For a woman, often chocolate means the same thing."

I smiled.

"If a man or a woman says they tend to have serious and long-term relationships, and the software sees they buy condoms or spermicide every week, we know they're bullshitting."

"I find this hard to believe. This still has to be incredibly complex."

"I provide the real-life savvy, and he writes the software and tweaks it on a regular basis. It's obvious the program works. The safeguard is when we throw these people together on a cruise, we put together people who came out closely plotted on spread sheet, as it were, so that if the people we thought were the closest to taking the plunge together still don't hit it off, the second choice is there, and the third and so forth. Our 'activity directors' actually have the compatibility ratings cross-referenced so they know who's supposed to be hitting it off with who… I mean whom"

I think the adrenaline rush was starting to sober him up, so I poured two drinks and handed him one. He sat down like he was drained, but he wanted to finish.

"You take one part sociobiology, one part game theory and one part data mining, mix it all together and, wallah! A match every time."

I knew I had my story and now I was at the point where I needed to make an exit or I would be too woozy to depart gracefully. I rose and shook his hand.

"It's a great story, and you're a real genius and business success, I must admit. Nobody in the world could ever duplicate such an ingenious program."

Powell gave a shit-eating grin and leaned back in his chair. I nodded to Catherine who looked like she had just lost a winning lottery ticket. I hustled myself out and left without looking back. I didn't even hail a cab, but went around the corner and caught one there. I went back to the hotel, fell on my bed and put my hands on my head.

Dansko just kept saying "holy shit, holy shit, holy shit" softly over and over again after my recording finished. "I can't believe he admitted this."

"Do we really, really want to go through with this?"

Dansko looked me square in the eye. "Warnings have been sounded for years about all this personal data collection and its potential for being used for manipulation and even fraud. Now we have a clear-cut example of how it can be abused."

Deep down I knew he was right.

The graphics department came up with a neat little animation showing a man and woman as marionettes and Powell as the puppet master. In the corner, a scraggly cat leapt from a sack.

"Master Matchmaker Lets the Cat Out of the Bag!"

Needless to say, before and after the story ran, Silverado and Powell's Pardners threatened dire legal action. Dansko basically told them "My lawyer can beat up your lawyer," and with a company the size of News of the Nation, that's true.

Armstrong escaped relatively unscathed in the story. Because I never spoke to him first-hand, he couldn't be named much in the story. To this day I've never spoken to the man. I understand he's had a great career subsequently working on other software development.

The sheets sold out at the newsstands and downloads topped a half billion. There may have been a camel driver in Baluchistan who didn't read the story, but he probably ordered a printed copy in the mail.

The news media soon picked up on the story. I saw videos of the Pardners office dark and empty in Dallas. The Silverado office in Plano was padlocked. I was interviewed for a few pieces myself.

I thought there might have been some hostility directed towards me for writing the piece, but Powell's words hung him. Another reporter said the topic reminded him of menstruation; it may be true and it may be a fact of life, but no one likes to talk about it, and no one likes anyone who makes money from it.

A couple of days after the story broke, another reporter hailed me in the newsroom.

"Well, we lost a great subject today."

I was ready for the worst. "Has something happened to J.R. Powell?"

"Oh, no, haven't you heard? Michael Jackson kicked off in California."

The realization I had staggered me and I had to sit down for a minute. That precog moment I had so long ago came back to me. What was the reporter's name? Martin Bashir? I just pulled the same trick. Reeled out the rope and watched a fool throw it over the beam and hang himself. Why didn't I see it coming?

It was a week later when Dansko called me into his office and gave me the news. "I'm afraid the pendulum of public opinion might be ready to swing against you. Powell's dead."

I got a cold feeling in my gut. "Did he commit suicide?"

"No, he was out drinking in a Dallas bar and woman walked up and shot him."

"Was it an ex-wife?"

"Umm, actually from what I've heard, it was his senior prom date. Like when he was in high school."

I just sat there.

"Take some time off, stay home, and I'll call you in a few days."

He nodded with a wry smile for me to head out the door.

I was almost out. "Don't beat yourself up, by the way. It was my idea."

"I know, it's just like the saying goes. Be careful of what you wish for."

"You might just get it," and he looked away

#

Two days later the little food I had in my bachelor's refrigerator had run out, so I ventured down to the market.

I was standing in line at the checkout, waiting to wave my index finger at the scanner, so it could debit my bank account and log what I had bought.

The tabloid sheets with their changing screens sat in the racks. All had the latest headlines.

"Powell dies in Data Mine Collapse"

"Cupid's Arrow Smites Sociobiology Snitch"

"Loose Lips Sinks Dating Ships"

And so forth.

An old lady in front of me looked me in the face, looked at the rack, and then back at me, shaking her head. I half-turned and the middle-aged lady behind me looked at my face.

"You're the fellow who let the cat out of the bag." She had obviously seen News of the Nation the week before.

I just gave a tight-lipped smile. I scanned and scooted as fast as I could with my groceries.

Back in my apartment, I sat down and just vegged for a minute. I was numb. The Powell story was the biggest expose in my professional career. "Well, certainly got what I wanted in a big way," I thought. "When I let that cat out of the bag, he had rockets on."

Now I knew the Powell story is what caused the deja vu when I saw the Michael Jackson interview years ago. I thought back to when the Columbia exploded, and that deja vu. What does that prefigure? Whatever it is, it hasn't happened yet. A plane crash.? Another spectacular national disaster?

I think it's time for me to take one of those government jobs, and in the meantime get the training to hone my skills. They say skilled precogs can recognize events in their future which they have foreseen sweeping up on them. I didn't enjoy the feeling I got when I realized I should have recognized the Powell interview for what it was.

Maybe I can get away with only being a junior grade freak. I don't want any more surprises. Cats can be very sneaky, too

\*   \*   \*

Well, as you read along, any number of problems probably came to mind. Gardner returned the story in August 2003, and this is what he wrote:

"Thanks for letting me see 'The Rocket-Powered Cat'. This makes good use of your journalism background, which is good, but the precog idea seem loosely attached to the plot, not really necessary at all—and without it, the fantastic element is really kind of thin.

"So I'm going to pass on this one, but, of course, let me see more when you have it."

Ouch! As I've said before, if a comment in a rejection resonates with you, it's probably true. I knew in my gut Gardner was right; I had grafted together two incompatible story threads

I felt grateful he was still encouraged me to submit, though, so he still had faith in me.

I made a few minor tweaks, but I suspected the story would need a substantial rewrite. Before doing a major overhaul I tossed it into the slush pile of an Australian magazine, *Andromeda Spaceways In-flight Magazine* in October 2003.

It passed the slush pile reader and was forwarded to the editors and a second round for consideration. However, they ultimately rejected it in November.

The panel of editors almost exactly duplicated Gardner's comments.

"It's a good solid story that's well told and quite interesting," said one.

*But*, said another, "The author seems to have tried to write two stories here, one about precog, and one about data mining, and they don't sit together very well for me—I felt that the story in here was muddied, and it lost focus at the end."

That did it, I acknowledged I would have to bite the bullet and do a major rewrite, and I did. The pre-cog business has to go. This is the only case of all the stories reprinted in this book where the original and final versions of the story are different enough that I am printing both versions.

So here is the revised version of "The Rocket-Powered Cat":

\* \* \*

I was standing in the supermarket checkout line when I saw a half dozen tabloid poly sheets sitting in the racks. All had different takes on the killing.

"Powell dies in Data Mine Collapse"

"Cupid's Arrow Smites Sociobiology Snitch"

"Loose Lips Sinks Dating Ships"

"Powell's Pardners Ends in Tragedy"

"Hell Hath No Fury..."

And the headline for *The News of the Nation*—where I worked—"We Let the Cat Out of the Bag!"

An old lady in front of me looked at me, looked at the rack, and then back at me. She recognized me and shook her head.

In the St. Petersburg area, all the tabloid newspaper headquarters were in the same general vicinity. *The News of the Nation* was a typical large windowless boxy office building. There were parts of it I had never ventured into. The Editor-in-Chief's office was not a place I would normally pass by, so he called for me.

"How would you like to interview J.R. Powell?"

He cracked his neck and looked away.

"Like he needs any more publicity?"

Dansko fixed his gaze on me. "He's hard to ignore, you know."

"Any intern can interview a publicity hound like him."

John Dansko was a journalism veteran. He started in the business when major newspapers were still ink and paper, and he took the job at *The News of the Nation* so he could gather a little nest egg for his retirement. Despite the long hours and sedentary lifestyle, he still had a formidably stocky build.

"Yes, he's been overexposed. We need a new angle. That's why I think you should interview him."

He lowered his voice and wagged his bushy brows. "You're still young and uncorrupted!"

"Screw you!" I laughed.

"Honestly, I think you have the sensitivity to snoop out a fresh angle on this story."

He sucked on a nicotine stick and looked thoughtful. "It would be a real coup if you could find out, at the risk of using a cliché, *the secret of his success.*"

I guess Dansko could tell from my body language I was interested.

"What we —you—could contribute to the big picture is to find out how much of this is the software system—really, despite what Powell claims—and how much of this is just old-fashioned bullshit and razzle-dazzle. In other words," he put his arms around my narrow shoulders, "this is one those special times when what we are looking for and real journalism happens to coincide."

*OK*, I thought, *so Powell is fair game for an exposé.* "Sounds good," I said.

Dansko smiled and rubbed his hands. "Take a couple of days and do some serious research, and then we'll fly you over to Dallas."

I nonchalantly gave him the traditional one-fingered journalism salute as I left.


I spent a couple of days downloading and reading everything I could find on the dating service. I needed some serious research if I was going to get any special insight into Powell and his system.

Matchmaking goes back thousands of years. Only a century ago, the most reliable of operations would be an umbrella-carrying *shadkan* strolling down the block on the Lower East Side. We had one in my family. Just a generation ago, computer databases and video archives tried to improve on that record, with little success. I remembered the hilarious "Lowered Expectations" parodies on *Mad TV* when I was a kid.

Then John Roberts Powell did a cannonball into the nationwide pool of singles.

I had a ton of material to go over, and I was still reading on the flight to Dallas. The usual languages and software used in data mining went by as I read: Intelligent database management systems, link analysis tools, automatic systemic analysis—the tools of so many cyber sweatshops.

As we crossed the Texas-Louisiana border, the captain pointed out Lake Columbia below us, the reservoir which had been created where the remains of the space shuttle fell to earth more than 40 years ago.

DFW Airport was shrouded in a steady drizzle, and it spritzed the whole way into the city. You could see along the highway the new growth forest rising up as a result of the increased rainfall.

Dallas' economy was picking up as businesses fled Houston, fearful of what the rising Gulf of Mexico might do. Galveston and Texas City were already under the waves, and the booms protecting Houston were creaking and ready to blow.

As I walked through the lobby of the North Dallas Radisson, I saw boxes of filters lying on a pallet. I knew they had to run the AC constantly to keep the humidity at bay.

My room was clammy but not too bad. I put the portable dehumidifier on the desk as I opened my laptop and propped up a few holopages.

J.R. Powell was 60 and basking in the success that had come to him so late in life. I spread out on my bed all the video sheets and printouts put out by Powell's Pardners itself. The applicant interview checklist, which Dansko got somewhere and had forwarded to me in Dallas, covered the kind of personal questions that have been standard with matchmaking services for years. Nothing special here, just a way of making sure you didn't match up cat people with dog people or Mozart fans with Goth head bangers.

For almost 30 years now, actual and virtual commerce sites have been directly downloading their log files to data warehouses. The customer contract with Powell's Pardners demanded a complete release of a person's consumer database for their use and analysis; of course, it promised the strictest confidentiality, but it was still fairly unusual in its scope.

Even with what little specialized knowledge I had, I could tell data mining and analysis was secondary to the way Powell played game theory. *What's your game, John Powell?* I thought as I scratched my chin and began to doze off.

Before the cab arrived the next morning, I googled more on Powell, and found he had a much greater background in data mining and game theory than first appeared. I also knew I would probably have only one shot at him. When he realized I wasn't doing a puff piece, everything would implode. I don't mind burning a bridge or two if it serves my purpose, but I can't afford to take them out before I cross them.

The Pardners corporate office was only a few miles from the Radisson. It had the hokey Powell's Pardners western motif on its walls. Other than a bandanna neckerchief, the lead receptionist was dressed professionally.

"Mr. Powell is expecting you, Mr. Yakir."

Powell's office was a walnut-paneled den full of western prints, shadow boxes, and small bronzes. His bright shirt and florid face made him stand out like a light bulb.

"I am honored to be interviewed by a reporter from the largest newspaper in the nation," he said, as he squeezed my hand into putty.

*Bullshit*, I thought, *and this guy is seriously schnockered at 11AM.*

He had the genial affability of someone who spends his waking hours liquored up, and was actually very personable during the first half hour, as he went over his personal and business background and how he founded Powell's Pardners. He continually sipped "orange squeezings" in a juice glass.

Some oranges.

"I used to operate a travel service here in Dallas that would book on cruise lines that did weekend excursions in the Gulf of Mexico," he said. "You know, making lazy 8s in the water while everyone had a fun time. I kinda segued through that into the dating service. I found when I used the right software and put the right people together on a first class fun cruise, happiness happened."

*I never knew Texas produced so much cheese*, I thought. *I'm gonna hurl.*

Powell looked at his glass wistfully, and I realized he was probably holding back a bit. I had a thought.

"By the way, can I have something to drink? I'm getting a little dry."

"What would you like?"

"Well, what you're having looks good."

Powell's eyes lit up. "I'll pour you one."

I pretty much avoided any pointed questions while I had a couple of drinks; as I had supposed, Powell tripled my pace.

I wanted to tighten the noose gently. "I know you can't discuss the specifics of the software you use to organize and sift through your database."

I began to sip my third drink. "Like you say in your ads, 'the secret's in the software.' But I wondered if we could talk in generalities." I wanted to keep him talking. "It's obvious that your software has top-notch database analysis tools. Maybe you'd like to talk—only in generalities, of course—about your game theory components of the software, where the genius of your system lies."

I stressed the pronouns to play to his vanity. His eyes lit up in recognition at the mention of "game theory."

He began to pace the office, clutching his glass, and he talked very deliberately.

"Are you married, Mr. Yakir?"

"No, sir."

"I'm not married, now. I've been married three times so far. You know what, Mr. Yakir? None of these women were what I would have called the great loves of my life."

He turned to face me. "The problem was, the women—the girls, I was young once—that I loved the most in my life didn't want me when I wanted them."

He looked down into the glass like he expected to see something. "Then the years go by, and you run into an old flame, and you find they married some jerk who's ten times the loser you'd ever be on your worst day. Why?"

I shook my head and shrugged, and realized I was feeling the liquor, too.

Powell spread wide his arms. "I found the answer a while back, when I went to merge my cruise bookings with a dating service, which I thought would create synergy and greater efficiency."

I widened my eyes and looked as interested as I could.

"I had been working on my own, just for grins, on some software using intelligent automated analysis. The software I picked up with the dating service gave me an idea, made something click. If you got people to sign off on completely accessing their personal databases and plugged in the right game theory projections…"

Here he belched and staggered a bit. I smiled most innocently. "This is all so fascinating," I said.

"Ahh, where was I?" Powell scratched his head and then looked up brightly. "It all came back to me one day. A report I read years ago when I was studying at UT. It was a study on sociable… socialistically… socio…"

"Socio-economics?" I asked brightly.

"No, that's not it." Powell snapped his fingers clumsily. "Sociobiology! That's it!" He smiled rather widely. "I never forgot a particular sociobiology study I read in psych class. It was on how seriously people regard romances, based on their ordinal rank."

"You mean, first love versus second love and so forth?" I asked.

"Right. The survey showed that men and women play the dating game very differently."

I sat back and tried to look nonchalant. I knew he was on the hook.

"You see, if you dig deep and get honest answers, you find boys' and girls' first loves are totally different. We men are dopes. Our first love, our first crush, is the most serious. That's why it's called puppy love. We're as devoted as puppy dogs. You know it's true."

I gave as noncommittal a nod as I could.

"Women, girls, are the opposite. Their first romance is the least serious. A flirtation, a trifle. They don't take it seriously."

Powell grabbed a dry erase marker that was behind a collectible plate sitting on the credenza behind his desk.

"This is what I worked out."

He strode to a wall and made two big stars, one high and one low. He pointed to the lower star. "Here is the girl's seriousness and expectations for her first romance. And this," he said pointing to the higher star, "is the boy's."

He turned and faced me. "Now this line," and he scraped a descending line on the wall, "is the boy's expectations as he gets rejected in each successive love affair."

He scraped an ascending line from the lower star. "The girl, on the other hand, gets more serious each time."

Where the lines crossed, he drew a big circle. "At some point, the man will marry the next woman who'll have him, because he doesn't give a damn any more. And there's a point where the woman will marry the next guy she goes out with because she's frantic. If you can put together two people whose lines are ready to cross, at the point where the man's descending apathy meets the woman's rising desperation—it's true love!"

I must have gone completely blank, because Powell didn't seem to register a reaction from me. He looked at me and waggled his eyebrows. I had to say something.

"This still has to be incredibly difficult," I said rather weakly.

"Not as much as you think. Besides, in the old days, all we had to go on was the questionnaire the clients filled out. Now we have all this database collection going on."

He swirled the ice cubes around in his cocktail glass. "For example, my software can compare dates and see whether the client is bullshitting on the questionnaire—which is more common than you would think," he said. "If the client said he was deeply committed to a single relationship, and the data mine shows he was making multiple on-line gift purchases and sending them to different locations, it's obvious he's stringing more than one gal along at the same time. It also works the other way. If a guy says a relationship was only casual, and his liquor consumption spiked after the break-up, it might be he is covering up how much he was hurt."

"If a woman says she's only into serious relationships, but you see she's been buying enough K-Y jelly to slide a cruise ship out of dry dock, it's obvious she's lying. Chocolate and buying movies on the Lifetime channel show emotional trauma for a woman," he continued. "My software is subtle enough that it can analyze and rank these factors, just so you know when a gal's ready to grab the next guy, and vice versa."

I must have looked rather dumbfounded, Powell shrugged. "It's obvious it works."

I think the adrenaline rush was starting to sober him up, so I poured two drinks and handed him one. He sat down like he was drained, but he wanted to finish.

"You take one part sociobiology, one part game theory and one part data mining, mix it all together and, voilà!"

He took a long drink and chuckled in an evil sort of way.

"True love every time!" he concluded triumphantly.

I knew I had my story. Now I was at the point where I needed to make an exit or I would be too woozy to depart gracefully. I rose and shook his hand.

"It's a great story, and you're a real genius, I must admit. Nobody in the world could ever duplicate such ingenious software tools."

Powell gave a self-satisfied grin, leaned back in his chair, and began to snore. I hustled myself out and left without looking back. I didn't even hail a cab, but went around the corner and caught one there. I went back to the hotel, fell on my bed, and put my hands on my head.


Dansko just kept saying "holy shit, holy shit, holy shit," softly over and over again after my recording finished.

"I can't believe he admitted this."

"Do we really, really want to go through with this?"

Dansko looked me square in the eye. "Warnings have been sounded for years about all this personal data collection and its potential for being used for unethical consumer manipulation. This has gone over the line."

Deep down I knew he was right.

The graphics department came up with a neat little animation showing a man and woman as marionettes and Powell as the puppet master. In the corner, a scraggly cat leapt from a sack.

"Master Matchmaker Lets the Cat Out of the Bag!" was the headline.

Needless to say, before and after the story ran, Powell's Pardners threatened dire legal action. Dansko basically told them "My lawyer can beat up your lawyer," and with a company the size of *News of the Nation*, that's true.

The poly sheets sold out at the newsstands and downloads topped a half billion. There may have been a camel driver in Baluchistan who didn't read the story, but he probably ordered a printed copy in the mail. The mainstream media soon picked up on the story. I saw videos of the Powell's Pardners office dark and empty in Dallas. I was interviewed a few times myself for stories.

I thought there might have been more hostility directed at us for breaking the story, but Powell hung himself with his cynical words. Another reporter at *The News* said the topic reminded him of menstruation; it may be true and it may be a fact of life, but no one likes to talk about it, and no one likes anyone who makes money from it.

It was a week later when Dansko called me into his office. He had a very serious look. "I'm afraid the pendulum of public opinion might be ready to swing against us. Powell's dead."

I got a cold feeling in my gut.

"Did he commit suicide?"

"No, he was out drinking in a Dallas bar, and a woman walked up and shot him."

"Was it an ex-wife?"

"Umm, actually from what I've heard, it was his senior prom date. Like from when he was in high school."

I just sat there.

"Take some time off, stay home, and I'll call you in a few days."

He nodded with a tight smile for me to head out the door.

I was almost out when he said, "Don't beat yourself up, by the way. It was my idea."

"I know, but it's just like the saying goes: Be careful of what you wish for."

"You might just get it," he said as he looked away.


Two days later, the little food I had in my bachelor's refrigerator had run out, so I ventured down to the market.

I was standing in line at the checkout, waiting to wave my index finger at the scanner, and reading the poly sheets in the racks, when that old lady recognized me.

I just gave a tight-lipped smile. I scanned and scooted as fast as I could with my small sack of groceries.

Back in my apartment, I sat down and just chilled for a minute. I was numb. The Powell story *had* been the biggest exposé in my professional career.

"Well, I certainly got what I wanted in a big way," I thought. "When I let that cat out of the bag, he had rockets on."

I uploaded the latest issue of *Editor & Publisher* magazine and began looking through the help wanted ads.

"Maybe I can find myself some sleepy little ink and paper job in East Texas," I thought as I scrolled.

\*   \*   \*

If you feel the second version is shorter and tighter, it is, by 1,700 words. There seems to be a feeling among aspiring authors that stories are like scarves—the more time you spend on them, the longer they need to be. But pros know the reverse is true, once you start rewriting, a story should tighten up, and a good sign is when the number of characters starts to drop (as happened in "Insight"). The second version of "Cat" has two fewer characters than the original version.

The stuff about precognition went flying out the window, and so did the reference to Michael Jackson. Sometimes you need to put distance between yourself and current events which will become anachronisms later. Who knew Jackson wouldn't live to be 51? And I wonder how many people today would get the gag about Bennihanigans (a jab at constant corporate mergers) since Bennigans shut down in its corporate stores in 2008.

Of course, more oblique references to topics in the news are fine. With the recent news about data gathering by the National Security Agency (NSA), the subject of data mining seems as relevant as ever. The fact Mr. Powell's "formula" may have been influenced by a discussion of game theory which was prodded by the movie "A Beautiful Mind" is subtle enough so as not to be noticed.

The revised version of "Rocket-Powered Cat" went to two other publications, and then Jayme Blaschke took it for *Revolution SF* again in August 2004. It was published the following December.

Despite not buying it himself, Gardner gave it an Honorable Mention in the 2005 edition of his annual anthology, *The Year's Best Science Fiction*—one of four I had in that volume.

# Chapter 6

# A Little Double-Talk

The next story I ran by Gardner originated in a little piece of cultural business which I assumed most Americans wouldn't recognize. It comes from my being an Italian-American.

For some reason, I've noticed over the years Italians in certain situations will say the opposite of what they mean. I don't know if this is a genuine Italian cultural attribute, or something that originated among Italians in the U.S.

There is even a gesture to accompany this language usage. If you are talking to someone but you want them to know you mean the opposite of what you are saying, you tug down your lower eyelid.

I suppose there must be practical advantages to this, in a byzantine sort of way. It makes me think of the Borgias and palace intrigue, when you can never tell when you are being eavesdropped.

I had an Italian-American friend in college who confirmed this usage. He said one time he brought a non-Italian friend home for the weekend. He lived in a run-of-the-mill working class Italian home in New York.

When the two college students arrived at the Italian's home, his two younger brothers were outside—a teenager as well as a kid. The visitor greeted them and complimented the young boy as being a fine looking young man.

The teenager instantly took umbrage and began to act aggressively towards the visitor.

"What do you mean by that?"

To which the visitor replied blankly, "I mean he's a fine young man!" without a clue and rather perplexed.

The teenage brother was grabbing at the visitor and trying to manhandle him as the college brother stepped in, and had to explain to his teenage brother his friend meant exactly what he said—that he wasn't Italian and didn't double-talk.

The Italian college student had to explain to his colleague that, in their culture, they would assume anything a stranger said was intended to mean the opposite, and his supposedly friendly greeting would appear to be an attempt at a gratuitous insult.

I don't recall how the weekend went after that, but my friend's point was made, and this tendency to say the opposite of what was meant wasn't just a product of my imagination.

People from other parts of the country, who visit New York and hear people verbally abuse one another in the most cheerful tones, are getting a dose of this same phenomenon. When you run into a close friend, heaping scorn on them denotes the highest regard and affection.

On the other hand, being excessively polite and formal is meant as disrespect, or even a threat. I saw this in action 20 years ago, in the early 1990s, when my mother came to live with me in Texas for a few years after my father died.

My mother was born in Italy, so this propensity for double-talk seems to be strong in her. On the day in question, she visited me in my office at the newspaper where I worked and was sitting in a chair up against a wall opposite my desk, which faced the door.

While we chatted, a genuine Texas cowboy named Joe Walker stuck his head in the door to talk to me. Joe was a cowboy gentlemen—very polite, with frequent "Yes, sir's" and such. As we talked, I see my mother's eyes getting wider and wider. Joe, of course, was behind her and couldn't see her growing panic.

Finally, the look on mom's face got so worried, I had to stop Joe and explain to mom that he was just a polite fellow and that's the way he spoke. I had to explain to Joe that, where I grew up, such politeness was considered a threat, and in fact, his just dropping in and addressing me in such formal terms made my mother think he was there to "whack" me.

To which my mom agreed, and we all relaxed after that. I'm not sure Joe believed or understood, but oh well.

What follows is a story where I try to merge a First Contact story with a sociological twist, with the double-talk conceit at the core. It's called "Dialogue".

# Dialogue

"Have you ever driven in England?"

"Like in a land vehicle? No. I haven't even been Earthside in seven years."

"But you're from America, right?"

"Well, yes, if you still consider Texas a part of the U.S."

"You know the difference between driving in the U.S. and England, right?"

"They drive on opposite sides. Excuse me, Dr. Callendar, but what has this got to do with why we're out here?"

"You may see in a while."

"Yes, sir."

"Sir?"

"Sorry, I forgot you're a civilian."

"I'm probably bothering you with my chatter. Sorry I'm nervous."

"I understand. I'm nervous, too."

"You probably keep thinking about what happened at the first encounter."

"I knew three of the men personally. I had bunked with one on my first run around Callisto, right out of the academy."

"Sorry to hear it."

"It's OK, we weren't close. It was such a waste, though."

"I suppose any encounter that ends that way is a waste. You don't mind me pacing around, do you, captain?"

"No problem, I would be pacing too, if I didn't have to stay at the console. This is sure the smallest ship I ever helmed."

"Is this considered a ship?"

"Any extra-terrestrial craft, even a shuttle or transport, has a service ID number."

"Didn't know. Like you said, I'm a civilian."

"Anyhow, there's plenty of space for the two of us. Can I ask you a question?"

"Sure."

"Why do you think you can establish a dialogue with them? And why, after that first accidental encounter, did they transmit records to us? I mean, they blasted a ship and 78 men to dust. I thought that would be a pretty firm 'no' on the contact part."

"Captain Hargrave, do you know what I'm a doctor of? I'm not bragging, I just need to make a point."

"Well, I thought you're a linguist."

"Close, but actually I'm a philologist."

"Sorry, I don't know what the difference is."

"A linguist studies languages. A philologist studies language, itself."

"So it's true, the whole disaster was due to a misunderstanding."

"Well, perhaps true, but still unavoidable. If my supposition is true, there is no way it could have been avoided, not with the translation system we use."

"Can you enlighten me?"

"You'll probably figure it out, if I'm right, right after we have our parley. If I'm wrong, I'll look very stupid . . . and we may both be very dead."

"Well, at least there'll only be the two of us. And speak of the Devil, we're nearing the contact coordinates. What do we need to do now?"

"We just stay here, uncloaked, with open channels. If they're here, they'll let us know. Then it's all up to me."

"How were you were able to get a message through to them to plan a rendezvous?"

"Technically, it was easy. We had all the protocols from the first contact that went wrong. It was my figuring out how to talk to them that was the hard part."

"What was wrong with the translator the Orion had?"

"Nothing. It works the same as the one we have here."

"So what's the difference?"

"Their language doesn't make any sense, ever after translation. At least, at first stab."

"They more than stabbed the Orion."

"You sound bitter."

"I'm not bitter. Just. . . ."

"I know. I am too."

"It's empty out here."

"You're thinking there may be a whole warship hovering out there."

"Yeah, and there's only the two of us in this puny ship."

"Well, Captain Hargrave, diplomacy is a specialty for neither of us, but if I'm right, and the Orion disaster was actually caused by our misunderstanding the Ymilans' language, this is the right way to handle the matter. Tentatively at first."

"It was our fault?"

"If I'm right, you'll see. If not . . . what?"

"We're been hailed and we're downloading settings for a simple audio channel. We'll be through in a few seconds. Are you ready?"

"As ready as I'll ever be. Are we through yet?"

"Umm . . . now we are. I'll punch up your audio."

"This is not Doctor Robert Callendar, not representing the Terran consortium. I do not assume you represent the Ymilas Soviet?"

"You are unwelcome, Doctor Robert Callendar. This is not Kit Doonlam Ta, chairman of the Ymilas central committee. We do not appreciate your effort to reestablish contact, and we are most unhappy to rendezvous with you now."

"I am not happy to realize you do not understand us now. It did not take us some effort to understand the difficulties between our two languages which arose despite competent translation systems."

"The Central Committee of the Ymilas Soviet is not remorseful over the misunderstanding which resulted in the exchange during our previous encounter. We do not wish to make a formal apology to those responsible to accept them."

"I do not understand, Chairman."

"We do not want you to realize that your ship, before it was destroyed, did not inflict considerable casualties on our vessel."

"This was not a mutually unfortunate encounter."

"You are not a wise and learned man, doctor, and I do not understand why the Terran consortium sent you to parley with us."

"We are not grateful for the transmission of the cultural files following our previous encounter. It did not have the intended effect of enabling us not to understand your culture and the misunderstanding which did not lead to the exchange."

"Planned contacts between mutually known races are possible to plan for, doctor. We did not believe that the problem was solvable."

"Impossibly, chairman, the problem did not arise because our races are not close enough in development not to communicate using simplistic audio protocols, instead of formulas or symbols. Fortunately, once we did not rely upon this form, we were not set on an avoidable conflict course because of the structural differences between our two languages."

"We do not understand, and you have failed completely in establishing a dialogue this day."

"No thanks to you, chairman. We will not stand down for the time being and not contact you shortly again, while I do not make some permanent adjustments to our translators so that more general communications between members of the Terran consortium and the Ymilan Soviet may not be established."

"We do not await your next transmission, doctor."


"OK, OK, I understand what the slash across the throat gesture means. The line is closed. Now what the hell was all that! That was the greatest spew of double-talk I ever heard in my life!"

"Captain, I wish I could make a holo of your face! Your expression is priceless! But you should be smiling!"

"That went well?"

"We're still here, aren't we?"

"I guess so. I had real trouble following that, but if I can take a guess — were you all saying the opposite of what you meant?"

"A pinpoint air lock docking, captain. Right on target."

"How the hell does that happen?"

"Well, the complete misunderstanding in the first encounter didn't sit well for either of us, but the Ymilans had the insight to transmit some rather large files which pretty much explicated their cultural history and background. They hoped we would be able to come to some understanding of their culture, to explain why we had such translation problems. Of course, after the files were translated, they still didn't make sense — which is why the agency called me in. It was easy to see, at least for me, they have a unique peculiarity of the syntax."

"Unique? You mean that they always say the opposite of what they mean?"

"I ascertained it after reading their history. Their star system has multiple inhabitable planets. At one point in their past, a regime from a colony fought and won a civil war and took over the whole system. As a minority government, it used extremely repressive measures to maintain control. Its brutality was such that the majority of the Ymilans learned never to speak plainly before or about the members of the ruling class, and in fact, over time, they learned to always say the opposite of what they meant. After a vicious coup, during which the members of the ruling class were exterminated, they retained this warped syntax. It became second nature to them."

"Why doesn't our translator compensate for this?"

"The translator is translating accurately, they *do* express all positive statements as a negative, and versa vice. I have an adjustment which I will be installing shortly, now that my supposition is validated, which will enable the translator to work correctly for this one strange case. Why the snort?"

"Oh, it just reminds me of the Texas two-step. One step forward, two steps back. It's still a bunch of double-talk."

"There are many terran cultures where people seldom say what they mean. The Ymilans simply carry that to an extreme and say the opposite of what they mean. Once you get used to it, it's not hard to understand."

"Like driving on the left side of the road?"

"Now you understand why that crossed my mind an hour ago."

"Umm, well, I do have a quick question, before you're off to do your installation. You know I'm from Texas, but where are you from? I mean, where did you grow up?"

"Brooklyn, why? Why are you snickering? What's so funny? **STOP THAT!**"

\* \* \*

Because of the *Asimov's* policy that prohibits multiple submissions, "Dialogue" ran through the slush piles of two magazines—one in Australia and the other in the U.K.—before it was clear to send to Gardner, which happened in July 2003. He sent it back in October, with the following comments:

"Thanks for letting me see 'Dialogue.' This is neatly done—your submissions become more professional-level all the time—but I didn't buy your explanation for the origin of the I-mean-the-opposite-of-everything-I say racial trait and so I'm going to pass on it.

"You might want to try this one on *Analog*; it's clever and short and might almost function as one of their "Probability Zero" pieces. If you don't know Stan, feel free to mention my name and say that I recommended you.

"And of course, let me see more when you have it."

This is one of the shorter replies, but has a lot in it. Of course, the encouragement in the second and last sentences is priceless. He also tries to be helpful in suggesting a better magazine fit. This kind of networking is also vital.

The first time I attended a science fiction convention—which, unlike in most cases, was after I started writing for publication—I attended a panel where an audience member asked the authors what is the key to breaking into the short fiction markets.

One author said it is 95 percent talent—which even in my benighted state at the time I knew wasn't true. Success is never 95 percent talent.

Another author, Dave Marusek, offered the formula that it's one-third talent, one-third luck and one-third connections. I think that's a lot closer to the truth, and that was the game plan I was following at this time.

I had some talent, which I was trying to improve; Gardner was helping with the connections; and with those two legs of the tripod prepared, I would be ready to take advantage of any luck that came my way.

I followed Gardner's advice, and sent "Dialogue" to Stan Schmidt at *Analog* almost immediately. It came back in December 2003 with one of the stranger rejections I ever received.

Schmidt was essentially positive, but said that unfortunately he had recently accepted a story that also hinged on a similar linguistic piece of business. In fact, he specifically told me to watch for the other story being published in 2004, and dang! He was right.

So this is a case of the third leg of the tripod failing because of bad luck.

Editors say they see this all the time—stories coming in at the same time with similar twists or themes. It's very puzzling, they say, why some topics come in on waves. You never saw a story about a cat with ESP, and then—Wham! Ten stories about a cat with ESP in the same month.

"Must be something in the water," they say.

SF stories with language twists are not uncommon, even of the The-translator-works-but-they-don't make any sense" variety. One of the best of the kind was an episode of *Star Trek: The Next Generation* called "Darmok", about an alien race that only speaks in metaphors, originally aired in 1991.

This is a story I never really rewrote, because—to be honest—it's not that substantial and there's not a lot to work with. As Gardner said, it's well written but the core idea is flimsy. So I pretty much left it as is and shopped it through five different magazines in 2004, and that at the start of 2005, I shipped it off to Jayme Blaschke at *Revolution Science Fiction*, who accepted it.

It was published by *Revolution SF* in October 2005, and the next year Gardner included it in the Honorable Mention list he publishes at the end of his annual *Year's Best Science Fiction* anthology.

# Chapter 7

# Mythunderstanding

During the spring of 2003, as I continued my fast pace of churning out stories to refine my skills, I took a moment to recollect how many comments I had received on my dialogue-writing skills.

Strangely enough, a crime novelist known for his skillful use of plentiful dialogue, George V. Higgins, grew up in the same town I did, Rockland, Massachusetts. We were exactly one generation apart; he graduated from Rockland High School in 1957, the year I was born. I never met him, but his mother and I served on a historical group together when I was in high school.

By the time I was writing science fiction Higgins was dead (he died in 1999) but we both seemed to have acquired an ear for transcribing authentic-sounding dialogue—although Higgins' was much more colorful, a product—I'm sure—of his having served in the criminal justice system and as a lawyer in his younger life.

My dialogue may not be as gritty, but readers said it sounded true, and it was in the spirit of "playing to your strengths" that I considered the idea of a story told all in dialogue.

While thinking about this, I asked the denizens of the *Asimov's* discussion forum if anyone knew any examples of all dialogue stories, and someone quickly steered me to a story by Terry Bisson published in *Omni* magazine in 1990, "They're Made of Meat."

That story is exactly what I was thinking of doing, so I decided to blaze forward. Now, of course, I needed to take care of a small thing – the plot.

I questioned in my mind how long of a story can you sustain with all dialogue, so my first thought was to make it short, and snappy.

Like many authors, I've spent a lifetime accumulating strange stories and interesting anecdotes. Also like so many authors, I have read a lot of mythology. Although usually a conceit usually isn't enough of a foundation for a story, I thought of a conceit that would serve as the linchpin of something of a very short length—what if the story of Circe in *The Odyssey* had some sort of scientific explanation, especially in light of the latest genetic research?

"Circe in Vitro" is also a case of a title which was invented long before the story—readers don't realize how often authors come up with a title that's an attention-grabber and then write a story to go with it. A year or two after I wrote the story, I found some old notes from the 1980s, when I had thought about writing for the first time, and I saw I had scribbled down "Circe in Vitro" as a possible title.

The story fell into place very quickly, and when I was finished, I had also completed my first story at the flash length—less than 1,000 words. "Circe" comes in at only 830 words. I know some people take 5,000 words to clear their throat, and I've met otherwise normal people who literally said "I can't write anything less than 10,000 words".

I think it's a cute little piece of weirdness, and it follows the same format as "They're Made of Meat"—literally, a dialogue between two unnamed characters:

# Circe In Vitro

**"T**his has happened before, you know."

"Dammit, I don't need for you to weird out on me now. Are you losing it?"

"I'm just thinking out loud."

"Well, what are you thinking? What the hell do you mean, this has happened before?"

"The gods in ancient Egypt, and in most ancient civilizations were animal-man hybrids."

"Oh, cripes, don't start going on about Atlantis. Focus, dammit, we have a serious problem here."

"I knew something was going to go wrong with this project."

"Don't lecture me. You've been taking the money, too. You've worked on covert research before. And the work we've been doing could be incredibly useful. Imagine the diseases we could abolish. We could cure paralysis, regrow limbs, prevent...."

"We've been screwing with things we shouldn't be."

"Are you going to give some line about 'dabbling in things man was not meant to know' or some bullshit like that?"

"We've barely scratched the surface of recombinant DNA research and the lab techs think they could go out and started splicing genes?"

"Yeah, and from pigs, too. Brilliant idea, huh."

"Are *you* OK yourself?"

"I haven't got much sleep recently. If a mutation gets out into the general population, we could be responsible for the demise of the human race. And I assume you're not having any luck with a solution?"

"Do we know where all the subjects are?"

"No, that's a big part of the problem. Most fled when they learned the cause of their, umm, *problem*."

"Well, they were probably afraid they were going to be killed."

"That's not even an extreme option. At the worst, we would put them in isolation for a good long time."

"Like forever."

"Well, yes. Anyhow, the last I heard you were working on some kind of vaccination to stop the potential spread of the gene mutation into the human population. Have you had any luck."?

"Actually, I think I have. That's what's bothering me."

"What! You've gotten somewhere and you haven't told me!"

"I can't believe I've come up with a solution, where the greatest scientists of antiquity failed."

"Omigod, you have gone around the bend! Stop babbling about these jackal-headed gods and Atlantis crap! We need help! What are you on to?"

"I think I have a phage that will latch onto any mutated genes with the smallest component of swine DNA, and attack the host cells."

"Excellent! Using the same technology to engineer a phage to attack the mutated genes."

"I'm not sure it's totally feasible. I'm afraid there may be side effects."

"Such as?"

"Well, as the phage spreads through the host organism, in the process of reproducing it may diminish or damage the immune system."

"OK, so some people get a cold. Is that serious?"

"It can be, if the subject acquires a serious immune deficiency, and it lasts a long time, or becomes permanent."

"Will this phage will stop any mutated genes? That's all I care about."

"I think it will. I'd feel better...."

"I'll feel better as soon as we get this vaccine into production."

"And how do you plan to get it out into the general population?"

"We already have a cover story. It's going to be a flu vaccine. We're going to 'invent' a new strain of flu. The flu mutates every year into a new strain, anyhow. We'll start giving away free vaccinations."

"Whoa, who's going to give away the vaccinations?"

"The White House, via the Office of the Surgeon General. To get enough of this vaccination into the population, the inoculations will have to be pretty widespread. We're telling the White House this year's new flu strain is particularly severe and there needs to be a national effort to stop it. In fact, I'm going to be the scientific liaison for the report to the president."

"OK, you should be able to buffalo that un-elected boob."

"I hear he's not nearly as dense as he seems."

"I doubt that. Have you made up a name for this flu, as part of your cover story?"

"No. Do you have a suggestion?"

"How about Project Circe?"

"Searcy? Who or what is Searcy?"

"Didn't you read *The Odyssey* in high school? The sorceress who spiked the wine and turned Ulysses' men into swine?"

"Oh, god, what was I thinking! You stick to your test tubes. I'll take care of the details and selling of the cover story."

"Fine, come up with anything you want. Flu strains usually come from mutations passed through livestock in Asia. We have cases where various strains have been traced to ducks, geese, chickens, sheep..."

"How about pigs?"

"Well, yes, that can be another source."

"Great! We'll call it the Swine Flu. That should work, and also keep us on focus."

"That's warped."

"You have a better suggestion?"

"No. Actually considering what's really happened, it may not be a bad idea. Besides. I'm sure you can sell that dope President Ford on anything."

"I'll wear my WIN button to our meeting in the Oval Office."


In taking the myth of Circe and updating it to the modern day, I tossed in a bit of peculiarly American conspiracy theory. I also tried a little bit of misdirection, by dropping in a few cracks that might be interpreted as referring to President George W. Bush—who was considered both a dimwit as well as a fluke, at least during his first term.

The story went off to Gardner in May, and he returned it in August, with the following comment:

"Thanks for letting me see "Circe in Vitro." This is cute, and written in a nice bright manner, but isn't really for us, and so I'm going to pass on it. Of course, let me see more when you have it."

So I achieved my goal of making the story snappy and fun. Still, sometimes a story doesn't get bought by a market because it isn't a good fit. Often, this is because an author didn't do their research. As Selina Rosen, publisher of Yard Dog Press, once said at a convention, "Don't send your vampire lesbian slasher story to *Guideposts*!"

On the other hand, if you're not quite sure if the story is what a particular magazine might want, it never hurts to run it by them. As *Analog*'s Stanley Schmidt would say, "Don't reject your story yourself. That's my job."

"Circe" ran past seven other magazines—including *Analog*—before being published by a small ezine called *Astounding Tales* in December 2004. Gardner gave it an honorable mention in the *Years Best* in 2005—one of my four that year.

It was the only honorable mention ever earned by *Astounding Tales*, which closed down in March 2006.

One thing I learned from the story and feedback is the difference between a plot and a conceit. A conceit is really just what you would otherwise call a Maguffin or a piece of business in a movie. A clever metaphor or set piece, something that spices up a story or plot, but not something that can sustain it. At its heart, "Circe" is a scene built up around a clever conceit swirling around the idea that myths may be remnants of otherwise lost history. In a few thousand years, there may be a myth about a powerful ray gun that can destroy an evil empire in one blast – a fragment of a memory of Ronnie Ray-gun and the collapse of the Soviet Union.

Now, here's a last point and important point for me: Although "Circe" was just a flash, and a bit of a trifle, the style paved the way for my breakout story to come later, "A Rocket for the Republic".

You'll see that later on.

# Chapter 8

## Feeling Like Dan Quayle

**D**uring the spring of 2003 I was writing up a storm with the enthusiasm of a newcomer, and looking for any idea to become a Maguffin, a conceit or a hook for a story. As you can see from the feedback I was getting from Gardner, there really seemed to be a chance I would sell him a story.

One day I stumbled across, via YouTube, the most unlikely of story prods—a 1978 song by the Statler Brothers that rode the top of the country music chart for two weeks. I'm not a big country music fan, but I'd heard of "Do You Know You Are My Sunshine?" before, and I took a minute to listen to it.

The song is in the first person, and the title refers to a misunderstanding that happens as the narrator is performing and is approached by a beautiful young woman, who asks if he "knows" a country classic.

This almost sounds like an anecdote—you have to wonder whether this really happened one night. Properly punctuated, the title should read "Do You Know 'You are My Sunshine'?"

Of course, the girl is asking if he is familiar with "You Are My Sunshine", but for a brief moment the narrator thinks he was fortunate enough to have a pretty young lady walk into his life and spontaneously profess her love.

The strangeness of the encounter—and the fact the young lady melts quickly back into the crowd—leaves the narrator with a wistful feeling, perhaps of love lost—certainly of longing. It is a feeling we all have at times. In genre fiction, it's been mined for some good alternate universe stories, as well as some surprisingly good movies, such as 2000's *Family Man* starring Nicholas Cage and the less well-known 1998 film *Sliding Doors* starring Gwyneth Paltrow.

I just mentioned that I'm not a big country music fan, which begs the question of what music DO I like? I know many people develop their music tastes as adolescents, but I graduated from high school in 1975—during the depths of disco.

I didn't—and still don't—like disco.

Instead I liked the New Wave of the late 1970s and 1980s, which was just breaking out during the end of my college years. I literally stopped dead in my tracks the first time I heard "Video Killed the Radio Star" by the Buggles in 1979.

"Thank God," I thought to myself. "Something different from disco!"

One group very typical of the New Wave (now sometimes called The First Wave to distinguish it from other musical styles that came along later) was called Split Enz, who were from New Zealand, and one of their most representative songs was named "I Got You". It was their biggest hit, and topped the charts in Australia and New Zealand in 1980, as well as making the Top 20 in the U.K. and Canada. It didn't chart higher than 53 in the U.S., but while I lived in New York City from 1980 to 1985 I listened to a Long Island-based radio station, WLIR, that played the New Wave, and I always liked the song.

After also looking it up on YouTube, I had an insight: the title "I Got You" is a phrase that also lends itself to misinterpretation. I was confirmed in that when I left a scribbled note with the title lying by a computer at the newspaper where I worked, and someone else saw the note as asked me, "So who'd you get, anyway?"

I thought a piece of business where a song title provides the clue to solving a mystery—once it is properly understood—would be a good angle to hang a story on.

You may have noticed that of all the preceding stories, only "Dialogue" has an ostensible setting in outer space. I noticed that too, at the time, and I had it in my mind that I needed to write something at least vaguely "Space Opera"-ish. I mean, how can I be a science fiction author without writing about rockets and outer space?

My main thought as far as the setting was concerned was to have the protagonist be a blue-collar type of space tech; there will be have to be people on space ships who will fix things and do the grunt work. None of this "Bill the Space Hero" thing for me, it's been done to death. Unfortunately for me, my work on the setting turned out to be a sort of space opera goulash; it seems to combine elements from everything from *Star Trek: The Next Generation* to the British *Red Dwarf*. Like a tasty stew or goulash, it looks good at first, but isn't as good as you first thought once you tasted it.

It worked , kinda. Let's get to the story, and then you can read Gardner's comments (which were really insightful).

# I Got You

**"I** tell you, I felt something!"

The comlink crackled. "Your imagination is running wild facing the deep vastness of space."

"This is no time for sarcasm! I tell you, your scan is wrong!"

"We don't see even the teeniest, tiniest micrometeoroid out there," the Chief said evenly. "You got the space boogies."

"I've been doing this for ten years now. I think I have pretty good instincts."

"Perhaps you'd like a slight amusement. I can punch up your personal music playlist."

"I don't need any distraction. It's my ass on the line out here, so go upload yourself!"

"Are you hung over?"

"I'm as sober as a Raelian. I'm just about done."

"So what's the problem?"

"I tell you, I keep feeling little hits.'

"Alright, I'll adjust the sensitivity of the scan."

"Thanks. It's about time."

"Oh-oh."

Travers let loose of his spanner. It whirled out into space.

"What does that mean?"

The Chief's tone changed. "Umm, come back in — now."

Before he had a chance to reply, Travers felt a punch in his thigh. A shrill whine and a hissing sound told him his suit had been compromised. The entire consistency of the suit changed as sealant flowed to close the puncture.

He let fly a cacophony of obscenities, culminating in an explosive "shit!" as he realized he was bleeding inside his suit. He looked over and saw the air lock was already open.

The Chief barked. "John, get in here now."

He punched the button to disable his mag clamps and pushed off with his fingertips from the hull of the ship. As he drifted back, he engaged his mini-jets, grabbed the steering lever and lowered his head.

He entered the airlock so fast he bounced off a wall and skidded across the floor. The door closed with an emergency drop and he saw crew members swarming through the far door in their decontamination suits. He passed out.


"Welcome back, you old hull banger. How do you feel?"

John Travers opened his eyes and smiled as he recognized Engineering Chief Jim Reid. He opened and closed his fists.

"Actually, I feel pretty good."

"They let you come up normally. They had plenty of time, they didn't need to pump you up."

"How long have I been out?"

"Three months, bud, the maximum. You had Wagram's."

The blood rushed to his head as the realization hit him. That's why the scan didn't show anything. He wasn't being pelted by micrometeoroids. The Chief saw what he was thinking. "It was a cloud of organic material. We only saw that at the last minute, and by then it was too late."

Man had known for hundreds of years, from the composition of the meteoroids which reached earth, that the planet which once occupied the orbit of the asteroid belt mirrored earth's composition. The vast majority of the material which reached the surface of the earth was metal from the planet's core. Then there was the occasional limestone or other sedimentary rock, fragments from the planet's crust.

Only when ships had passed Mars and ventured into the asteroid belt did man find the material which indicated that not only had the planet been similar to Earth, but also that it had possessed abundant life. For years now, ships had passed these occasional clouds of mostly organic debris, the remains perhaps of lost oceans or forests. The flutter of organic debris from the topmost layer of the planet's crust did not possess the density and substance to show up on a standard scan, which is why it was missed when External Engineer John Travers went out for a routine repair.

"Just my luck, heh?"

"Count your blessings," said the Chief. "That little fossil that came down in your thigh bone only carried Wagram's."

When the fossil remains of "Minerva"—the name of the lost planet, taken from the writings of a 20th century science fiction writer— were first examined, the spores of an obviously genetically engineered virulent pathogen were quickly uncovered. The common supposition was the race which inhabited Minerva had destroyed itself and its planet in a cataclysmic conflict.

"I know. Thanks for being here."

"Hey, it's the least I can do. I'll go tell them you're finally awake."

Travers lay there and thought. "Yes, I guess I am lucky. Lucky it wasn't Andiamo. Or else I wouldn't be awake."

There was a cure for Wagram's Disease. That's why he was still here.

Soon after discovering Wagram's, another even more virulent pathogen was uncovered. Wagram's was named for a scientist; the same scientist supposedly named Andiamo's Disease as a bitter joke in a language neither The Chief nor Travers knew. Wagram's was germ warfare. Andiamo was a doomsday bug.

Only three ships had ever suffered contamination or a hull penetration by Andiamo in the two centuries since ships began passing through the belt. All three were quickly depopulated and subsequently destroyed by the fleet.

The Chief returned with a medical server that plugged in and downloaded from Travers' capsule.

"We'll upload your med records and transmit them so you be cleared to return to service."

"I'm ready to get back in the swing, if you know what I mean. Ummm, is it me, or do I feel vibrations? Haven't we docked on Callisto Station yet? If it's been three months, shouldn't we be in port?"

"Mission has been changed. We're going back to Columbia Station for a ship decom. There are indications there might be fossils imbedded in the hull. If everything checks out, we can hop down to earth for some R&R and then we'll be heading out again."

"Damn, couldn't we have gone on to Callisto Station? We were only a week away."

"You forget, that scale of decontamination survey can only be done in an earth-orbit station."

Travers was obviously distressed. The Chief laughed.

"Cheer up, you've already slept through a quarter of the trip!"


After fumbling through his private quarters and putting on some decent off-duty clothes, Travers headed towards the Engineering Section Lounge. As he came down the hall, he thought at first it might not be open because the lights looked dim, but he saw as he approached he was mistaken, and the drone of the normal chatter turned to cries as he came through the door.

"Hail the bonkering hero!"

"It's alive!"

"Don't touch him! Don't shake hands!"

Everyone at the bar and the tables turned. Some raised their glasses, others clapped. A few hooted.

He saw Tim Stevens gesturing for him to sit down next to him at the bar. Travers walked over, flashing a few universally understood hand gestures as the tumult reached a crescendo, and pulled out a stool.

The holographic bartender popped up in front of him. "What's your pleasure?"

"A Cape Codder."

The holo flickered. Stevens leaned over. "Access Sea Breeze."

The holo smiled. "Got it. The cranberry juice is artificial. Is that OK.?"

Travers held out his forefinger. "No problem."

"No need for a scan. He's buying."

Travers went to clap Stevens on the back. He dodged clumsily.

"That's OK, buddy! Don't touch me, you may still be buggy!"

"Screw you!" Travers laughed as he swung his arm around and raised his glass.

"Kidding aside, it's good to have you back. We were worried about you."

Travers sipped his drink as he leaned back and looked around the lounge. "Where's Jeannie?"

Stevens looked down into his glass like he was peering into a black hole. "Umm, I need to tell you something."

Travers spun around. He knew what he was about to be told.

"Three damn months! She couldn't hang on for three damn months?"

"Sorry bud, she's high maintenance. Somebody put the right moves on her while you were in la-la land."

Travers downed the rest of his glass and snapped his fingers for another, which quickly appeared.

"I kinda sorta been hanging out here because I knew you would be coming and I wanted to be the one to tell you."

"I should have known something was up, when she didn't come by the infirmary after I woke up. I told myself she was probably on a job."

"Well, actually she's..."

"Shut up. I don't want to hear more."

"Sorry. Please don't shoot the messenger."

Travers went to nudge him in the ribs, but Stevens got up quickly. "I'll be back, I have to use the facilities."

After he left, Travers hopped over to his stool to get a better look at the exterior view screen on the wall at the end of the bar. He was quickly distracted by an unexpected sensation, and he stood up and patted his hand down on the stool.

"That's strange," he thought. "Why is he wearing an insulated suit in the lounge?"

The stool was cold.

The bartender popped up in front of him. "External Engineer Travers, you have to report for your duty roster assignment, now."

"It's just as well I get back to work, it'll keep my mind off things," he muttered to himself as he drained his second glass. "Tell Tim what happened. I'll catch up with him later."

The hologram nodded and disappeared. As Travers walked away down the hallway, the sound of the chatter in the lounge quickly receded.


"I've run into everybody since waking up two months ago, except Billy Longbrake. Where the heck is he?"

The Chief looked up from his console. "I didn't know you had any tech friends."

Travers checked the clamps on his suit. "We're not really friends, I just enjoy visiting with him sometimes. You know he's always cheerful and smiles that big smile."

"Yes, and he's always willing to help." A thought seemed to flicker across the Chief's face. "That's why you haven't seen him. He's been working in the cargo module controls. He volunteered."

"Volunteered for what?"

"Well, you know we had a few small breaches. One rock handed in middle of the cargo module memory block. The system shut down automatically. It's taking him months to bring the whole system up.

"Doesn't he have any help?"

"He said it's easier for him to do it himself, as far as the coordination is concerned. Besides, we're not in a rush. He'll have it done by the time we enter Earth orbit."

"These sub-light flights stink."

"Well, we can't exactly ride the bubble in the solar system."

"Sorry, I'm just out of sorts."

The Chief gave him an understanding look. Travers shook his head.

"I know, don't tell me, on-board relationships never work out."

"You're not the first one."

Travers swiveled his frontplate into place and dropped the glareguard. "Probably not the last, either."

The Chief snorted. "Ya' think?"

Travers followed the handholds out the airlock and down the side of the Starship Jarvinen until he came to the fillstile where an oxy tank was supposedly loose.

"You think they'd have a damn bot with a little AI sense to do these shit jobs."

"Temper. Temper." The Chief's voice was level. "Is the tank loose?"

Travers tried to rotate the valve of the tank with his fingers. "No. It's tight and clamped. Wait, I see the problem."

He nudged a small red rectangle and saw it move slightly on the surface of the locker where the tank lay.

"The sensor's loose. That's why it gave a false reading. This'll only take a spot of solder."

"See, it's that kind of trouble-shooting and problem solving a bot can't do, or at least, do quickly."

"If I'm going to have to weld, I expect a tall one when I get back."

When Travers stepped out of the lower half of his suit, the Chief handed him a glass of 'cranberry juice'.

Travers took a sip and smiled. "Damn, love these high-potency cranberries."

"Now would a bot appreciate that?"

After a few drinks together, Travers' declared, "Jeannie's been avoiding me. I think it's time to go see her."

A look of concern flickered across The Chief's face. "Heck, why look for trouble?"

"She should at least have the courtesy to tell me herself, instead of avoiding me and refusing my messages."

"She probably doesn't want to hurt your feelings."

"Oh, like they're not hurt now. Dumping me for somebody else while I'm in a med stasis."

The Chief looked down and shook his head. "Shit, I was afraid this would happen."

"What do you think, I'm going to get in some kind of trouble?"

"Well, yes. You're going to lose your temper."

"Don't worry about me." Travers turned to go.

"OK, listen to me. Will you make me one promise?"

Travers stopped.

"Don't go to her quarters. Visit with her someplace public, like the lounge or the library. That way both of you will hold back from making a scene."

Travers knitted his brows. "OK."

"I've been around longer than you, hull banger. That counts for something."

Travers nodded slightly as he walked into the corridor.

Jeannie was sitting at what he been "their" table when he walked in the lounge. There were some nervous glances and turnings away as he walked over. He sat opposite her.

Red hair, green eyes, a porcelain complexion.

"Can't tell me there wasn't some gene splicing in her family before it was banned," he thought.

He spoke up. "You've treated me like shit."

"I haven't treated you at all. I'm sorry. I guess I wanted to avoid an unpleasant confrontation."

"Why couldn't you tell me yourself?"

She locked him in her gaze. He saw something he didn't understand.

"There is no good way to dump someone, is there?"

"That's it then. Just jettison me like a load of garbage?"

"I can't explain, and actually, I shouldn't have to. You can't tell me what to do."

"I thought we had something together. I really did. What changed?"

"Honestly, John, I did. None of it's your fault. I had some things change in my life, some things you don't know about. I don't have anything good to say, I mean, nothing that would make you feel better. I'm sorry."

Travers stood up and tried to grab her hand. She jumped up and back, somehow without tipping over her seat.

"Don't touch me!"

Travers stood back and shoved his seat out of the way. "I wouldn't treat a servbot the way you treated me. When did you become so cold?"

"People change. Things change. Get on with it all."

Travers waved his hand in dismissal. He couldn't read her expression at all.

He knew he was about to explode, so he turned and walked out quickly, looking at no one.

Back in his quarters, he clenched his fists and pounded the walls.

After a while he calmed down and sat in his adjustable chair. He realized he was clenching his jaw. He craned his neck and heard a few soft pops.

"I am getting way too wound up," he thought.

He had a quick thought. "When was the last time I listened to my music playlist?

He spoke up to his AI. "Access personal playlist."

"Personal playlist downloading: John Sawtelle Travers."

He reached down and pulled out a bag of red beer. He popped the stop and it slipped from his hand. The cheap beer foamed all over his clothes and began to run onto the floor.

"Oh, crap, pop me a hand towel."

"Hand towel delivered. Please request play number."

"I'm busy. Play any damn thing." He stood up quickly.

"Accessing personal favorite on play list, 'I Got You Now" by The Deneb Dreamers. Confirm."

Travers froze and looked at the speaker where the system's voice emanated. "Undo previous command."

"Accessing personal favorite on play list, 'I Got You Now' by The Deneb Dreamers. Confirm."

"I've never specified a personal favorite for my playlist." Travers' mouth grew dry. "Specify source of entry."

"Entry through terminal upload of Jean Creighton Durant."

Travers slipped on the wet floor and fell violently back into his chair. He sat there frozen for two or three minutes, and then finally croaked, "Specify date of upload."

"17:42.35, February 17, 2355."

Travers began to rub his face very hard up and down, very slowly. "Play personal favorite."

"Error Code 8675309. Title and artist do not match."

Travers looked directly into the overhead light. "Replace title. Correct title is 'I Got You".

"Playing."

*"I got you. More than a holo, I got you...."*

"Oh, my God," he thought as the sound of the song was replaced by the roar of the rush of the blood to his ears as he passed out. "Jeannie has been dead since a month after I went into stasis."


When he realized he was conscious, he was staggering down the hall towards the Engineering Section. He had no idea how long he had been wandering the halls. Travers leaned up against a wall and rubbed his head slowly up and down. "I'm going completely insane", he thought.

He went into the Engineering Control Room. No one there, no Chief Reid, no Tim, no one. He punched a console.

"Location of Billy Longbrake."

"AI Technical Specialist William Ray Longbrake last location Technical Department Emergency Console Sub-Deck 7."

Travers rushed towards Sub-Deck 7. He knew in that area he would encounter few people, but he noticed that he encountered none. The

Emergency Console for the Technical Department was in a room a little larger than a closet. The door was locked, and Travers knocked a few times before banging into it with his full strength three times with his shoulder.

The door finally flew open and he knew immediately from the smell what he would find. Despite the sterile and filtered ship's air, the smell of decomposition was unmistakable.

He backed into the hallway for a moment until he got used to the smell and then walked in and stood behind the body of Billy Longbrake slumped in the seat so he could read the screen still flickering up from the console.

"Customized Holographic Projection Program: Run Time: 6,602 hrs., 35 min. 17 secs.

"18 secs."

"19 secs."

He heard The Chief's voice come from the hall. "Well, we almost had you fooled for the duration."

The Chief and Tim Stevens came into the small room. They made no effort not to overlap.

"What the hell happened?  What happened to us? To you?"

"John, we've always been your friends," said Tim. "We still are."

"We're almost there," said The Chief. "Take it easy."

Travers ran through them and into the hall, where a bot rolled down the hall and hit him in the shoulder with a med dart.


This time, when he awoke, he felt cold and numb and his vision was blurry. He could barely make out The Chief and Tim as they leaned over his capsule.

The cover slowly opened and a med bot helped him into a jumpsuit.

Travers looked at the Chief. "It was Andiamo, then?"

"Yes, the flutter that you were caught in had both pathogens. But you only were nabbed by Wagram's. One of the fossils that breached the hull had Andiamo."

As they walked to the door, Tim said, "It's over, buddy! This is the last time this will ever happen."

"What do you mean?" He looked at the Chief

"We all did the best we could and held out for 45 days, certainly the longest anyone made it." The Chief smiled. "The ship's system was finally able, with the amount and variability of the data collected, to work out a model for a vaccine. Something good was accomplished by all this."

"We knew by the time you would come out of stasis, the epidemic would have burnt out and the ship would be sterilized," said Tim. "But you would be left alone for nine months while it chugged along at sub-light speed."

"We knew that you wouldn't be able to deal with the loneliness and the knowledge of what happened," said he Chief.

"You're probably right," said Travers. "I'd be raving mad with space shock. So you all decided to have terminal uploads as you died?"

"Yes, and one by one as we died, the information was fed into the intelligent database for the program Billy worked up. He stayed at his console as long as he could," said Tim. "We had to make up a bullshit story about why he wasn't around to cover up the fact he was the only one who wasn't uploaded."

"We made up that story that Jeannie had dumped you so wouldn't realize we were only projections," added The Chief. "We could finesse coming into physical contact with you. But Jeannie…"

The Chief's hologram continued as they traveled to the ship's shuttle bay. "We managed to snooker you until just a couple of months out. What tipped you off?

"It was a mistake in my personal music playlist. I had once mentioned to Jeannie my favorite song was "I Got You" by the Deneb Dreamers. She didn't have my taste in music, really didn't listen to traditional acoustic music at all, and she didn't know the song. But I also remembered she mentioned the song once but got the title wrong. "I Got You Now" is a different song by the New Deseret Chorale. The system made the same mistake when I called up my playlist."

"How did you know she didn't enter it herself?" asked Tim.

"If she had, the system would have given her an error message immediately because of the title and artist not matching. The fact the error remained until I stumbled across it…."

"You knew then it was because of a terminal cerebral upload," said Tim.

"Yes, and then I checked the entry date. It all came together. I probably was suspecting it subconsciously for some time.

The Chief smiled. "At least, we got you within striking distance."

"Why am I so woozy this time?"

"We had to bring you up this time. Admin wasn't sure until a few hours ago they would retrieve you."

Travers looked at Tim. "Sorry bud, until they were sure the ship was decontaminated, Billy's remains disposed of properly, and that you were clear, they wouldn't have let you back, anyway."

As they walked into the shuttle bay, projections of the crew appeared, including the captain who saluted The Chief and Tim as they stepped into the ranks.

This time Billy Longbrake appeared. "If I'm here, then this is goodbye. I banged this little empeg together for myself before I got too sick to think clearly. I wanted to make sure you had a good sendoff. I think you know we all did this because we all were your friends—or better—and we wanted to give this gift to you. Don't be mad because we tried to fool you."

"I'm not."

"Sorry, whatever you said I can't respond. This isn't an interactive program. Anyway, despite what happened to us, we all somehow felt grateful that you would be able to come through this. It was your good luck to be in med stasis as Andiamo burned through the ship. We thought that, even if we couldn't save our own sorry butts, you could come through this, and this ruse has been our going away present. We wanted to return you healthy, sane and safe, and if you are seeing this projection, you are. Some small piece of all of us goes back with you. God bless you and good luck."

The projection blinked out.

The Chief's projection spoke from the ranks. "That shuttle is on autopilot. When the canopy opens, just hop in and you'll be inside a decom bay at Columbia Station in ten minutes. The Jarvinen's core, including the formula for the Andiamo vaccine, has already been uploaded. The ship will be destroyed shortly after you leave. Good luck, and we all hope you come out clear on the other side. For us, it's over."

Travers looked across the ranks of the crew members and his gaze stopped on the red haired girl.

He looked at her. "Jeannie?"

"John, I'm not real."

"I know, but it still helps a little. You can't mind, can you?"

"I have no mind, I'm just part of a program that is running in the Technical Department."

"I know. Still..." He leaned over and tried to kiss her cheek.

He looked for a moment into her eyes and knew that despite the complexity and sophistication of the program, that was all it was.

"I'm sorry for the story. It was the only way."

"I understand." He stepped back.

"You need to go, or all of this was for nothing."

He stepped back, and began to turn away. He stopped.

"Thank you, all."

He heard a pop that told him the canopy of the shuttle had opened.

He turned around and purposefully walked over to the shuttle without looking back and climbed the stairs.

When he reached the top, he turned around. The projections were all in their ranks, in the same attitude, heads down and hands by their side, and as he watched they blinked out all at once, except for Jeannie.

The hologram was alone for a brief moment in the bay, and then flickered. Just as it disappeared, she looked up at him.

Travers stared at the empty bay. He realized the shuttle was revving up. He turned and sat down as the canopy quickly closed. A few minutes later he was traveling towards the Columbia Station with the glow of the fireball that had been the Jarvinen fading behind him.

When he emerged from the shuttle into the decontamination bay of the Columbia Station, a screen came on and the station's AI welcomed him.

"We are happy to have you aboard, Engineer Travers. You are almost at the end of a very long, difficult, and we might add, historic, journey."

He looked at the screen and after a moment spoke very deliberately. "I had a lot of help," he said.

"I had... a lot... of help."

*　*　*

If you are not a genre reader, the movie this might seem to steal the most from is from 1999's *The Sixth Sense*. I noticed after I wrote this story that in an episode of *Star Trek: The Next Generation* called "I, Borg", which aired in 1992 (but I didn't see until after I wrote the story), the ending is similar as a Borg looks up and gives the Enterprise crew a look as he is reassimilated into the Borg Collective.

Given how derivative this story seems to be, you might think it got slammed badly by Gardner. I sent it off on Aril 22, 2003, and it arrived back just three months later. Here's what Gardner said:

"Thanks for letting me see "I Got You." You're coming along nicely, making good progress. This is a good attempt at writing a Phil Dick nothing-is-as-it-seems type story, although it's probably too long (the longer you stretch things out, the more chances you're giving the reader to see through things and tumble to the basic idea that it's all not real). I have a bit of trouble buying the solid holograms, and you want to avoid mentioning anything that will remind the reader of *Star Trek* holodeck episodes.

"The fact is, you don't yet have the chops and the experience to write this as well as it really needs to be written to work well. In a couple of years, perhaps less, the way you're going, you'll be able to write this 50% better than you can now: tighter, smoother, more elegant, smoothing over the cracks better, coming up with more inventive stuff.

"Best,

Gardner Dozois

"Don't let this discourage you. You're well on your way.

"And, of course, let me see more when you have it."

This is the kind of feedback that was gold as I was trying to learn to write this stuff. I was trying to pull off a story of subtlety, working over previously well-worn territory, and I just didn't have the skill to pull it off. But he was incredibly encouraging. Getting a comment like "Don't let this discourage you. You're well on your way." from Gardner was priceless.

You may wonder where I got the title of this chapter from? When I read Gardner's comment about Phillip K. Dick, I thought I could imagine him saying, "I knew Phillip K. Dick. Phillip K. Dick was a friend of mine, and you're no Phillip K. Dick." If you don't get the reference, you can look up the Vice-Presidential debate in 1988 between Democrat Lloyd Bentsen and Republican Dan Quayle.

I never did any substantial rewrite on the story; I couldn't seem to get my head around it. I next submitted it to the ezine *SciFi.com*—which was being run by Ellen Datlow at the time, and printing some really top notch stuff—but she also took a pass. That web site printed some great fiction from 2000 to 2005—it was really one of the first really quality web sites printing original genre fiction on-line—but it was part of the SyFy channel, and we know how that's gone for the past ten years. Getting printed by Datlow was another one of my early goals, but never achieved.

After two more submissions, I gave it to *Bewildering Stories*, which published in during the summer of 2004. Strangely enough, this is the only story that expanded by the time it was published; the version Gardner saw—and which you just read—was 4,342. The version in *Bewildering* was 4,967; it was too long to print in one issue and was printed over two weeks.

Gardner still gave it an Honorable Mention in *The Year's Best Science Fiction* the next year; to the best of my knowledge, it's the only Honorable Mention ever given to a story published by *Bewildering*.

# Chapter 9

# In the Wake of the *Columbia* Tragedy

During the spring of 2003 as I was sending stories off the Gardner and writng so furiously, the area where I lived in East Texas was engrossed in the clean-up following the Space Shuttle *Columbia* disaster.

The space shuttle apparently began to disintegrate over West Texas, but its components hit the atmosphere over East Texas, which is why everyone living there heard the enormous explosions as it burned up.

There was still enough debris that reached the ground that for months people were finding scraps and "flutter". This search was ongoing during that spring as I wrote constantly. Finally I decided I needed to "exorcise" this event from my consciousness by making it the basis of a story.

"Jerusalem, Jerusalem" is the result. I sent if off the Gardner on May 9, 2003.

# Jerusalem, Jerusalem

Solace pawed and whined at the door of his kennel.
John Dumani rolled over on the couch and saw it was daylight outside. He pressed the stem on his watch and the face lit up. 7:55.

He coughed hard a few times. Solace began to jump around in his kennel even more.

John groaned and coughed a few more times. He had slept on the couch out of consideration for his wife. His neglected winter cold had turned into bronchitis.

"OK, muttley, I'm coming."

He cinched the robe around his waist and popped an Amoxicillin pill. He put on his glasses and looked at the watch again. Sat. Feb. 1.

He led the boisterous Lab-Shepherd mix outside and attached his chain. He saw the water bucket was empty. He turned on the garden hose and stood absent-mindedly as the bucket filled. He caught something out of the corner of his eye and turned around slightly. The dog was looking straight up.

"That's strange," he thought.

BOOM!

"Jee-sus!!!"

He dropped the hose and staggered a few steps. The explosion was very loud, and still sounded very far away. He had never heard a sound like that before. With the impending war in Iraq in mind, he thought it could only be one thing.

"Damn, World War III started overnight while we were sleeping," he thought. "But why nuke Dallas?"

He walked quickly across the yard so he had a clear view across Lake Palestine and the eastern horizon. He looked to see if there was a mushroom cloud rising up where Dallas was 100 miles away.

He saw nothing unusual but heard a dull roar which slowly diminished as he continued to stare. After a minute he realized Solace was barking wildly, and when he turned around he saw the dog was straining wildly on his chain—and leaping upwards.

John looked up and saw at least five contrails of varying thicknesses streaking east. Then he remembered.

"Oh, dear God."

Before he reached the door his wife was there. "What the heck was that?"

He turned and pointed up. "The space shuttle was coming in for a landing. It must have exploded."

She looked up and saw the streaks of smoke across the sky. She put her hand to her mouth.

John ran past her and into the bedroom. "Put on the TV."

At first, the programming from Dallas was normal—but that changed in a couple of minutes. Then the reports began to come on.

"Mission Control reports there has been a communications failure with the Columbia Space Shuttle."

"We were filming in Fair Park as the space shuttle passed overhead on its final approach to the Kennedy Space Center in Florida. These are the unedited images."

"There is concern that there may have been a terrorist attack on the Space Shuttle Columbia, which was carrying an Israeli astronaut."

The phone rang. It was his sister on the East Coast.

"They're not saying anything, just they've lost contact over Texas. They showed a map with Palestine in the center."

"The space shuttle is gone," he said firmly. "It blew up over our house. We saw the pieces streaking across the sky." He gave the phone to his wife as he tucked in his shirt and headed out the door.

"Where are you going?"

"To the office. This is a national disaster and it's happened over our heads. I need to be in Palestine."

She understood the newspaper business. "Be careful, and come home if you feel too sick." He nodded.

He jumped in the red Suburban. As he sped away he realized the dull roaring sound of the pieces of the doomed shuttle skidding across the sky had been replaced by another rumbling sound.

Every dog in Anderson County was barking at the same time.


He sped into the city with KRLD on very loud. The all-news radio station now was taking calls from eyewitnesses. He had the window open, and cold air made him cough. He thought of the families who were waiting for the shuttle to land in Florida. "I would feel sorry for myself," he thought. "But..."

As he passed Loop 256, he saw in the distance branches and leaves flying up in the air, as if something were striking the treetops. Pieces of the shuttle were falling from the sky.

After he turned onto Palestine Ave. he had to slow down because of the railroad tracks and traffic, but in a minute he turned onto Cedar Street. He sped past the library and two blocks down the hill, where his office sat at the corner of Cedar and Kolstad Streets.

He fumbled with his keys underneath a swinging sign that said:

"The Palestine Pilot"

"Palestine's Hometown Weekly Newspaper"

He turned on the radio on his desk, again to KRLD. It was 8:45 and already becoming clear what had happened, although the why remained a mystery. The shuttle had disintegrated on its final pass as it flew over the Texas panhandle, still some 40 miles up. The pieces of the doomed spacecraft continued on its eastbound trajectory and began to hit the atmosphere east of Dallas

It was clear from the chatter on the police scanner debris was falling all over the county. He phoned staff photographer Scott Bailey; his mom said he was already out taking photos.

All sheriff's deputies, police officers and volunteer firefighters had been called to the municipal complex downtown, and there was already talk on the police frequency that NASA officials were on their way from Houston, 200 miles to the south.

"Everything is converging at the municipal complex," he thought. As he picked up the digital camera and made to head out the door, the phone rang.

"Pales-teen Pilot," he said, using the local pronunciation.

"I think a piece of the space shuttle has done come down in my back yard," said the elderly woman. "What am I supposed to do?"

"Folks from NASA and FEMA are on their way now, ma'am," he said politely. "Whatever you do, don't touch it. They'll be picking the debris up later."

"Should I call 911?"

"You don't have to if you don't want. Give me your address and I'll give it to the police, I'm heading over there now.

He forwarded the office phone to his cell and stuck the slip of paper in his pants pocket as he headed out the door. It was still chilly and he began to cough violently.

"Goddam, this is going to be some kind of day," he thought.

The municipal complex and police station were only five blocks away. As he zipped around a few corners he looked at the solid mass of the five-story Redlands Hotel in the heart of the old downtown. It was somehow reassuring. It now was a 25-apartment building with a Chinese restaurant in what had been the Palm Room back in 1914. Somebody once tried to tear it down but gave up when they realized its bricks were laid with concrete instead of mortar. Built to last.

He saw a state trooper he knew as he crossed the police station parking lot. The trooper shook his head. "They say they're coming down Hwy. 287 like buffalo."

John could just envision the procession of microwave tower trucks and Jeeps with media logos rolling out of Dallas.

The police station was already in a commotion and Chief David H. Wheat was in the middle of the office with people walking to and from him.

"NASA is going to set up temporary operations as soon as they get here," he said to John. "But no one is to touch the debris or bring it there."

"What are we supposed to do with the stuff?"

"A guy from Oncor brought us markers like those used for marking gas lines, those stiff little wires with flags. We're just marking them for now until the feds pick them up."

The state trooper told the Chief Department of Public safety officers were stationed along Hwy. 287 where debris had fallen in the median and along the roadside. On a television in the corner of the room they could see a helicopter's view of the scene being broadcast from Dallas.

The Chief muttered a long drawl of a short obscenity as he took a quick look at the screen.

John caught a glimpse of himself in the mirror on the lobby wall and saw how pale his face was contrasted with his dark hair and beard.

A shock of red hair appeared in the mirror a full head below his. "We're getting calls from all over the world now, I wish you could talk to them."

"Hello, Trudy, they've called everybody in, huh?"

Dispatcher Rios was endowed with freckles and bright red hair which contrasted with her blue uniform.

"I've been here since 8:30. I've been spelled for ten minutes. I'm not kidding, I wish you could answer the phones, I'm sure you know better how to handle the media."

Behind them, another dispatcher called out. "It's the folks at Mattoon's. They say there's a piece of tile on their roof."

"Tell them not to touch it," the Chief called back. "Someone from the fire department will come out."

John turned to Trudy. "I wonder whether it's on the Bible book store, the auto repair shop or the sporting goods store?"

Trudy snorted. "Wherever it is, I'm sure they're already trying to sell it."

Another dispatcher, obviously in some kind of distress, was waving at the Chief.

"I can hardly understand them, but I think they said they're from the *Jerusalem Post*."

Another dispatcher piped up. "Jerusalem, Texas?"

The Chief popped. "No, you damn fool, Jerusalem, Jerusalem! There was that Israeli astronaut, remember?"

Trudy and John looked at each other. "Oh, my God," said Trudy. "I wonder what they must think in Israel? I mean, when they see the shuttle has come down in a town called Palestine, uh, Pales-teen?"

"I think they'll see God's hand in Colonel Ramon coming home to Palestine," John said. "We won't tell them we pronounce it differently."

The Chief fobbed off the call from Jerusalem to a lieutenant and as he turned around and calmed down, he saw John and waved him over. He put his arm around his shoulder.

"Can you give me a hand?"

"Jeez, Dave, of course, anything. What is it?"

"Are you still on the volunteer fire department roster?"

John knitted his eyebrows.

"Well, yes, I am, I've kept my dues paid up. But I haven't been active for years, ever since I came down with diabetes."

"FEMA has said we need to inspect public property immediately for debris. Schools and other public buildings are not supposed to open Monday unless it's picked up."

"Do you want me to help pick up debris?"

"No, the feds already said they're going to do that themselves. But we have to locate and mark it all, and I'm already spread pretty thin. Nobody has been able to look over the sewer plant property."

John began to cough again.

"Hey, I'll help wherever I can," he said between wheezes.

The Chief leaned back.

"Are you up to it?"

"Oh, I just sound bad," said John. "I don't feel as bad as I sound."

"That's because if I felt as bad as I sound, I'd be dead," he thought.

"Well, I'd be grateful," said the Chief. "I'll feel better the sooner we can tell FEMA all public property has been inspected."

"No problem, I'll take care of it for you."

"Thanks, I owe you again."

John gave a mock salute and as he headed towards the entrance, he passed Dispatcher Rios.

"Where are you going?

He slowed down a little and explained.

"It isn't the first time the Chief has given you shit."

He smiled as he turned back around and headed out.


He saw the media rolling into the municipal complex parking lot as he left.

"Damn, they must have done 90 all the way from Dallas," he thought. The news on KRLD was dismal and confirmed the worst; debris was fluttering down like confetti all the way to the Louisiana border.

The reports were that a piece of insulation had broken loose and struck the underside of the left wing when the shuttle lifted off 16 days earlier. Sensors detected abnormal heat spikes on the left wing before contact was lost.

As he drove out of the city he could see a yellowish gray haze high in the sky. The smoke from the morning had spread into a dull smudge that covered half the sky.

"I hope no one ever has to see this again," he thought.

His cell phone buzzed and he saw it was Scott Bailey.

"There's a helmet in the front yard of a house on Douglas Street. Do you want me to take a picture?"

"Of course, why are you asking me?"

"The head's still in it."

John sucked in his breath.

"Yes, we need it for the record. But it won't be running in the paper."

Along the way he saw a state trooper standing guard on the side of the road where what looked to be a piece of panel lay. It had already been encircled with yellow tape; 20 feet away three carloads of gawkers snapped pictures.

Palestine's wastewater treatment plant was on the fringe of the city. He turned on the narrow service road and stopped at the gate. It had a heavy chain and padlock. Chief Wheat had forgotten to tell him the combination, but John guessed it was the same from when he was an active volunteer fireman. It was.

"It helps to have a good memory," he thought as he pulled through and jumped back out to lock the gate.

It was past noon now, and the sun began to draw some warmth. As he hopped out of the Suburban, John thought to take something in case he needed to poke or prod a piece of debris. He pulled a heavy right-angled tire iron out of the back, and with the little wire flags sticking out of his hip pocket, headed out.

The grass was short and hadn't begun to grow yet, so it was easy to look over the flat landscape. He quickly found a few pieces of frayed rubber and stressed plastic, and pressed the little flags into the ground.

He saw what looked like a wedge of cheese coated in a thick black wax, but the cheese was snow white.

He flipped it over and saw it was a shattered fragment from the corner of a ceramic heat tile. The other side clearly showed where it had been glued to the shuttle. "They were right about how light these things are," he thought as he put down a flag. It seemed lighter than foam plastic; he didn't even feel it when he poked it.

He began to cough, and reaching into his pocket, he realized he was out of sugar-free cough drops. When he looked up he thought he saw something move on the other side of the sedimentation pond.

He thought it looked like an especially large cow patty at first.

"I wonder what the heck that is?" He walked around the end of the pond.

A closer inspection didn't enlighten him. It looked like a horseshoe crab, but its shell was in one piece and oblong. It was also much larger than a horseshoe crab—almost two feet on the long axis—and it didn't have a tail. The rim of the shell was perhaps two inches thick and grooved.

When he got up close he saw a long depressed path in the grass, and ten feet away a gash in the sod.

"Oh, crap, this is some kind of experiment that was on the shuttle," he thought. "But what is it?"

It was clearly alive because it moved slightly even as he looked. He took the pointed end of the tire iron and flipped it over sideways.

When he was a boy growing up on Long Island, he once found a horseshoe crab on Jones Beach, and he had flipped it over. He never forgot the unsettling appearance of the flailing trilobite legs and how ancient and strange the creature appeared before it flexed its hinged shell to right itself.

That was instinctively what he expected to see when he turned this creature over. Instead, he gasped and raised the tire iron.

The underside was a mass of irises opening and closing, rimmed with tentacles and spicules, imbedded in a mass of ridges and tubes.

He staggered back and thought to run. But he saw the unintelligent creature was simply trying to right itself. As he looked on, his conclusion that it was not a terrestrial organism was confirmed in his mind as it slowly but methodically folded itself over sideways until it was lying on the ground shell topmost again.

As it righted itself, he saw a black and white fragment of a heat tile snap off the end of a tentacle and land a few inches away.

"This damn thing is what caused the heat tiles to fail," he thought.

In a moment as the blood rushed to his head, he thought of the seven astronauts, and more, of what the disaster might mean to the future of the space program. He brought the tire iron down and in complete anger cursed the thing.

"God damn you!"

He barely held onto the tool as it glanced off the shell with a clang. He raised it again and looked at the creature in amazement. It was metal.

In a flash of intuition, he saw how function follows form, and he realized what the gasping irises and flailing tentacles denoted. He saw fleets of starships manned by an ancient and unknown race traveling for eons between stars, autonomous and self-sustaining, giving rise to their own cybernetic parasites. He looked at the ancient creature and knew all this, from its form and its behavior. And he exploded.

He began hitting the thing again and again with the tire iron, repeating the same curse over and over: "God damn you! God damn you! God damn you!"

After perhaps a dozen blows he saw he hadn't made a dent and it had moved an inch away. He stopped.

"What am I doing?" he thought.

He wiped his forehead with his hand. Three drops of sweat landed on the shell of the creature, and began to sizzle. The shell began to throb.

He drew his hand across his brow and shook more sweat on the shell. Every place the moisture struck sizzled and it began to quiver violently.

What had his chemistry teacher called it years ago in high school? "The universal solvent," he thought, "this thing can't take water."

He looked over to the sedimentation pond only six feet away. "Adios, asshole, " he said, as he reversed the tire iron, holding it by the straight end. He bent over double and took a nice low swing with the bent end of the iron.

The space parasite flew through the air and plopped into the pond where it quickly turned into a mass of bubbling foam. John stood on the edge of the pond and watched the scum dissipate. In two minutes there was no sign anything had even been there.

He took a deep breath.

"What the hell have I done?" he thought. Before he had his next clear thought, he began to cough. His hand holding the tire iron shook wildly.

"I probably got the frickin' Andromeda Strain now," he thought.

He tossed the tire iron into the water.

"Rest in pieces, you bastard."

Still coughing, he stumbled back to where he was parked. He looked up where there was still a grayish-yellow haze high in the sky.


The municipal complex parking lot now looked like a hybrid between a media circus and a gypsy camp. He knew where there was a parking space in the alley behind Eilenberger's Bakery across the street. He was still coughing when he walked into the police station.

"God almighty, John, you sound horrible."

"I'm sorry, Dave, I guess I overestimated how I was doing. I need to get back home and in bed and take more medicine."

"Were you able to do anything out there?"

"I spotted about five pieces, but I wasn't able to get over most of the property."

He put a handful of the flag markers on the counter.

"Sorry."

The Chief looked tired but somewhat more relaxed.

"FEMA's set up in the conference room, and volunteers are pouring in from all over," he said. "By nightfall they'll have a complete command center set up."

They both turned to watch as the television in the corner put up a map that showed the extent of the debris field, all the way from Anderson County past Nacogdoches and Lufkin and Longview to the Louisiana border.

"What's with the podium out front?"

"They're going to have a press conference at 6 p.m."

John looked at his watch. "I'm sorry, I'm not going to last another hour. I'll watch it at home myself.

He saw Trudy smile.

"Hey, what's so funny?"

She turned around. "John, you've said yourself you're as stubborn as an Italian jackass. You looked like five miles of bad road when you first came in here. I was wondering when you were going to pitch it in."

"I'm not complaining, you know...."

"Yes, I know" she said softly.

Another dispatcher called out. "Cancel that call on Arrowhead. It's not a piece of heat shield tile after all."

The Chief hunched his shoulders in a gesture of inquiry.

"Uhh, it was a piece of toast her husband burned and threw out the window this morning."

The Chief just shook his head, looked at John and rolled his eyes.

John started hacking worse than ever. Trudy looked concerned.

"You go home and get better, hear?"

He looked out and saw all the law enforcement, FEMA and NASA personnel swarming outside. "I think everything's under control," he rasped sarcastically to himself so she would hear. He was starting to lose his voice.

He kept coughing all the way out the building. One of the sheriff's deputies who was being pestered by journalists in the parking lot pointed him out.

"He's the newspaper editor, and he was out looking for debris."

Three reporters with microphones, two with notepads and one lug with a camera perched on his shoulder jogged towards him.

He tried to restrain his coughing, but he was almost choking. One reporter ran up.

"Did you find any debris? Did you retrieve any remains of the space shuttle?"

John could only nod, and then he looked at their stupid faces. "This'll teach the jackals!" he thought.

He opened his eyes wide and clasped his throat. "Yes, I found some of the debris from space," he croaked. "And look what happened to me!" He started to cough horribly.

Half of them looked startled and the others puzzled. He turned and walked away quickly.

Back in the Suburban, he tried not to laugh as he coughed all the way home.


He took a double dose of Amoxicillin and sat watching the depressing news on the television from the couch under a throw. The chicken soup cooled down as he thought about what had happened that afternoon. His wife sat on the loveseat and alternately watched the television and him.

"Somehow, I have to let NASA know what happened, but if they believe me, I'll be in a cell in Area 51," he thought. "And if they don't believe me, I'll be in Terrell State Hospital."

His wife looked at him. "What are you thinking?"

He snapped out of it and then something popped into his mind.

"Do you know if there's a Jerusalem, Texas?"

Unlike her New York-born spouse, she was a native Texan. "I know there's an Athens and a Paris. And a Rhome, too. And Palestine, of course. But I don't know I've ever heard of Jerusalem. If there is, it's pretty small. Why?"

"Something I heard in the police station reminded me of something. When they got a call from the newspaper in Jerusalem, in Israel. It's made me think of something."

She tucked a leg under her knee. "Like what?"

"For thousands of years, each Passover, the Jews said 'Next year in Jerusalem.' They never forgot their expulsion by the Romans."

"Why does this make you think of the shuttle."

John slouched down under the throw. "I hope this isn't our expulsion—from space."

She frowned. "You're being a typical gloomy Italian. I'm sure they'll be flying the shuttle again soon. "And besides", she said turning back towards the TV. "The Jews found their way back to Jerusalem."

She didn't hear a reaction and after a while she turned to see he had slumped back and fallen asleep.

He woke up and heard a banging and scratching sound. He pressed the stem of his watch and the dial lit up. 12:30.

He looked at the television and saw it was on mute. He heard a whining, and the fog parted.

"Oh, she forgot to take Solace out before she went to bed."

He got up, put on his glasses, cinched his robe and grabbed the leash. The rambunctious dog pawed at the door until he arrived.

As Solace relieved himself profusely on a large Pin Oak, John looked up at the clear sky and saw the bright stars.

"God, what a day" he thought. "I had no idea what was going to happen when it started. And now..."—Solace dragged him to another tree—"I have no idea what I'm going to do with what I know."

He took a deep, clear breath. "The medicine, and the adrenaline, must be working."

Solace slowed his pace, so John reined him in and steered him back to the door. As he stood on the steps, he looked up, and this time Solace looked up with him.

He rubbed the dog's large floppy ears—-and noticed he was shaking.

"That's OK, boy, it's all right," he said. God, how loud that explosion must have sounded to those ears.

He looked up again. "We'll be back. We're made of tough stuff."

Solace leaned up against him and gently moaned as he rubbed his ears.

"We'll be back."

And the man and the dog went to their beds and slept well that night.

*   *   *

Gardner returned the story almost four months later, at the start of the September, and ironically (the irony will be explained shortly) this story prodded the most lengthy and in-depth appraisal of a story he ever gave me:

"Thanks for letting me see "Jerusalem, Jerusalem." This may be your best and most professionally handled story yet, but I'm going to pass on it for a number of reasons.

"One, I'm afraid that the shuttle tragedy is still so new that people are going to react badly to your handling of it here, feeling that you're exploiting the tragedy just to get a sale.

"Two, there's been so much on television, in such specific detail, about the causes of the explosion that nobody's likely to find your explanation very credible. Three, that explanation, the robot crab-creature, is pretty unlikely in a broader sense—if there were creatures of this sort attacking vehicles or structures in space, you'd think that it would have shown up long before this, and everybody would know about it—or at least the government would know about it, even if they were trying to cover things up.

"You're still hampered a bit here by your journalistic training. The protagonist doesn't have to be sobbing and bursting into tears every five minutes, but you get almost no sense here of what he feels about what's happening, of what his inner emotional responses are.

"You see him instead almost entirely from the outside, as an observer would, rather than living through the day along with him, feeling the emotions and the sensory data he experiences as he feels them. This is something you need to work on, I think.

"So I'm going to pass on this one, but, of course, let me see more when you have it. See you in Texas, the Lord willing and the creek don't rise."

This critique is a good example of the many possible ways a story can go wrong. First, after some very nice comments about my writing skills in general (a great encouragement), he starts with a practical point—sometimes the real world impinges on your fiction.

I learned of a very good example a few years later, when I was participating in a writers' workshop in Austin (I attended my first writers workshop *after* selling a story to *Asimov's*). Austin author Brad Denton wrote a book called *Laughing Boy* and had been ready to have it published when 9/11 happened.

Brad's story dealt with a brutal incident of domestic terrorism—a massacre at an outdoor music festival in Kansas City, and—worse for him—one of the characters muses how much more effective it would be to commit an act of terrorism against a big symbolic target—like, say the World Trade Center.

Brad's book publication was shelved until 2005 and the pain of the 9/11 attack lessened.

The first scene of "Jerusalem, Jerusalem" is completely factual—that's what happened to me that morning. In using it as the jumping off point for a story, I think I was being self-centered. Gardner gave me the insight to realize how the story might seem to other people.

Gardner's second criticism—that the story didn't meet the Suspension of Disbelief test—is of course, one of the most common difficulties in creative writing, and again, he brought some perspective to my attention with his observation. It's a problem—I think—that could have been overcome, if I did a major rewrite of the story.

His final criticism—that my journalistic objectivity is an impediment to *my* creativity—is a particular problem I've always had to cope with. If "Jerusalem, Jerusalem" had a lasting effect and caused a permanent improvement with my writing, it was to help me realize how much I have to work to overcome that.

He closed with his usual encouragement to send more, with a final note which refers to the ArmadilloCon convention. He was among the guests in 2003, and I was looking forward to seeing him. Unfortunately, at the last minute I developed car troubles and was unable to drive to Austin. I missed the chance to meet him in person, and I lost my registration fee. This also established a pattern—which remains unbroken to this day—that I have never been able to attend any convention where I paid the registration in advance. Thankfully, for years now I have been invited to conventions as a panelist, but for some time afterwards, any time I paid the fee beforehand, something happened to keep me from attending. When I attended ArmadilloCon in 2004, I paid at the door.

I later sent "Jerusalem, Jerusalem" to a couple of small markets, but ultimately I decided it needed too much work. In addition to the problems already outlined, it was just too personal; it reads like a first-person newspaper story. It remains a snapshot of my life at the time—which is nice for me, but ultimately fails as a story. Rather than attempt a complete overhaul, I published it on my blog in August 2005, and that's the only time it saw the light of day. Of all the stories I sent to Gardner during this breaking in period, it's—ironically—the only one that was never published.

Although when the story was written it was the shuttle disaster that affected me personally, now looking back it's the fact it featured my dog Solace. In the years after the story was written, he developed what seemed to be mental problems, and started to have bouts of aggression. We tried to have it treated, but they got worse, and in January 2006 he attacked my wife. He mangled her hand and she lost her right index finger as a result. There was nothing to do but have him put to sleep. I still have a dog biscuit of his that I've saved all these years, and when I die I will have it put in my hand so I can give it to him when I cross the Rainbow Bridge and tell him I always loved him.

# Chapter 10

## Returning To Space

For my next story, I thought I'd return to the protagonist of "I Got You", the space engineer John Travers. I thought it would be interesting to use a character a second time—something I hadn't done yet—and it also gave me an opportunity to write another story in an outer space setting.

The title came to me after reading a story in the 1976 anthology of Texas-themed science fiction *Lone Star Universe* by Glenn Lewis Gillette, "Fiddle Ess". The "fiddle" there refers to—as it does in my story—to FTL, Faster Than Light travel.

The story starts off with a set-up very similar to the beginning of "Silence is Golden". Two-person scenes lend themselves to dialogue because it is easy to keep track of who's talking, and since my skill at writing dialogue obviously seemed to be a strong point, that kind of set-up allows me to show my skill at that to best effect.

# Double-Crossing the Styx

"**H**ave you ever done any fiddle work?"

Travers looked at the Engineering Chief and knitted his brows. He made a sawing motion across his forearm.

"You mean like an Old American square dance?"

The older man burst out laughing.

"That answers my question!"

Travers sat back on the bulkhead bench and leaned up against the wall. His eyes were as glazed as the gray non-reflective paint.

The Chief chuckled as he sat down next to him and crossed his arms. "Enjoyed the juice bar last night?"

Travers rubbed his forehead and groaned. "Those geeyem berries have too much alcohol in them."

"I told you to stick with the hops juice."

The Chief turned to him. "I didn't expect that you would have, but I thought I'd ask."

"Would have what?"

"Experience with FTL shuttles. Faster Than Light."

Travers groaned again and nodded in recognition. "I'm just a mid-grade hull banger, sir!"

"You do have a basic level pilot's license, right?"

"To pilot a small transport, sure. But I've only driven around a ship or two doing maintenance. Never really done any recoveries or transports."

"Would you do a small recovery job at double time and a half?"

Travers turned to face the Chief. "You've got my attention."

Engineering Chief Ron Remede stood and began pacing the air lock floor. "We've got a special FTL shuttle coming in from Adrienne's planet in the Sirius system."

"What's so special about it?" Travers stood up and leaned up against the bulkhead.

"It has a corpse—plus a live experiment."

Travers didn't look up as he checked his straps. "I thought anything that went through the light barrier died anyway."

"But the man whose body is being transported sent along a mouse as one last experiment."

Travers turned to the Chief as he pulled on his safety harness. "I heard about this. The doctor who worked so many years to break the light barrier."

"Dr. Dickey Beasley. He spent 150 years trying to come up with a way to get living organisms through the light barrier."

Travers was running through his EVA checklist and punching on his wristpad. "I saw that the Service agreed to his last request. He wants his body buried in Texas."

The Engineering Chief shrugged his shoulders. "We get ashes transported all the time. But he's a Christian and wants a traditional subterranean interment in his family cemetery."

Travers cocked his head. "He *was* born on Earth, wasn't he?"

"Yep, I think he's the last of the original colonizers. Spent 20 years in transit on a half-light ship. He was 194."

"I guess the Service felt they owed him."

"Well, he did a lot of the work that got us up to light speed transport—and beyond for cargo. He just never could get living organisms over that light speed threshold."

"And he's got one last experiment with him, huh?" Travers grabbed his helmet and checked the glare shield for cracks. "Stubborn SOB, wasn't he?"

"Certainly persistent." The older man cracked a wry smile.

"So what's the problem that you need my help? Don't you just drag the shuttle in with a mag drone?"

"Yeah, well, that takes a few hours, at least, if not a day."

Travers rubbed his ungloved hands. "Okay, I see where you're going. Because of this stupid experiment, you need someone to grab the shuttle and bring in with one of our transports." He cracked his knuckles, and winced. He was still a little groggy from the previous night.

"It's a waste of time," he continued. "You know the rat will be dead."

"It's a waste of double time and half," the Chief smiled. "And it's a mouse."

"What about your console jockeys? Can't one of them handle it?"

"Right now, I don't have a single internal engineer EVA certified. So I have to use you."

"I'm so lucky."

"Hey, when you transfer to your next assignment on the Jarvinen, you'll have a little saved up." He patted him on the shoulder. "You can afford better drink."

Travers gave him an oily smile and put his helmet on with the glare shield up, so he could still be heard through the thinner plexi.

"Hey, I'll do it, don't worry," he yelled. He dropped the shield.

Remede gave him a thumbs up as he left the air lock. The inner door dropped slowly and when the outer seal pivoted open, Travers began his climb along the handholds to check for micro-meteoroid corrosion on some solar-directional panels—a regular chore for any external engineer hullbanger serving on a ship in the Asteroid Belt.


"Why is this transport nicknamed 'Jenny'?"

"I have no damn idea." The Engineering Chief's voice came through loud and clear.

"It has something to do with its ID number."

Travers looked over the holo readout. "8675309. So what?"

"Got me. I think it has something to do with a really old song. It's over my head."

Travers was looking over the cockpit carefully.

"This thing's hardly bigger than a Luna shuttle. You sure it has a near-light drive?"

"We'll have you by your pet rock in ten minutes."

"Very funny," Travers snorted. "Another really old joke. When do I actually get to pilot this thing?"

"Oh, you'll be on your own for few hours until we know the shuttle's in the system. You can just putz around and blow smoke rings out your ass to kill time."

"Double time and a half, haha."

"Did I say double time *and a half*?

"Hoo, hoo, hoo, don't screw with me. I'm starry-eyed today."

"Damn, I only thought I got you to do this because your ass was hung over the other day."

"Fiddle my ass."

Travers checked all the console controls and a few minutes later "Jenny" exited the station on auto-launch. Eight minutes later he was a 16th of a solar unit from a nondescript asteroid on the fringe of the belt.

When the near-light engine kicked off, the Chief came back on. "Just relax until I come back, it shouldn't be more than three or four hours."

"I'm well stocked." Travers patted a pocket on his personal "kit."

"Uhh, John, you didn't take a beer pouch or two, did you?"

"Shit, no, I got something a lot better than that. I got a sack of jalapeno-crossed frankenplums."

"The sweet kind?"

"Yep." Travers popped one in his mouth.

"Damn, those *are* good. I've had them before."

Travers passed the time reading some holo-pops. He finished *Asimov's* and was halfway through Strosstime *Station* when his attention began to wander.

He cleared the projection window and zoomed in on the asteroid. He squinted and tried to think of what the irregular piece of space detritus looked like.

"A hog with only three teats," he finally concluded.

"Now listen up or one of those teats will slap you upside the head."

Travers sat up in his seat. He didn't realize he'd spoken out loud.

"Crap, I dozed off."

"So you talk in your sleep. More bytes for your personnel file." The Chief's voice became serious.

"I don't blame you, it's been six hours. But the shuttle's coming in."

"I'm ready." Travers rubbed a hand over his face.

"Don't snap on the shields until you see the rock pop. A small transport like that can't take the drain of keeping shields up for long."

"I got you."

He saw a ripple in the star field.

"Here she comes!"

The irregularly shaped asteroid shattered as it absorbed the momentum of the shuttle dropping back to sub-light speed. Travers grabbed the manual controls.

"Bang!"

He punched on the shields and peered through the projection window.

"Hey, Ron, I think this sucker landed right on the rock. It's a cloud of dust."

"Their accuracy through the wormhole is getting better all the time."

"By the way, how big is this thing?"

"Just a big box twelve by six by six."

"It looks like a coffin," thought Travers as he slowly glided it in the transport bay a few minutes later. "I guess it is."

But it was sharp and metallic, covered in that same gray paint used on the exterior of Service ships.

After the clamps were in place and the pressure equalized, Travers opened the bay door.

After a few twists and pulls and yanks, the lid of the coffin swung up and the internal atmosphere swooshed out.

"Damn waste," he muttered.

He saw the body of the scientist in a form-fitting plastic case, and on an inside wall, a shiny box with slits, labeled "Experiment."

Travers took the box and raised it. He heard no sound and felt no movement. He put the box down on the edge of the coffin and popped open the lid.

He looked at the lifeless body of the mouse.

"Poor little dude," he said. "Stupid waste. Like it would prove something."

"It proved a lot."

Travers jumped back and dropped the box. The mouse's soft body made a little plop as it hit the floor.

The man in the case turned his head and looked at Travers.

Travers' throat was tight. "Holy shit."

"Pithy but appropriate." Dr. Beasley raised an arm. "Can you help me sit up?"

"I thought you were dead."

"I was."

Travers reached out mechanically and Dr. Beasley grabbed his hand to pull himself upright.

"I did it.

Dr. Beasley put his hands on the sides of the coffin and sat up straight. He looked at Travers.

"You have no idea of what you've seen, do you?"

The whiff of condescension began to blow the fog away from Travers' mind.

"What con have you pulled, cocker?"

Dr. Beasley scowled. "I can see from your insignia you're an mid-grade external engineer. I wouldn't expect you to understand."

Travers' attitude rose. He crossed his arms and leaned forward slightly from the waist.

"Try me."

The old man looked at him with an almost religious intensity.

"Physicists thought for centuries that time was an absolute. Then over three hundred years ago, Einstein showed that it wasn't. Then we thought the speed of light was an absolute."

Dr. Beasley saw that Travers was listening.

"Then we learned that the speed of light wasn't absolute, except for living creatures."

The doctor slammed his palm on the edge of the coffin.

"I spent a century and a half on Adrienne's planet, trying to punch through that barrier. It would be the culmination of a lifetime of study."

The doctor continued. "When my medical diagnostics told me I would be passing away soon, I had a flash of insight. Soon I would be facing my mortal absolute, death. And in a flash of intuition it came together. I realized that death is timeless—all our tentative metaphysical research has shown that time does not flow in the afterlife.

"The speed of light is an absolute, but only to living things," he continued. "When living things die, time stops flowing for them. So I posited that the light barrier kills living things because it halts time for them. That's why FTL travel doesn't affect inanimate objects."

Travers was following along as best he could. "OK, so what's this got to do with your supposed death?"

"I realized nobody had ever done what I proposed to do—transport an intact body back to the sol system using an FTL shuttle. I thought I'd try one last experiment.

"Our friend down here," he said as he picked up the mouse, "was not the experiment. I was."

"This was my last shot at solving the problem that had bedeviled me for decades, and left my scientific legacy incomplete," he continued. "The mouse was only an excuse to put a life support system in this carrier."

A slow realization began to creep across Travers' face. The doctor smiled slightly

"My theory was, if a living thing dies when it hits the light speed barrier because time stops, whether time would restart for the dead crossing that barrier."

Travers slowly shook his head.

"I arranged so that my body would be preserved untouched, and then loaded into this crate with the mouse and the life support system, which was supposed to be for him. Because when we came out of light speed, I revived. Without life support, I would have quickly suffocated."

"This is some kind of hoax," Travers spat out. "Even if time began to flow again for you, you still would be dead. You died of *something*."

"Ah, my friend, time hasn't just begun to flow again. For me, it has begun to run *backwards*. In fact, I am beginning to feel younger already! Give me a hand up, will you? Help me out of this box."

The doctor extended his hand. Travers hesitated and then stepped forward. The doctor shoved his palm up against his grabbed it firmly.

His free hand came up and he pressed a small stun gun against Travers' chest. Travers staggered back as the dart plunged through his suit.

Dr. Beasley raised himself up and stood in the case. He jumped out and grabbed Travers.

"Now, my friend, it's your time to journey to that undiscovered country from which no man, once bidden, may return."

He shoved Travers roughly into the coffin.

"Sweet dreams—whatever dreams may come," and he slammed the lid shut.


"How do you feel?"

Travers realized someone had been speaking to him for some time.

"Everything's numb," he mumbled.

"That's so you don't feel the pain."

"Ron?"

"It's me. You're in the med lab."

Travers remembered what happened. "Where's Beasley?"

"We were going to ask you the same thing. How the hell did you end up inside the shuttle instead of the doctor?"

"He put me there. He must have. He tazed me."

"This is crazy. The transport's missing and the FTL shuttle was floating out there with you inside. What in the hell happened?"

Travers took a deep breath. He could tell that, even under the deep anesthesia, his chest hurt badly. "The SOB shot me point blank with a stun dart. He could have killed me."

"He would have, except for the potassium level in your bloodstream. It caused a mild short circuit."

Travers had to think for a minute. "The plums!"

"You're lucky. You are also lucky that when the shuttle closed up, the life support came back on. Are you telling me when you opened it Beasley was alive?"

"Are you ready for the craziest story you ever heard?"

The Chief rolled up a stool and looked at him steadily.

Afterwards, Travers rolled his head and looked at him. "I swear to God, that's what happened."

The Chief rocked back and forth slowly. "Jeez, I wouldn't believe you, but I know from your med readings you're clean, and the transport's missing—along with the doctor's body."

"What now?"

"Well, you stay put and recover. I'll have to think about a report, and what to say in it."

"Good luck."

The Chief went back to his office and slammed shut the hatch. He brought up his personal assistant.

"I need you to do a sub-space google. I need to see any inter-relations between faster than light transport residual radiation, frankenplums and cheap beer."

The image hovered over his console. "Are we looking for anything in particular?"

"Yeah, how an overworked external engineer gets to see visions—and loses a corpse."

Remede poked at the soft body of the mouse with his laser pen. "And I need a forensic scan on the body of this mouse."

"The creature is inanimate. There is no proximate cause of death."

"That doesn't tell me a thing. Are there any DNA or fingerprints on it."

"Yes."

"Well, who's?"

"There are fingerprints, but they are not on file for any member of the crew of this vessel or the Solar Service."

"That doesn't make sense, again. Are they on record anywhere."

"Scanning."

"That's strange," thought Remede. "I could see there being no fingerprints, or Travers' fingerprints. But who else's?"

"File found. Dickey Leakey Beasley, Ph.D. Last residence—Adrienne's Planet in the Adrienne System."

"Of course, the mouse must have belonged to the professor," he thought, and he raised his finger to punch the console.

He had a thought.

"Ah, can we tell how old the fingerprints are?"

"Residual thermal traces indicate two to three hours old."

"Holy..." Remede rubbed his forehead.

"Get me the RSSS out of Callisto. Code Sentinel."

In a moment the image of an RSSS officer appeared over his console.

"To what does the Regional Secret Service Staff owe a Code Sentinel call?"

"Encrypt and secure this channel, and sit down. I don't believe it myself, but this is what I know."


While Remede was briefing the RSSS duty officer, a scientist was paged and covertly brought in to listen to the conversation. After Remede was done, and advised to sit tight until security officers arrived, the scientist sent out a message to a few key colleagues.

"The Asgard Equation has been independently solved by a scientist on a colony, who just re-entered the home system. He is being sought by the RSSS. Strongly advise immediate secure conference to discuss the long-term of the rainbow bridge issue."

Remede meanwhile stashed the mouse's body in a hermetic box and went over his duty roster, making adjustments to compensate for Travers' absence for the next few days.

"I might as well take care of this while I can," he thought as he looked over the rolls, "the fireworks will be starting soon."

*    *    *

As mentioned earlier, I leaned on my dialogue skills in writing this story; there are only three essential characters, and only two people in any scene at one time.

The piece of business about smashing into asteroids to slow a Faster Than Light transport is something I borrowed from Gillette's story in *Lone Star Universe*. I had never heard of that theory before, and I thought since it isn't well known it would seem like a fresh idea.

The idea of how life and time would flow backward and forward depending on which direction you crossed the light barrier is something I thought up. I have no physics to back up the theory, but I've been told more than once by "hard" science fiction editors that my science is "rather rubbery".

I used a few tricks of the trade in the narrative. If you noticed the reference to the Starship *Jarvinen*—the ship where "I Got You" is set—you realize this story is set earlier than "I Got You", which lets me duck the question of how Travers might have been permanently changed by his experience in that story.

I used the extrapolation trick when mentioning Travers' reading material. That's when you reel out a list of names—one unfamiliar—but you know what the unknown one is like because of the others. "Like Earth leaders of the past—Genghis Khan, Napoleon, Hitler and Colonel Green" or something similar in an episode of Star Trek, lets you know whoever Col. Green was, he was a nasty. Since Travers mentions "*Asimov's*" and "*Strosstime Station*" in the same breath, you can assume "*Strosstime Station*" is also a science fiction magazine—and obviously named, like *Asimov's* was, for a famous SF author, in this case the Scottish Charles Stross.

I sent the story off to Gardner on June 14, 2003; it arrived back on October 30. (I didn't think much of it at the time, but you may notice the return time on the stories was getting longer and longer—from just over three months to now over five months.)

He said: "Thanks for letting me see 'Double-Crossing the Styx.' Some good solid work here, but the motives and actions of the Mad Professor seem a bit dubious to me, and so I'm going to pass on it. You might want to try this one on *Analog*."

His pithy reply was essentially that my core motivation in the story didn't pass the "Suspension of Disbelief" test. At the time I couldn't think of what I could do in a rewrite that would fix the problem. I didn't inflict it on Stan Schmidt at *Analog* (Gardner, like many editors, would suggest other markets if they came quickly to mind.)

A few months later, right after the start of the new year—on January 2, 2004—I sent the story to a small print magazine, *Continuum Science Fiction*. It was published in the fall of 2004 by Editor Bill Rupp.

*Continuum* was one of those small labor-of-love magazines. It published its last issue in 2009.

One last word, about Glenn Lewis Gillette. After publishing only three stories between 1972 and 1976—including "Fiddle Ess" in *Lone Star Universe*—he took a real paying job in the private sector and stopped writing for over 20 years. His next short story publication was in 1996. Once he became active in the genre again, he spent a lot of time volunteering for the Science Fiction Writers of America.

All told, his bibliography in the International Science Fiction Database (ISFDB) has seven short story entries. By comparison, I have 30 (and two collections and one award). The ISFDB doesn't list the smallest of publications, especially if they are ezines. Ironically, "Double Crossing the Styx"—because of its publication date—is my oldest entry there.

Despite not being a prolific author, Gillette was apparently well liked by everyone who knew him, and when he died of cancer in 2010, he was missed. I'm sorry I never met him.

# Chapter 11

## An Alternate To Dallas

"**R**ome, If You Want To" was both a landmark and signpost in my development as an author. It clearly showed my progress in becoming a better writer, as well as the direction my fiction would trend.

As is so often the case in fiction, it is firmly rooted in personal experience. I lived in Dallas County, Texas, from 1985 to 2002—almost all of that time in the suburb of Cedar Hill. That's the longest I've lived in one place. Because of Texas laws that grant municipalities a great deal of legal autonomy—including the ability to resist incorporation into larger neighbors—Dallas is one big sprawl where cities seem to merge seamlessly into one another without any noticeable change. Often the only way to tell you've crossed a boundary is the change in the design of street signs.

The City of Cedar Hill could just as well be called far Southwest Dallas. Certainly all the years I lived in Dallas County, the City of Dallas loomed large across the horizon. By the spring of 2003, when I was engaged in this writing frenzy, it was just finally sinking into my consciousness that I was no longer a Dallasite. At the time I lived in Winnsboro, a full 60 miles east of Dallas.

A free-floating sense of nostalgia seemed to evolve into a conscious attempt to do a tour—a travelogue, if you will—of the city. I also already began to realize I was being thought of as a Texas-based writer, and I thought people from other parts of the world might find some of the details of the city interesting. Unfortunately, the city is damned to everlasting fame because of the assassination of President John F. Kennedy—and that's about all most people know about it.

Rather than overthink the subject, I quickly realized the simplest way to achieve my objective would be to be have the protagonist BE a tour guide.

To create some sympathy on the part of the reader, I set him up as a lonely, one-man operation. Then I had to actually come up with a plot.

The hook of the title—as in the case of "I Got You—comes from a 1980s song, in this case "Roam, If You Want To" by the B-52s.

In retrospect, "Rome, If You Want To" seems to be where I began firmly along the path of writing alternate history—an effort which was recognized in 2013 when I was a finalist for the Sidewise Award in alternate history. The transformation of "roam" into "Rome" may have been what punched my alternate history button; the literary speculations and alternate histories that dwell on different outcomes for the Roman Empire are legion (pardon the pun). In that unfathomable creative churning that goes on in a writer's mind, I began to work out a plot that would allow me to use that title, and spin a tale of paths not taken and worlds not won.

The business I developed—the motivation behind the tour guide's customers—is hardly original, but it does the trick I needed.

I need to let you read the story before I spoil it and give away too much in advance.

# Rome, If You Want To

Thom Burns looked out his office window. He could see the nearby Dallas skyline wavering in the vicious heat. He could feel the heat radiating off the heavy blue tinting.

He could hear the air conditioning straining. "Goddamn, maybe this summer really *is* the beginning," he thought.

It was 1980, the year before he was born, when Dallas saw its previous record set. It was over 100 degrees for 40 days straight, and that was when Dallas saw its all-time high—113 degrees.

But nobody was talking about Global Warming then. Now, after 30 years, Thom knew, that record was about to be broken.

The dark navy stretch Lincoln which *was* Burns Limo sat outside soaking up the rays. A few more years in this sun, he thought, and she'll be baby blue, dammit.

He couldn't even afford a garage or car port. It took all his money when he came back from Operation Iranian Liberation to buy the ride and a small manufactured building.

Burns Limousine Service sat in a small rented corner of a strip shopping mall on Industrial Ave. across the highway from the American Airlines Center. They still called it that even though the airline was long gone.

"No business today," he thought. "I can just stand here all day and play pocket pool for all the damn good it'll do me."

It was the middle of June and the end-of-the-school-year rush was over. Lots of times he felt like little more than a glorified pimp. It took him hours each day during the prom season to clean up the interior of the limo. The teenagers splattered drugs, booze and bodily fluids until it looked like the inside of an office microwave.

He couldn't afford any help or a receptionist. "I guess I can use the break," he rationalized.

He had a B-52s CD playing softly in the background. He liked the upbeat music; it reminded him of when he was young—and he thought he might amount to something when he grew up.

He went to sit back behind his desk and stopped to turn up the CD player so he could better hear it over the roaring AC unit hanging in the back wall. Instead, he lowered the volume as he heard the bells on the door jangle.

He turned to see a couple of young ladies, smiling and well dressed "Oh, what now?" he thought. He hadn't heard anybody pull up.

"Can I help you ladies?"

Both were tall, but the one with auburn hair was taller than her blonde companion.

"We're sightseeing in Texas and visiting Dallas," she said. "We wanted to rent a limousine for a day tour."

Despite looking as if she was in her early 20s, her speech had the cadence of a middle-aged woman and spoke very precisely.

"Where y'all from?" he said slathering on a Texas drawl.

"We're visiting from Luxembourg," said the blonde.

"Yeah, well, shit, I had to ask," thought Thom.

"Welcome to Dallas," he said. "Do you have anything special in mind?"

"We thought we'd rely on you," said the auburn-haired one. "We like to get off the beaten path."

"Well, I've lived here all my life," he said. "We can start downtown and work our way around. I'll go over our rates."

"Oh, don't bother," said the blonde. "We are well-to-do," she enunciated precisely. She pulled a bundle of hundreds from her small handbag. "Will this cover it for a start?"

"Crap, yes," he blurted out without thinking. "You two ain't into anything illegal or kinky, are you?"

They both laughed loudly. "No, sir, not at all," said the auburn-haired one. "We're just rich."

"Nice to know somebody's doing well these days," he thought. "Then again, you're not Americans."

"Well, then, can I know you two little rich girls' names"? he asked.

The blonde held out her hand in a well-bred manner. "You can call me Annie. Annie Gerson."

Her tall companion pumped his hand. "You can call me Julie. My name's Juliana, Juliana Anselmo."

Thom grabbed a remote control device and stuck his hand out the door. It was like sticking it into a convection oven. He started the limo and punched the remote AC start.

He turned and faced the young ladies, smiling. "That way it will be cool when we get in," he said. "Meanwhile we need a little paperwork."

"Will you be driving us yourself?" asked Julie.

"This is a mom and pop operation, without mom," said Thom. "I'm one of those hard-working American entrepreneurs you hear so much about."

Julie smiled, but a strange sort of sad look flitted across Annie's face.

After reviewing some very neat IDs and filling out paperwork, he pulled on his jacket and plopped on a cap. When he turned around he saw the pair was looking at the muted local Weather Channel on the television which sat on top a filing cabinet in the corner.

"New Dallas Record Set," the scroll said. "Temp hits 114 at 11:10 a.m."

He would have cursed but he didn't want to offend his customers. "The limousine is nice and cool," he said. "You'll be very comfortable."

"No doubt, Mr. Burns," said Julie. "We're sure a Texan knows how to deal with the heat."


The first place they wanted to visit was the first place everyone visits—Dealey Plaza. He drove them slowly down Commerce Street and then back around the triple overpass and into the parking lot that overlooks the grassy knoll.

There they got out and looked over the tight white fence where the second gunman supposedly drew his aim. Thom hung back a bit; their demeanor was reverential, and they didn't pull out any cameras.

It was a short walk in the searing heat to the County Office Building, the former School Book Depository. Thom had been through the Sixth Floor Museum many times, but his clients were hushed and downcast at every exhibit. Sometimes Annie seemed on the verge of tears.

It was almost past lunchtime when they emerged. "You ladies said you wanted some local color while you're here," he said. "Does that include lunch?"

It was an old trick, but it always worked on out-of-towners. He took them up Central Expressway to Northwest Highway. The limo barely fit under the awning of Keller's Drive-In.

He cranked the AC up as high as possible and Julie and Annie giggled as the waitress hung the tables off their windows and plopped down two cheeseburger baskets with onion rings and a couple of ice cold beers. Thom just had a beer and a chili dog and tipped the waitress very well.

"Any suggestions as to what you would like to visit next?" Thom asked as the tables were being cleared off and taken away.

"We have seen someplace sad and then someplace fun." Annie leaned forward. "What about someplace beautiful?"

"I have just the place."

He winced as they drove down Garland Road past a bank that flashed the time and the temperature. It was almost two and the temperature was already 116.

It was a struggle to walk the short distance from the Dallas Arboretum parking lot to the DeGolyer Mansion. Julie and Annie paused briefly to admire the beautiful blooms which had yet to wilt under the onslaught of the Dallas summer.

Inside the pair walked slowly as they admired the art and décor of the mansion which had been the home of the respectable family whose donation was at the core of the Arboretum.

Thom hung back a bit. At one point, he saw Annie put her hand to her mouth in front of a painting. The portrait showed a young man in a WWII Army Air Force uniform.

He thought he heard her say to Julie that she knew the man—but that was impossible, given the obvious age of the portrait. Besides, the last heir of the DeGolyers died in WWII.

"That was a good choice, Mr. Burns," said Julie back in the limo. "The flowers and the mansion are both very beautiful. But from now on, we stay in the car."

"Well, then again, any further requests?" he asked cheerfully.

Annie sat back up against the back seat while Julie sat up straight. "We want to see your slaloms."

"I'm sorry, Miss Julie, we don't ever have winter sports in Dallas. You can't mean like snow skiing, do you?"

"No, I mean where your poor people live."

"Ah-ah, now we get to the pervy part," though Thom. "I guess to rich people *slums* must be kinky."

"I got you," he said. "We'll be in Mexico in 30 minutes." Both Julie and Annie looked puzzled.


Thom went straight down Singleton Blvd. His clients were plastered up against opposite windows, making alternating sounds of amazement and sympathy. The ramshackle homes and dilapidated shops, with jalopies and low riders in front and in between, were within sight of the towers of downtown Dallas—but really a world away: The Third World.

Thom had refrained from any commentary, but he felt compelled to say something now. "This is where the people who do all the work, the dirty work, in Dallas live. Folks like to run down the Mexicans, but honest to God, they need them."

He thought about himself as a white person and added, "We need them."

"This is really so sad," muttered Annie.

"You don't have slums in, uh, Luxembourg?"

Luxembourg? Oh, no, there's nothing like this where we come from."

Thom turned the limo around before they entered Grand Prairie and headed back towards the city. "I'm open again for suggestions, ladies," he said. "We aim to please."

Julie leaned forward. "We want to see something really, ahh, unique."

Thom set his jaw. "You want we should go up Harry Hines Blvd. into the Red Light district?"

Julie smiled a thin smile. "Not quite. We have sex in Luxembourg, too. No, I want to see what you call a housing addition."

Now Thom was puzzled. "I don't quite get you?"

"You know, hundreds of houses all the same, long streets, little yards, packed together." She turned to her companion. "What am I trying to say?"

Annie piped up. "You know, what you call ticky-tack."

"Snobs," thought Thom. "Well, whatever floats your boat."

"I know just the place," he said. "Ladies, we're heading to suburbia."

The real estate developments in southwest Dallas sprawled across invisible city boundaries. The names were marketing ploys—The Woods, Mountain Creek, High Pointe—but it was all one big cancer.

Julie and Annie seemed just as appalled—if not more so—by this. "It's so sad, the sameness and dullness," said Annie. "I can't believe people live out here. They must think they have a life."

Julie saw the expression on Thom's face. "I'm sorry, if we offend you."

"Oh, heck, don't worry. I live in a condo on Abrams Road. I don't live out here."

They stopped at the Southwest Center Mall. The pair seemed flummoxed at the shops and noise. "They probably don't have all this shit in Luxemburgie," thought Thom.

They did do a little shopping. Julie bought a sack of music CDs, while Annie found a gold necklace with an iridescent crystal. Julie held her sack up as they left the mall. "Loot for Luxembourg!" she laughed.

The shadows were beginning to lengthen as they got back in the limo. "The temperature's finally beginning to drop," said Thom in the car. "I wonder what it got up to?"

As they drove back into Dallas, Thom turned the radio on. The new record set was at 117 degrees.

The culmination of the day was dinner at Sonny Bryan's on Inwood Road—the best barbecue place in the city, if not the world, Thom declaimed. Julie and Annie took a little time getting into the spirit of things, but after they noticed the other patrons dealt with the ribs, they dug in and had a good old time.

"Do you ladies want to see some night life?" Thom asked as the table was cleared.

They looked at each other, and Julie spoke. "Perhaps another day. We have to be getting back."

"Where are you ladies staying. Obviously I'll drop you off."

Julie looked puzzled for a second. "Oh, we've arranged to be picked up from your business."

Thom thought that was strange. "Well, the customer's always right."

When they got back to his office, Julie said, "I have to make a phone call. I'm going to wait outside where the reception's better."

Annie came inside and paid in cash after Thom tallied up everything, and threw in a good 25% extra. "It's been a pleasure," he said. "Come back tomorrow, or whenever."

Annie looked around. "Umm, where's the facilities?"

"The bathroom? Right through that door."

Thom turned on the CD player again and the B-52s started playing. He walked behind the window. He saw Julie standing there, talking on a cell phone hanging off her ear, the mouthpiece in front of her mouth. He gave her a thumbs up.

She didn't react, and he realized the security light out front was so much brighter than the indoor light that, combined with the tinting, she couldn't see him.

After a little more talking and a few nods, the conversation was obviously over. Julie pushed the mouthpiece sideways. It retracted into the piece which hung on her ear. Then it dropped onto her shoulder like a spider.

The "cellphone" grew little black legs and ran down Julie's arm. She opened her handbag and it jumped in.

Thom staggered a few steps backward. He heard a gasp and turned to see Annie behind him. "Oh, my God, you shouldn't have seen that."

She ran to the door. "Julie!" she hissed, nodding towards the blue expanse. "This is a window!"

Julie ran in and saw Thom's face. "I'm sorry, we need to leave." She spun around with Annie right behind.

Thom grabbed a remote off his desk. The deadbolt dropped in the door as Annie hit it. She shook the door a few times until she realized what had happened.

"An anti-robbery device," Thom said as calmly as he could.

The pair turned and faced him. They looked at each other, and then Julie spoke.

"Are you going to hold us for ransom?"

"Should I? If you're aliens, can't you bust out?"

Annie actually gave a little giggle. Julie snorted. "We're not aliens. We're just as human as you are."

"OK, time travelers, then?"

Annie seemed somehow more relaxed. "There's no such thing as time travel."

"Well, what was that crawling down your arm?"

"A specialized communications unit in the form of a genetic construct," said Julie.

"Wow, they must really be up to date in Luxembourg."

Annie smiled. "We're not from Luxembourg. We live here in Dallas."

"Well, then, I'll give you a lift home."

"Not unless your limousine can cross dimensions as well as traffic," Julie said curtly.

Thom clicked the remote and the door unlocked. "I appreciate your coming clean with me. You're free to go, if you want. You see, I'm not a thug. I really would, however," he said plopping into his chair, "love to hear your story. But I can't force you."

Julie looked at Annie, who shrugged. "Why not," said Annie. "Nobody would believe you, anyway."

"I'm sure that's true."

"The kind of cross-dimensional travel that we're doing is, well, kind of looked down on, where we come from," said Annie. "They call us 'Bummer Slummers'."

"Our timeline had much more technological development in the 20th century than yours," she continued. "One thing we learned is that time travel is impossible. Instead, there was the discovery and perfection of dimensional travel."

"If that's true, isn't there some kind of rule against scooting around the way you do? I mean, to avoid screwing up history?"

"Well, ordinarily, yes," said Julie. "But you see, this timeline is considered fair game. It could hardly be screwed up more than it is."

Annie looked apologetic. "I'm sorry Mr. Burns, but this timeline is close to ours, but it went seriously wrong in the last century. It's our guilty pleasure to see what our world managed to avoid."

"Can you enlighten me as to what went wrong?"

Julie knitted her brows. "Actually, the divergence is less than a 100 years back. There is no difference up until the end of World War I, or as we call it, the Great War. For us, it really was the War to End All Wars."

"Unfortunately for this timeline, after that war, a secretive group of industrialists who made a fortune from the war decided they'd insure their future profits," Julie continued, "by managing wars and manipulating economies .

"The first thing they did was to take control of the American government behind the scenes, by destroying key national leaders. They poisoned both Theodore Roosevelt and Woodrow Wilson in 1919. Roosevelt died and Wilson suffered a massive stroke."

"In your world, the U.S. never joined the League of Nations," said Annie. "Which is what these industrialists wanted, so that there would be no potential challenge to their control. They heated the economy up in the 1920s, then crashed it and started the process of industrial consolidation."

"Yes, and while everyone was suffering, the German accomplices pushed a psychopath to power who was sure to get Germany agitated enough to launch another world war," Annie said. "You really don't think a crackpot like Hitler did it all himself, do you?"

"In our timeline, Wilson got the votes to join the League of Nations, but Roosevelt came back to win the White House in 1920. He was unhappy that the U.S. had joined the League, but he couldn't go back on it—so he made it work.

"With his energy and attitude he *made* the league work. Yes, he had to break the two-term tradition to do it, but it was worth it," she continued. "We never had a Great Depression, a second great war, or that stalemate you called a Cold War."

"Oh, heck, I forgot about that," snorted Julie. "Those industrialists ran that Communist scam for years. You poor suckers. When that ramshackle mess finally ran out of steam, they began putting together wars one at a time like ad campaigns. Your military-industrial complex makes up wars now. Desert Storm, Iraqi Freedom, Iranian Liberation—neat little media packages."

"Instead of fighting other nations overseas, or pitting class against class at home, *our* 20th Century America turned its fight to science and technology," said Annie. "You landed on the moon in 1969. For us, that's when we had our first colony.

"You're right, ordinarily this kind of excursion is prohibited," said Julie. "But for a large, and I mean large, fee, the DOD, Department of Dimensionality, takes money from fools like us to help defray their costs so we can visit this timeline."

"Wait a minute, if there's no time travel involved," asked Thom, "why did Annie here recognize the young man in the Air Force uniform at the DeGolyer Mansion?"

Annie rocked her head back and forth as Julie raised an eyebrow. "Hmm, you know, maybe I underestimated you."

"There's a simple explanation, actually," she continued. "How old do you think we are?"

"Umm, early to mid-20s?"

"I'm 86 and Annie here is 79."

"Jeez, you're two old ladies on vacation!"

"You'd be amazed at what not eating adulterated food and getting occasional telomere treatments can do for you," said Annie.

"Even the people in the timeline where Joe McCarthy was used to set up a fascist dictatorship aren't as bad off as your people here," said Julie. "Because the nationalist regime didn't allow all its jobs to be shipped overseas. Plus the oppression there is obvious and heavy-handed. You are all brainwashed and clueless in this timeline."

"Thanks a lot. OK, why me and why now?"

Julie looked at Annie. "Be nice," she hissed.

"Don't be," Thom said. "Tell me the truth. You've come this far."

"We picked you because you are isolated and meaningless. We picked now because, well…"

Thom saw she was glancing over at the muted TV with the Weather Channel still on.

"Oh, jeez, this is the beginning!"

"I'm sorry. Our projections say in a few years your Dallas will probably be uninhabitable. We just wanted to see what Global Warming would be like."

Julie looked down. "I'm sorry. We have to go now."

They began to turn away.

"Please tell me…"

Annie stopped and turned around. Julie tried to nudge her out the door, but she waved her off.

"Tell you what, Thom?"

"About your world. Have you visited others, too? Please tell me." And for the first time that whole long damn day, Thom Burns' façade cracked.

"Please?"

Annie leaned on his desk. "Thom, there are beautiful places out there, worlds where humans never split into three races, worlds where Atlantis never sank beneath the waves, worlds where the laws of magic were uncovered instead of science. Many wonderful worlds."

"In one timeline, Athens defeated Sparta and the industrial revolution happened before Christ. Now, in that timeline, they're building rings around stars. We once booked a vacation to Sirius on the Starship Theodora."

"If you're into pomp and circumstance, there's a timeline where Rome never fell and the Eagle Standard rises over Trinity, which is what Dallas is called," said Julie.

They realized Thom looked very sad. "I think we've done enough damage," Annie said softly. They turned to leave.

Thom raised his voice to be heard above the B-52s CD. It broke.

"Did I do a good job today?"

Annie had her hand on the door. She looked at Julie. "Thom, you were the best tour guide we've ever had. I mean it. That's why we feel bad for you."

She pushed the door open. Julie was right behind her.

He raised his voice, pleading. "Can I keep the job?"

Julie turned around and Annie followed her back in.

"That's a very tempting offer, Thom," Julie said. "Would you really come work for us permanently?"

"We can even take the limo. It's paid for."

Annie raised her eyebrows. "Hey, you know, that thing can pass for a customized vehicle in a bunch of timelines."

"You can never come back. We'll be paying an enormous fine because of you," Julie said.

"I really don't have anyone I care about, and I don't have any close family. Nobody will miss me. Besides, I'd be rather be anywhere than here watching Dallas dry up and blow away."

Annie suddenly frowned. "Juliana, wouldn't we have a doppelganger problem?"

"Oh, I forgot to tell you I noticed something when I was researching this trip… There is no Thom Burns in our Dallas, or any other of the 1,142 immediately adjacent timelines, for that matter."

"Sorry Thom, although this timeline sucks, it's the only one you exist in. Your grandfather met your grandmother while he was stationed in England during World War II."

"OK, then, no holdups," he said hopefully. "Let's go."

Julie looked at Annie and set her jaw. "You're right. Let's go."

She opened her handbag and reached into it. The "cellphone" ran up her arm like a ferret, hung off her ear and swung its "tail" out.

"Cheddar, it's time. Yes, open the gate, and maximum aperture. We'll be taking a vehicle through."

Just to show off, Julie held her handbag out in front of her. The "cellphone" leaped in like a seal.

"Who's Cheddar?"

"Oh, that's our mook. He's the personification of our AI. You have to call him something."

As they stepped out into the steaming early evening air, Thom automatically turned to lock the door. "Oh shit, who cares!" He threw the office keys through the door. They hit the CD player in the corner and it stopped.

"Do you have the B-52s in your Dallas?"

"My goodness, funny that you mention that. We went to their concert just a few weeks ago," said Annie. "They never broke up."

As they walked to the car, she also said, almost to herself, "we also don't have AIDS."

Once inside, Thom turned around. "Well, ladies, where to now?"

"Just pull onto Reunion Blvd. You'll see it," said Julie.

He gave a little cry when he realized all the traffic and motion had stopped around him.

"Don't worry, we need a slight temporal stasis so people don't see us go through the gate," said Annie. "Go straight ahead."

At first he thought he saw a gap in the skyline, but then he realized there was a rectangular star field directly ahead in the roadway. He slowly braked.

"Are you sure about this?" Julie asked.

"Yeah, I am," he said quietly.

Annie leaned over the seat and smiled at him. "Think about where you want to go next. There's a whole wide multiverse out there."

Thom thought. "For grins, how about that eternal Rome? Like you said, it must be impressive."

"Hey, big fella, no problem," she said. "We can go to Rome, if you want to."

Thom set both hands on the steering wheel and hit the gas. "Goodbye, Big D," he said.

The stars came towards him. "What was it that kid said?" he thought. "Oh yeah."

"Second star to the right, and straight on 'til morning."

*  *  *

The trick of having cross-dimensional travelers visit an alternate reality that happens to be our world—or accidentally creating an alternate reality which is our world—is hardly new. That's essentially the plot of the seminal alternate history novel *Bring the Jubilee* by Ward Moore. Having them be tourists out essentially slumming was my special insight for this story,

The story was sent off to Gardner on June 23, 2003 (yes, only nine days after I sent off "Double Crossing the Styx"—I said I was writing fast!). However, it came back over a month later than "Styx", on December 10, 2003. In general, the longer a story stays at a magazine the more it is being considered, so that was essentially a positive sign.

On the other hand, and in retrospect, it may have been a sign Gardner was getting snowed more and more under his burgeoning slush pile.

He wrote back:

"Good to see something by you again, and thanks for letting me see "Rome, If You Want To." This has got some very nice stuff in it, and your level of line-by-line craft grows with every manuscript I see by you, but the problem with this story, published in a genre magazine, is that everybody in the audience is going to know they are time travelers almost from the beginning of the story, long before Thom tumbles to it."

He signed off with the usual encouragement, "So I'm going to pass on this one, but, of course, let me see more when you have it."

This was good feedback for a couple of reasons. First, he didn't say there was anything wrong with the story per se, just it wouldn't work for the audience I was pitching it for. Sometimes writers have to be reminded publishing is a business, and you have to create a product people will pay to buy. If I had the knowledge then I have now, I might have tried to pitch it to a general short fiction magazine.

Second, he noticed that my prose was becoming polished. The dialogue was getting crisper, the writing tighter. This was an effect of my constantly writing in the pursuit of the proverbial "honing my craft", and it was nice to know it showed.

I went back over the story and tightened the travelogue aspect a bit by dropping some of the locations visited, and a week after receiving the rejection from Gardner, I sent the story to John Thiel, who runs—and still runs—a small fanzine called *Surprising Stories*. He accepted it a week later. I don't recall, almost ten years later, what my thoughts were on submitting it to such a small market. The only supposition I can make is that, being in such a writing frenzy, I must have had a story in every slush pile of every important magazine at the time. Most magazines strictly forbid multiple submissions—Gardner was an exception.

Surprising Stories published "Rome" the following spring, in May 2004. This was only my fifth story ever published, but it was the first time I ever received any critical notice.

British author Patrick Samphire gave it a generally positive review in some short fiction capsules he used to do on his web site. It was a great encouragement at the time, and made me realize people out there were actually reading my stuff.

Samphire wrote:

"'Rome, If You Want To' is set in near-future Dallas, as global warming begins to bite. A limo driver is approached by two strange women asking for a tour of the city.

"The writing in this story is rather clumsy, particularly at the beginning, but you shouldn't let that put you off. Antonelli's story opens up to show visions of other presents and futures, and it is tinged throughout by a beautiful sense of sadness at what might have been had we made different decisions in the past. The protagonist of the piece, Thom Burns, is a lonely figure who seems lost against the background he finds himself in, and the final redemption the tale offers him is both inevitable and satisfying.

"Although this appears to be an earlier story, his potential is clear in it. Worth checking out for someone who may develop into a significant writer."

This was very encouraging, and also heartened me, because Samphire saw in the story what I put there. In the end, it came out a very wistful piece.

I had thought, as I was writing it, that somehow my writing skills had sharpened, and I realized I was right when, towards the end of the story, I was proud to be able to drop in the title as part of the dialogue.

If in the process of developing as a writer I was uncovering depths about myself, I learned I am a rank sentimentalist. The direct reference to *Peter Pan* at the very end is a dead giveaway.

This story contains the seeds of the alternate history body of stories I would develop later, in the scene where one of the travelers explains alternate worlds to Thom. "Worlds where the laws of magic were uncovered instead of science" became "The Witch of Waxahachie", which was published in *Jim Baen's Universe* in 2008.

The world where "Athens defeated Sparta and the industrial revolution happened before Christ" became "The Starship *Theodora*", which was published in *Nova Science Fiction* in the summer of 2012.

# Chapter 12

# "I Don't Like Football Very Much"

Following the old vaudeville saying, "Never follow a banjo act with another banjo act," I decided my next story needed to be different in tone and subject from "Rome, If You Want To".

One segment of American culture I hadn't touched on as yet was professional sports. Having lived in the Dallas area for so long, I had soaked up a fair amount of the Dallas Cowboys culture—"America's Team"—and so I thought football and the Cowboys would be a good setting.

I also had written few stories set in the future, so I thought to stretch a bit and make that my setting. Finally, with modern trends being what they are, it was (and is) easy to write dystopian fiction. There's an old saying, "The past is a foreign country". These days, you can just as well add, "The future is dangerous territory."

Note that "Berserker" was written more than a decade ago, and things haven't taken much of an upswing, as far as American society across the board is concerned.

To be able to write something futuristic, I had to do some research—a process considerably facilitated now by the internet—and I tried to make my nano-babble sound convincing.

I wrote this story from the first person, and in addition to giving a good opportunity to exercise my dialogue-writing skills, I enjoyed the opportunity to write in this kind of tone.

# Berserker

My football-scarred ass was floating on a neat little maglev in a sonic whirlpool. I was just beginning to relax. I had to fill two piss pouches that day—the regular daily doping test, which was only going through the motions, of course, as well as a second one to show that the regen nanites I had taken for my ACL tear had washed out.

Everyone cheated. You were expected to. Those regen nanites I took for the ACL tear—yeah, the ones Doc gave me washed out, but I pumped in some silicon ones gray-marketed from Vilnus. I got them from a trainer. Those little Lithuanian buggers didn't react to anything. Of course, I'll probably never get rid of them. I'll be pissing out sand when I'm old. If I live that long.

Brad Carlisle sidled up to me and bent down. "The Hillman is going berserk tomorrow," he said quietly.

I didn't turn my head. "How do you know?"

"I heard him tell Coach we're sure to win."

"Shit."

The Hillman. That was his nickname, because of his name as well as because he was as big as a hill. Hylton Hawkins had been a defensive lineman with the Cowboys for ten years—a long damn time in pro ball, especially when you're constantly being doped with nutraceuticals, nanoparticles and GM-protein supplements. It took a toll.

The Hillman was really sort of dumb and sweet; he was just an East Texas big country kid out of Texas College in Tyler. For years after he hit the big time he threw away his money on drugs, whores and cars. Of course, team owner Joe Jenkins got a cut of it all.

It was Jenkins who spread the money around to pay off the police and the media. And it was Jenkins who sent the word down that a berserker payoff was available.

Not that it was very common, or people might have wised up. Even as corrupt as the U.S. and especially Texas was, you couldn't pay someone to go berserk very often.

The summer of '27 we were a tight race in the west division with the Raiders. Oakland was coming to town for the second-to-last game of the season and everyone knew it was an important one.

Tuesday that week Coach said it was a "must win". We all knew what that meant.

I thought we could win, anyhow, so I didn't give it much thought.

Then Carlisle dropped me the word.

He slid away as quick as he came. I muttered under my breath.

"Oh, Hillman."

Three years earlier he had met a nice gal and married. He really settled down, in every way. Had his mook block the drug dealers, stopped going to the titty bars. Christ, he traded in the candy apple red Viper for a fuel cell SUV.

Last year they had a sweet baby girl. His wife brought her to the sidelines during training camp. Adorable little booger.

I'll never have any kids. I went to a Big Ten school. The steroids I took in college turned my cojones to stone.

In the big leagues you didn't get anything as crude as steroids or performance enhancing drugs—unless and until you went berserk.

The news from Carlisle hit me like a horse dose of respirocytes. Goddamn, why didn't I think of it? Hylton has squandered millions over the years. Even from the nosebleed seats you could see he was struggling this year. His pro career was coming to a close—and he had a wife and a daughter he probably couldn't provide for in the future.

I was a strong safety slash cornerback. The shit I took to do my job would probably make me hobble and wheeze by the time I was 60. That was the tradeoff for being a pro. A big lineman like The Hillman—he'd probably be in an augmented wheelchair by the time he was 45.

Well, now he'd never have that problem.

I must have looked stunned when I got out of the whirlpool and went over to the physical therapist doing rubdowns.

He rubbed his mech-gloved hands over my calves and thighs.

"Marcos, man, you look puny."

Nanites are supposed to be too small to cause an immune reaction, but the silicon jobbers from Vilnus didn't seem to know that. Between the nanites and the bad news, I was sweating like a hog.

I faked a smile. "I had to give two UA samples this morning. I feel squeezed like a lemon. Sometimes it's awfully disconvenient, as Coach would say."

The trainer laughed. "You'll bounce back soon enough."

Hylton was already on the field by the time I was suited up. I slapped his shoulder pads as I ran by. He didn't turn or acknowledge me. With those carbon nanotube plates, he might not have even felt it.

He was subdued and held back somewhat from the other players during practice. There wasn't much of the normal macho chatter and cussing, and what there was sounded tinny. I think the word had begun to spread. The grunt trainers and second stringers might have thought we were all concentrating on the next day's game.

In a way, we were.

The locker room bullshit and bragging seemed forced. A few of the players hailed Hylton as they walked by; he only grunted or said "hey" in that squeaky voice of his. He showered and dressed quickly. He didn't look to the right or the left. He looked down, and then walked out.

A few of us shot glances at each other. We really couldn't say anything that might get back to Jenkins.

I just shook my head a little. "Goddamn Jenkins." I thought.

Running a pro football franchise was a big business. In an evil way, he was real smart. He made millions, but spread a lot around. The league and the officials were kept happy.

You know, by then, some people had begun to wonder why we were still using cash in the U.S. If you ever saw a ref pick up a fat envelope before a game, you would have known why. No smart chips in cash.

I was doing well myself. I had a big ICE machine that rattled the bridge over the condensation canal as I pulled out of the parking lot. That year the canal was almost overflowing all summer as the cooling towers sucked the moisture from the domed stadium. Welcome to the Texas Tropics.

And God bless Houston, the poor bastards.

I paid a fat fee for the right to drive that internal combustion engine. It was worth it to hear the roar and watch people turn as I rumbled down the streets in North Dallas. Other players lived in the gated community. Carlisle was one of them, and I banged on his door as soon as I got out of my car.

"You went straight home, too, I see."

"I guess I'm like you, I don't feel like going out tonight."

"Where's Melissa?"

"She's off with some friends at the Galleria."

We sat down with some microbrews.

"You know, when I was in high school and a player would drop dead, I thought it was like they said, stress, you know, and the strain of pro ball."

"It's not like it's common," said Brad. "Hard to see a pattern.

John Tomachevski with the Pats two years ago—from what I heard, he really did have an aneurysm."

"Yeah, but was it caused by drugs, anyhow?"

"Welcome to the Big Leagues. The point is, he didn't go berserk."

For the past few years, once or twice a season, a player had died either after being stricken on the field or in the locker room. When I was a rookie out of college, I thought it was the drugs and the stress, too.

"I've only been on the team a few years. I've never seen this happen with the 'Boys."

Brad smiled a crooked smile as he wagged his beer bottle. "Yeah, well. Money talks and bullshit walks. The Hillman wants his wife and kid cared for."

"You think she knows?"

"What do you think?"

"What will she think after the game?"

"She'll probably think he took one hit too many." He stared down the long neck of his bottle. "At least, that's what she'll be told."

Brad was an offensive lineman. The calcium-carrying nanocrystals he took for his bones had begun to affect his face. When he looked serious, it looked like a mask.

I stood up and looked out the window. "Do you think it's really his idea?"

"He probably thinks so. I'm sure Jenkins somehow dropped him a hint. Maybe he read the News on Sunday. You saw that story about J.J. Jervinis."

"J.J. was in a fight in a bar. That's just a coincidence."

"Yeah, well Jenkins knew about his contract."

"You don't think he'd arrange for somebody to beat J.J. up?"

Brad took a long swig. "Well?"

J.J. left the team the year before, banged up and broken after spending years on the line. He was killing the pain the previous Saturday night when he got in some kind of fight in a West End bar. The beating left him brain dead.

Usually people go years before passing away and having their organs harvested.

"Everyone knew he signed that organ contract so he's have some money for himself and his wife," Brad continued. "But he only collected a few months. Hardly got anything at all. His wife's screwed now."

"What do you think it would take to take J.J. down in a fair fight?" he asked bitterly. "It was obviously a set-up."

Also, J.J. didn't read the fine print. The company he signed with exercised its option once he was on life support. Instead of pumping him full of hyper-accelerated regen nanites, they parted him out.

"Shit, you think Jenkins would do that just to drop a hint to The Hillman?"

"Hey, he's not the sharpest guy in the world, but he knows what's coming at the end of the season," he said. "He sees someone like J.J. push off and leave his woman high and dry, and then a day or two later, a berserker bonus is hanging out there. A sure ten million dollars."

Something about quoting an actual dollar figure startled me. "Is that the going rate?"

Brad flipped open another bottle. "From what I hear."

"I wonder if he knows how much his wife and that baby girl will miss him."

"I think he sees it as a self-sacrifice, which it is."

The sun was setting over Dallas. The late afternoon monsoon rainbow was fading into the orange twilight.

"You know, what almost pisses me off the worst is that we can't say anything," I said. "You know what a businessman like Jenkins would do."

Brad shook his head in a short jerky kind of way. "There's not much guys like us can do."

He took a really long swig. "We're just 21st Century gladiators. Sometimes, you win, sometimes they drag you out by your heels."

"Yeah, well the gladiators were forced to do it. Or they did it for the glory. We do it for the money."

Brad gave a bitter chuckle and raised his bottle in a mock salute. "God bless America!"

I could tell how he was dealing with his feelings, so I left him to soak and slouched over to my apartment. I kept the TV on flat as I watched the news and sports; I wasn't keen to have the sports AIs jumping across the room at me. The old pro, Dale Hammond, was live and real, though, and holding forth.

"The Cowboys' game tomorrow against the Raiders is an important one, but both teams are in the playoffs. The only thing to be decided is who plays against whom, and for Dallas, whether they can put the hurt on a tough Oakland team which will try to keep them from making it out of the division."

"It's an important game, a big game, but let's get past the hype," he continued. "Nobody needs to go berserk, if you know what I mean. Cool heads will prevail."

I sat up like a shot. "Goddamn, he knows!"

"Troy!" I shouted. My mook came on.

"Yes, most worthy breaker of asses?"

"I need an e-mail to Dale Hammond. Just say, 'I saw your report on the 10 p.m. news. Hylton Hawkins is a player to watch in the Oakland game.'"

"Do you want to send this as 'anonymous?'"

I thought hard for a few seconds. I guess it was time to be a standup man.

"No, fuck Jenkins. Use my proper name. Marcos B. Taylor."

"Yes, sir. Sent."

I know it wasn't much, but it was something. If anything came down, well, shit, I could make a dash for the Pacifica Republic.

That would be funny-I might even play for Oakland.

I thought about Hylton as I drifted off to sleep listening to my restful playlist coming through my audio chip. I saw the face of his wife and daughter, who would not have a husband and father tomorrow night.

I thought about what Brad had said. "Yeah, bread and circuses," I thought. "Beer and football."

I rolled over. "Let's not forget about drugs and nanites," and after the endorphins kicked in I slept.


I saw the video bots circling under the dome like vultures as I looked out the runway. I had to wait my turn as we all were dosed with our protein/calcium supplement. I didn't see Hylton at all; he was in a back room probably being prepped like an Aztec sacrifice.

The supplement was supposed to be simple GM-proteins and minerals; we knew Jenkins, as well as almost all the other owners, paid off the league to look the other way. It was a witch's brew of nanoparticles and crystals that looked as ugly as swamp water and tasted worse; we bitterly called in Nanorade.

The linemen on both sides of the ball also got a shot of respirocyctes, to carry extra oxygen in their bloodstream during the game. One of the few things they dosed us with that was actually harmless, but still illegal. It was given under the cover of a vitamin shot.

I was on the sideline when Hylton came out right before kickoff. They obviously didn't want him talking to anyone. I saw the head trainer wave a little hand-held device alongside his head. He was disabling his MEMS chip so the medical staff wouldn't get an accurate reading of his vitals during the game. The doctor had to be in on this, too, for it to work.

I took my place for the opening kickoff. From behind I could see Hylton and tell the berserking was already starting. In addition to our normal pre-game preps, he was now full of nanites that increase his muscle metabolism, along with others carrying steroids. He also probably was pumped a few gallons of enhanced methamphetamines. His metabolism was speeded up to the point I could almost see the heat coming off his helmet.

He probably had a normally lethal dose of nutraceuticals to fuel all this, and probably some morphine-based happy juice for good measure.

I just caught out of the corner of my eye his wife with their daughter on her knee sitting in the third or fourth row on the 50-yard line.

The other cornerback took the ball and sprinted up the field as Hylton cleared a swath. He batted and banged away the Oakland line and secondary like so many toy soldiers. Our runner tripped over his own feet at midfield because he was running so fast.

On the next down, Oakland made a line shift. One of their largest linemen, Dexter Ward, lined up opposite Hylton. I thought, "poor chump, he doesn't know what he's in for."

On the next play, the pair hit squarely. The stadium almost shook. The play stacked up in the middle.

I couldn't figure out what happened. I looked over to Brad on the sidelines. His eyes just got real wide. I guess he got a better view from where he was. Then it hit me.

I hadn't cussed like that since I was in college and realized what the steroids had done to me.

That had never happened before, two players at the same time.

Oakland had a player going berserk, too.

I learned later the progression of the nanites and other drugs was accelerated by the increase in a player's metabolism and adrenaline as the game progressed—but normally a player went quarters before he got real sick because he was smashing his opponents.

Now with two equally enhanced and aggressive players facing each other, their berserking quickly went out of control. After a couple of downs our quarterback was shouting at Hylton in the huddle, who couldn't hear because of the blood rushing in his ears. The Oakland QB was screaming at Ward, too.

You could tell from the hush that fell over the stadium that the fans knew what had happened. All the players, both on the Dallas and Oakland side, were stunned and weak-kneed. To see a player go berserk was bad enough. To see two players killing each other on the 50-yard line was a horror show.

The pair began to hit each other so violently blood splattered on other players, who began to shrink away, afraid of being infected by the raging nanites. The refs looked like they were trying to walk backwards out the stadium.

And neither team was scoring.

After punting the ball back and forth a couple of times—both linemen were playing both sides of the ball, their owners wanting to get their money's worth—neither QB could keep either man in the huddle. They paced the line of scrimmage and groaned like animals.

At the seven minute mark of that first quarter, the pair hit each other so hard and evenly they both bounced back three or four feet from the line of scrimmage. The ref's whistle was futile.

They shouted and went after each other. Ward landed a crushing blow on Hylton's head that crushed the top of his helmet. Hylton's simultaneous blow, to the side of Ward's helmet, obviously broke his neck.

It was over.

Ward was dead, but Hylton was still breathing, and now the medical staff had to go through the motions of trying to help him. Jenkins meanwhile had come down from his skybox and, as he so often did, put on a show of fake concern over the injured player.

The doctors and trainers were mumbling and looking at each other.

Hylton began to convulse.

Jenkins stood next to Doc. "Can't you do something for the boy," he shouted. For the record.

He looked down and over at Hylton. In one gigantic spasm, Hylton's back arched in a violent thrust and the contents of his stomach erupted all over Jenkins.

Hylton's body relaxed and as his head turned sideways blood ran out onto the artificial turf and towards Jenkins, who stood there with puke all over his face and suit. You could see him raise his hands like he was ready to scream, but then he saw Doc's face and he froze.

Doc saw Jenkins had aspirated some of the vomit.

A trainer dumped a water bottle over Jenkins' head. Another began to wipe his face with a towel. Coach spun Jenkins around and told him to run towards the locker room, and then shoved him ahead of him as he ran.

Brad came up to me as everyone stood there stunned. We listened as the ref called off the game.

Brad took off his helmet. "Can you believe this?"

I thought I heard a baby crying in the stands.

I looked towards the runway where Jenkins disappeared, and said the most hateful thing I ever have said in my life.

"I hope he dies, too."

I meant it,

Hammond went live after the game, and bless his artificial heart, laid it on the line. Some of the other sportscasters, craven paid-off stooges, still couldn't get over being afraid of Jenkins and they hemmed and hawed and babbled from the sidelines.

Hammond was live and livid. Everyone who saw it remembers it. I was ten feet away.

"Two wrongs don't make a right, but it does make it over," he shouted as he began.

We knew then it was.

When he was done and the lights went off, Hammond muttered, "The suits can have me fired, but I don't care."

I went over to him. "We hold these goofs to be self-evident. There's no turning back."

"Thanks for the e-mail, Marcos." He smiled. "You confirmed what I suspected."

"You didn't know, for sure?"

"No, not really, but with my experience, I had a real good hunch. Actually, I was more sure of Dexter. There is much more freedom in Pacifica and I have good sources in the Bay Area."

He threw his bag over his shoulder. "In fact, I feel a trip to the West Coast coming on. I have a jet at Addison Airport.

He turned away.

"Hey, you old sportshound, can I come?"

He smiled a crooked smile. "What do you plan to do out there?"

I threw my helmet to the sidelines.

"Defect."


I was still wearing my uniform when we arrived in California. On the way to the hotel we watched the video as a representative of the Pacifica Council met the Oakland team at the airport. The coach was quickly in jail, the owner in France.

Of course things haven't moved as quickly in the U.S. That's why I have welcomed the opportunity to testify before this congressional committee. I think every intelligent and honest person in the U.S. supports the nanotech legislation proposed by the Administration. Although I am no longer a U.S. citizen, I urge its passage, and I hope my first-hand account of Bloody Monday has been enlightening

I hope you understand my reasons for not coming in person. There are still people like Joe Jenkins in the U.S. ready with bucks and bribes. I think I'll stay put in Pacifica for the time being.

Jenkins hasn't died, yet. They've been trying to purge the nanites, I understand. Apparently he's little more than a zombie.

Mrs. Hawkins and her daughter received a $50 million settlement from the court ordered sale of the team.

Because the reforms enacted by Pacifica after Bloody Monday, I have enjoyed playing football for the Raiders. I know the worst abuses in the U.S. are dissipating. Let's finish the job.

I have nightmares sometimes. Nightmares neural-interface chips can't control. I see a metal box designed to hold ashes, sitting on a mantel in a home in North Dallas. It's late at night, and there's not a sound.

And I see the box move just a little. And I hear it groan.

*　*　*

When I finished the story, I had second thoughts about sending it to Gardner, because he still had "Rome, If You Want To" and I reckoned it would be confusing at the very least, to have two stories closely identified and set in Dallas at the same time.

So instead, I thought to send it to Ellen Datlow, who was helming the top webzine at the time, *SciFi.Com*. I sent it off July 10, 2003, and Ellen replied on September 5:

"Thanks for sending me "Berserker" for *SciFiction*. It's not bad, but I just don't love it."

This is as good an example as any of the fact that many, many good stories get rejected every day, because of the stiff competition and the need to fit certain needs of the particular publication.

Five days later "Rome" came back from Gardner, and I dropped "Berserker" in the mail to him immediately.

In the meantime, I finally had the opportunity to meet Gardner in person. He was a guest at the convention in Philadelphia, Philcon, in December 2003, and I made the effort to fly out to the East Coast and see him. I had hoped to see him the previous August in Austin at ArmadillonCon, but I had car troubles and was unable to make it.

This time, things worked out. PhilCon 2003 was only the second convention I ever attended. When I arrived I introduced myself to Gardner and asked him to sign my copy of his collection of short fiction, *Strange Days*, which was published in 2001 by PhilCon when it was the World Science Fiction Convention that year and he was Guest of Honor. He signed it:

"For Lou,

"Someday maybe you can sign *your* collection for me!

"Gardner R. Dozois"

Which was nice, and six years later, with the publication of my collection *Fantastic Texas*, I was able to do exactly that.

When I returned to Texas, I shot him off an email:

"Oh Great One!

"Having traveled thousands of miles to have kissed thine own ring, this meager vassal is now gratefully returned to his home fief. (By the way, I *really* did kiss his ring!)

"Well, OK, enough of the baloney. It took me three hours to fly from Philadelphia to Dallas, and another two to drive back to East Texas, but I made it. Back to the sports desk in the morning.

"It was great to meet you this weekend, and I learned a lot and picked up a ton of tips at PhilCon. It was very worthwhile to me.

"I hope to make something of myself one day as a writer. Meanwhile, I'll just keep plugging away. Thanks for all your kind comments and encouragement.

"I am tired but inspired. As Red Skelton used to say at the close of his show, 'Good night and may God bless.'"

His response was: "Glad to hear you made it home okay! Next con, hang out in the bar more!"

It's amazing how much networking is done informally in social settings.

Gardner's rejection arrived in the mail January 24, 2004—which would seem to indicate, if the theory holds true that the longer the return time the more the story was under consideration, "Berserker" wasn't in the hunt very long.

His reply also makes me think it didn't get far:

"Thanks for letting me see "Berserker." This is a totally saleable story, as far as I can see, but I don't like football very much, and so didn't warm to it. Try *F&SF* with it, bit more of a longshot, *Analog*. So I'm going to pass this one, but, of course, let me see more when you have it."

At this point, email was starting to supplant written communication between authors and editors, and I shot Gardner an email commenting I thought *F&SF* was a really hard market to crack.

His response was: "You need persistence to crack the top markets. You may send fifty stories to a magazine and have them all rejected, and then they buy the fifty-first. Talk to James Van Pelt about that some time; he sent me stuff for several years before I finally bought something from him."

As far as the sports subject matter is concerned, I know there's a stereotype out there that science fiction fans are geeks, which I don't necessarily believe it, but it's not a genre that attracts a lot of jocks, either. Before I wrote "Berserker" I hadn't thought that sports-oriented stories wouldn't get sympathy from SF readers, but I learned that's somewhat true.

In May 2004, when I attended my first writing workshop—a session of

Turkey City hosted by Bruce Sterling in Austin (this was after I sold a story to Gardner, so I have the strange distinction of having made a pro sale before ever attending a fiction writing workshop), the most common observation of workshop participants about "Berserker" was that they didn't like the subject or couldn't judge it fairly because they didn't like its sports setting.

(The second most common observation was that my speculations about illegal drugs in sports wasn't speculative but true. Cynical bunch.)

Because of Gardner's suggestion I run the story past *F&SF* and *Analog*, Berserker is the only story from this period of my writing—and in this book—that was seen by the top four short fiction editors at the time—Dozois, Schmidt, Van Gelder and Datlow.

After I got it back from Gardner, I sent it off to Gordon Van Gelder at *Fantasy & Science Fiction* on January 26, 2004. His reply—dated a week later (*F&SF* has always been known for a quick turnaround of rejections) was a longer than Gardner's:

"Many thank for giving a look at 'Berserker', but I'm going to pass on this one. I like the game of football fine (I suspect Gardner was thinking of Robert Reed's 'Game of the Century' (May 1999) when he referred to recent sports stories), but I didn't connect with this one.

"I thought the narrator had too little stake in the story, which consequently made it hard to get caught up in the overall drama."

Van Gelder also thought the story lacked credibility. "It seemed unbelievable to me that such a lethal drug would be used as openly as it is in the story, esp. after the Ephedra-related death of that Orioles pitcher."

Pitcher Steve Bechler died of heatstroke at the beginning of spring training with the Baltimore Orioles in 2003. He was using the supplement ephedra, against the advice of his trainer, in an effort to lose weight.

Van Gelder's comment highlights how genre authors don't live in a vacuum, and how the real world sometimes intrudes. A sidelight to this whole topic is that, as the local newspaper editor, one of my duties was to cover county government. I regularly attended the meetings of the county commissioners, the county's governing body, and at the time the County Judge—the highest elected official in the county—made his living from a business that manufactured dietary supplements. The U.S. Food and Drug Administration (FDA) banned the sale of ephedra-containing supplements on April 12, 2004, and the Judge went bankrupt and later resigned his post.

I later also sent the story to Stan Schmidt at *Analog*, who also passed on it, saying it was "nicely done, but I'm afraid not my cup of tea."

"Sports stories rarely do much for me, unless they're quite a bit more than 'just' sports stories; this one does have some extra but for me it wasn't enough, and it's also a bit gruesome for my tastes."

I had wondered when I first dashed off the story if it would be considered a bit messy, but Schmidt was the only editor who commented on that.

As in the case of Gardner, both editors ended on a positive note. Schmidt wrote "Thanks for letting me see it, and good luck in placing it elsewhere." Van Gelder ended with "Anyway, I'm sorry this one didn't work for me—best of luck to you with it, and thanks for sending it my way." As an author trying to break in, it was nice to get these little encouragements.

Over the next couple of years as it made the rounds I simplified the plot structure and combined scenes (diminishing scenes, like diminishing characters, is a sign of better writing).

"Berserker" ultimately proved to be a hard sell, and after a total of 20 submissions it finally found a home in the second issue of a new magazine called *OG's Speculative Fiction* in September 2006 (which lasted six years and 35 issues, but finally folded in 2012.)

Editor Seth Crossman wrote in his acceptance: "Thank you for your submission. We heartily accept it! With the steroid scandals going on in sports these days, we thought this story was timely and well written. Plus, it was just my kind of story. Great to have a writer of your talent on board!"

One final note: With the story's close connection with the Dallas Cowboys, I wanted to do a bit of a tribute to a Dallas sportscaster who I always liked. "Dale Hammond" is a direct homage to Dale Hansen, who's been sports director at a Dallas TV station for 30 years now. Hansen is just the kind of guy to do what his doppelganger in "Berserker" does; in 1986 he broke a story about a massive scandal involving payments to players on Southern Methodist University's football team. Hansen's reporting led to the NCAA canceling the Mustangs' 1987 season, the so-called "death penalty."

As Wikipedia notes, "His reporting of the scandal garnered him a Peabody Award for distinguished journalism, a DuPont-Columbia Award, and several death threats."

Hansen was pulled off the Dallas Cowboys beat in 1994 after he and Cowboys Coach Barry Switzer and Cowboys Owner Jerry Jones got into an argument on the air during the team's spring training.

Of course, any resemblance between the evil owner in "Berserker" and Jerry Jones is, uhh (clears throat) unintentional.

# Chapter 13

## Pages From the Past

Early in 2004 the U.S. House passed legislation banning human cloning for any purpose (the bill did not pass the Senate). News of this got the proverbial wheels turning; cloning has been a subject of SF stories for decades, but I thought it was interesting that something that was once considered totally speculative now had prodded legislation.

I'm a bit self-conscious about my lack of science background for an SF writer. I was a history major in college, and I've worked as a journalist all my life. My scientific knowledge is very sketchy. But basic cloning technology seems to be simple enough I could skate through the subject with some slick writing and hand-waving.

Even in 2003, it was clear that the internet—which might have held so much better promise—was being prostituted because of the human tendency to want money and/or sex. Along the same lines, I assumed if cloning ever becomes common, it will be used to reproduce particularly pretty women as sex objects.

My first thought when approaching this story was to have a grave robber break into Marilyn Monroe's tomb, but then I realized cloning from dead tissue was somewhat complicated. That's why I settled on another pin up and sex symbol from the same era. But the idea of having a grave robbery, which would, of course, provoke a police investigation, led me to the path to make the story a police procedural.

# The Queen of Guilty Pleasures

Something made Bob the stockman stop.
He was absentmindedly loading a shelf with dollar pasta when something caught the corner of his eye.

Bob used to be a telecommunications specialist, but the gigantic corporation went bust and now he felt himself lucky to get a minimum-wage job at a Bargain Bucks store.

He turned and realized why his peripheral vision had tugged subliminally at his consciousness.

"How special," he thought. "The Trash Perfecta—Cheap Trash, Old Trash, Euro-Trash."

The astoundingly-dressed hooker was just picking up her yellow plastic bag full of junk food. An old overweight woman standing behind her stepped up.

The elderly woman was cheaply dressed but her clear and pretty blue eyes sparkled as she made small talk with the clerk, who took her cash and turned away.

Euro-Trash was behind her. Even in LA, this guy stood out—wrap around mirrored sunglasses, slicked back hair, olive complexion, a narrow white tie on a silver lame' shirt and navy blue chinos. All under a heavy dark long overcoat.

"This dope is a slave to fashion," thought Bob. "Wearing a coat like that in LA in July."

Before the old woman had a chance to withdraw her arm, Euro-Trash reached into a deep coat pocket and pulled out the god-damnedest big syringe Bob had ever seen. In one smooth gesture he raised it and pulled the cap off the large needle. Leaning around the old woman, he plunged it deep into the fleshy part of her upper arm.

It took a moment for the pain to register. As she turned and started the scream, Euro-Trash raised his forearm to block her head, and then pushed her away, letting the needle pull out at the same time.

With his free hand, he pulled a narrow black container out of the opposite pocket and he dropped the syringe inside as he ran out the door.

Blood ran down the old woman's arm and onto the counter as she sobbed. The clerk pulled a roll of paper towels out from under the counter.

Bob saw the whole business, which probably took all of ten seconds. He ran down the aisle and for a second thought to help the old woman, but instead sprinted to the door and into the parking lot.

Despite the heavily tinted windows, he could see Euro-Trash wildly turning the steering wheel as he sped into the street. In the split second the Porsche slowed as it entered traffic, he read and memorized the license plate. It was from Texas.

Bob went back into the store, where the cashier was holding the old woman.

"There, there, Miss Bettie, the ambulance is on its way."

The old woman pounded the counter with the fist of her uninjured arm, and clenched her teeth in pain.

"A kook, another damn kook! Jesus protect me!"


Agent Tersarius alighted like a crane on a branch. He perfunctorily flashed his badge.

"I'm glad to meet you, Detective Sloan, and I appreciate your contacting us."

The LAPD detective sat back. "I hope this isn't a false alarm."

"We evaluated your message. That's why I'm here."

"You think there may be something to this?"

"Ever since the Prohibition of Human Cloning Act of 2003 was passed, we've had an outline for potential enforcement."

The detective sat up straight. "I guess you have a serious forensics background. It must be interesting."

"Actually, I've been mostly stuck in a lab, and it gets boring as crap." He smiled. "I enjoy getting out of the lab. There are only a handful of us who know forensic microbiology at the molecular level."

The detective's eyes began to glaze. He raised his eyebrows and pushed a sheaf of papers towards Agent Tersarius. "Here's the full report from the attending physician who treated the subject."

Tersarius flipped though the papers as the detective spoke. "As an assault, it's fairly a-typical," Sloan continued. "There was no prior contact, no communication during the assault, no attempt to take any valuables, and there was no attempt on the woman's life. For now, it's still only an assault. The bells went off because of the comments the attending physician added."

"Yes, I see. *Wound indicates attacker used specialized tool normally used for taking tissue sample from cadavers.*"

Tersarius looked up. "That's the operative term, *tissue sample.*"

"When I came to where you first mentioned the victim's name, I thought it sounded familiar," said Tersarius. "Googled up a storm."

"She's lived in LA for many years. She was pretty famous in her day—they say she had 20,000 pin-up photos made in the '50s."

Tersarius looked up. "Maybe some rich old man wants to re-live a teenage fantasy?"

"Is that possible?"

"I doubt it, but someone may be running an elaborate scam. Anyhow, it's the thought that counts," he said with a thin smile. "I'll take the case from here."

"No problem, I wouldn't know where to start, if this is what you think it is," said the detective. "Now I have the good news and the bad news."

"Give me the good news first."

"A few minutes before the attack, while he was stalking the victim in the store, the perp stopped to make a cell phone call, and as he held the phone, a surveillance camera could see the key pad. We got the area code and exchange."

Detective Sloan handed him a slip of paper. "Outside Dallas," he said. "A town called Juniper Valley."

"Texas A&M has been in the forefront of cloning technology for years," said Tersarius. "What's the bad news?"

"The plate is untraceable."

"I guess that's not surprising."

With the corruption in Texas law enforcement caused by the Mexican drug cartels, more and more organized crime protection rackets were being run out of the state. Somebody in law enforcement probably procured the plate, thought Tersarius.

Detective Sloan showed him to the door. "You think someone is finally trying to clone a person?"

"You know the saying. I'm not paid to think. But if someone is trying to violate the law, it's my deal." He squared the papers. "By the way, how is the victim?"

"She's fine, but still shook up. I'm sure she would have been happier if someone asked for her autograph."

"Ouch." The agent dropped the papers in his briefcase. "I'll let you know what I find."

Agent Tersarius picked up a car at the Dallas FBI office and drove 30 miles to Juniper Valley, a small suburb on the southern edge of the county. He homed in on the City Hall with his GPS and drove around the Town Square.

Catty-corner from the City Hall he saw a rather dilapidated office building with a sign, "The Juniper Valley Journal—Your Hometown Newspaper".

No one was inside except a dark-haired middle-aged man behind a large desk. Tersarius smiled as the man stood. "I'm Ed Tersarius and I'm looking for information about Juniper Valley."

"You've come to the right place." The man shook his hand.

"I'm a microbiology forensics specialist with the FBI out of Washington, D.C.," he said evenly. "I'm investigating a suspected attempt of illegal human cloning, and I have a lead that's brought me here."

Tersarius could tell the man actually understood him. "How can I help you, Mr. Tersarius. Is that a Lithuanian name?"

"Yes, it is, my grandparents came through Ellis Island. A phone call trace has led us to Juniper Valley," he said. "How much do you know about law enforcement in this town?"

The man turned around and sat back in his seat. "We run the police log every week. Like everyone else."

"Who's the *coordinator* in this town? You know, the guy you need to go to get permission, to do stuff?"

The man glared at him. "I don't know what you mean."

"I assume whoever your local *coordinator* is might be involved—for protection."

Since the drug cartels had law enforcement officers working for them in every city and county, these 'coordinators' usually took advantage of their position to run little side rackets. Ordinarily, Tersarius wouldn't speak so plainly, but they were alone.

"We know Texas law enforcement is on the other side of the drug war. We've known it for years. Mostly all the local police and sheriff's departments have been compromised by the drug cartels. It's like during the '20s and Prohibition. And I," he said leaning forward, "am a G-Man. So I don't give a damn. I'm not here on a drug investigation, Mr...."

"Marcel, Tim Marcel."

"That would take thousands of agents, and quite frankly," he said, "with society's attitudes, the problem will probably be solved the way the first prohibition was."

"A former Playboy Playmate and pin-up star from the 1950s was attacked in Los Angeles," he continued. "The nature of the wound indicates the assailant may have been after a tissue sample."

He let the statement sink in. "We have a partial phone number that led me to Juniper Valley. The question is, why would an investigation into cloning lead to Juniper Valley?"

The editor looked wary. "What kind of businesses might be involved?"

"Reproductive services, artificial insemination, livestock cloning, perhaps? Microtechnology, cryogenics…"

"Whoa, stop right there. What's cryogenics got to do with cloning?"

"If you transport tissue samples, they probably would have to be cryogenically frozen for transport," said Tersarius.

Marcel walked over to a window and beckoned the agent. "You see that furniture store across the square?"

"Yes?"

"You remember the Superconducting Super Collider?"

"Yes."

"The Collider was being built next door in Ellis County, at least until the assholes in Congress cancelled the project ten years ago. The project's headquarters were in an industrial park here in Juniper Valley while the tunnel was being built."

Marcel turned to Tersarius. "The first people who came here were in cryogenics, because of the magnets they were going to install. When the funding was yanked, a number of people took retirement and gave up on government science work, including…" He pointed. "Jim and Jill Frame, who opened up that antique furniture shop."

"Thanks, that's interesting."

"Yes, and AirFlo Gases is still in the industrial park."

"What's AirFlo Gases?"

"An outfit that started up the same time as the Collider. They liquefy gases they pull out of the clean Texas air. Like liquid oxygen and liquid nitrogen."

"You've been very helpful, Mr. Marcel. I may stop by and visit with you later. By the way, do you own the paper?"

"Yep, I do everything pretty much. Owner, publisher, janitor-in-chief. This is a small outfit."

"Well, I know small newspapers don't make lots of money. You hang in there."

Marcel showed him to the door. Agent Tersarius turned before he walked out.

"By the way, you never told me."

"Told you what?"

"Who I was asking for?"

"Oh, yes." Marcel shuffled. "Lt. Scott Hitchens. He's the guy."

The temperature was already past 100 and the sun beat down in sheets of glare. Although the Juniper Valley Antique Furniture Emporium was across the square, Agent Tersarius drove out to the highway.

AirFlo Gases was in a medium-sized industrial park. He could see a large vacant building with the faint outlines of "Superconducting Super Collider Facility" still visible on the facade where the letters had once been.

"We only sell direct to industries," said the office manager. "You just can't walk in and buy liquid nitrogen."

"Really?" Tersarius was still holding out his badge. "This place is rather out of the way. How do we know if a terrorist came by and slipped someone in the plant some cash for a carry out deal?"

The woman cringed. "Please, I had nothing to do with it."

"Who did?"

The head of the shop where the tankers were loaded blubbered away immediately. "Probably an illegal, though I could care less," thought the agent.

"Just tell me who wanted the nitrogen and I'll be happy," he said.

"I don't know his name, he was a white man. He had a real lab flask, though, so I figured he knew what he was doing."

"Well, what he look like?"

The man hesitated. "If hope he's not going to tell me we all look alike," thought Tersarius.

"He was an old man, tall, bald in the middle with curly hair on the sides. He had a checked shirt on."

"Anything else?"

"He had a funny hammer in his belt, with a small square head."

"Relax, amigo, you're a small fish. Gracias."

Tersarius headed back up the highway and towards the Town Square.


He walked into the furniture store and saw a lanky man hammering away at the back of an old Victorian-era sofa.

The man's eyes twinkled behind his wire rim glasses. He unfolded his tall frame as his tucked the upholsterer's hammer in his belt.

"How may I help you?"

Tersarius pulled out his badge. "I understand you once worked for the government too, Dr. Frame."

The retired scientist stiffened.

"And if you are retired, why would you still need liquid nitrogen?"

"Am I under some kind of investigation?" He spoke very precisely.

"Yes. Liquid nitrogen is a very hazardous material, and you had no right to purchase it. The agency is very concerned about any possible terroristic threats against...."

The older man straightened. "There's no terrorist threat!"

"Then what about The Prohibition of Human Cloning Act? You're a little old to go to prison, Dr. Frame."

An older woman with stark white hair pulled back in a ponytail came from a back room. "Who is it, Jim?"

"Someone who wants to know how we paid for the Sebring convertible."

She stopped dead in her tracks and looked over Tersarius' thin frame and dark suit. "Oh, dear god."

Frame gestured to large couch against a wall. "Can we sit down and talk?"


Their story was simple and straightforward. Someone who knew about the retired couple's background had paid them a fine sum to prepare a kit for the transport of a tissue sample. Yes, it could have been used for a human sample, noted Frame. They never knew who paid them. An intermediary arranged the deal.

Lieutenant Hitchens.

When he was back in his car, Tersarius realized someone sitting in an unmarked car across the square was looking at him. They made eye contact.

They both got out and met at the gazebo in the center of the square. Tersarius sat down on the bench and spread his arms. Hitchens stood with his arms crossed on his chest just below his badge.

"I really don't care whatever else you have going," said the agent. "I know this couldn't have been your idea."

The lieutenant had watery blue eyes and a droopy cowboy mustache. "I don't know it's any y'all's business." He spat tobacco juice over the railing and into the geraniums.

"The boys in Washington want to nip this new crime in the bud," said the agent. "I'm sure you wouldn't want to lose your money from Matamoros. Nobody's going to care about protecting you because you got involved in some science project."

Hitchens glared at him. "You drive a hard bargain."

"Hard, but simple."

*Spit.*

"We're all divided up, like cells. Mah part was to handle the liquid nitrogen. After Frame got the kit ready, I turned it over to someone else, who's the real middle man."

"Yes, someone I imagine in the middle of things, who everyone trusts, and nobody would suspect. Certainly not you. Let's go."

Tersarius took off at a fast pace across the small park towards the newspaper office.


Marcel shot a quick glance down the hall as Tersarius and Hitchens walked in.

"I wouldn't bolt, if I were you," said Tersarius.

"He knows," said Hitchens.

Tersarius looked towards the credenza with a shelf lined with software packages. "I see you've already removed the box."

Marcel looked angry. "I needed the money!" he snarled.

"What box?" asked Hitchens.

Tersarius turned to the lieutenant. "He had an insulated container with the tissue sample sitting right on the shelf. In plain sight."

"I needed the money," Marcel repeated. "Why else do you think I'd work with this crooked bastard?"

Hitchens snorted.

"Well, you're not any better than him now, are you?"

"Can't we make some kind of deal? Like for immunity?"

"You've been watching too much television. You tell me where you were taking the tissue sample, and maybe, *maybe* we can talk."

"I had to wait until I was told to make the drop-off. This whole deal was set up with firewalls," said Marcel. "The guy at Cloverleaf, Jim Jervinis, contacted me. I passed along the information on what was needed to him," he said, gesturing to Hitchens, "he got the stuff from Frame, and then I passed it along."

Tersarius shook his head. "What's Cloverleaf?"

"That's a fancy horse hotel on the edge of the city, right on the county line," said Hitchens. "So that's where this was going."

"I assume there's a lab set up at Cloverleaf," said Marcel. "They host a stud service, and have been big into AI for years." He paused. "Of course, in this case, AI stands for artificial insemination."

"Have you already called Cloverleaf?"

"No, I called Scott."

"Did *you* call Cloverleaf?"

"I didn't know they were in on this. My connection was to him."

"Good, then we're going to this Cloverleaf place and you're both coming with me." He turned to the editor. "Would you like to retrieve the box?"

Marcel led them to a small shed behind the building where old bound volumes of newspapers lined the shelves. He pulled a box from behind some of the large books.

"Damn, you put the stuff out here?" said Hitchens, "with no air conditioning?"

"This sophisticated kind of package is totally insulated," said Tersarius, as he carried the old software box into the building.

"I wouldn't open it if I were you," said Marcel. "It's in there pretty tight."

Tersarius cracked the box just enough to see the zero-energy container inside.

"How did you notice the box?"

"Well, even though I don't use the software much, I know Pagemaker is an Adobe product now. And this box says Aldus, so I knew it was pretty old. I mean, why would a newspaper be using desktop publishing software ten years old. And then I realized the name."

"I tried to be too clever, huh?"

"I don't get it," said Hitchens, "what about the name?"

"This tissue sample is from a woman named Bettie Page. She was a top pinup in the 1950s and the Playboy Playmate for Christmas 1955. She became a Christian in 1959 and has been pretty much living a private life in anonymity since then."

"I get it. Page-maker. Shit." Hitchens wagged his head. "Well, somebody apparently remembers her."

Tersarius pointed a thumb towards the door. "Maybe your friends at Cloverleaf Farms can tell us who this somebody is."


Despite it being the middle of a Texas summer, the grounds of Cloverleaf Farms were bright green. It was gated and a voice squawked from a box after they pulled up.

"I'd like to see Mr. Jervinis."

"Do you have an appointment?"

"I don't need one. I'm Agent Ed Tersarius of the Federal Bureau of Investigation."

There was a pause. "May I see your badge?"

Tersarius held it up in front of the lens. The gate swung open.

They drove up to a large and long building, where a chunky man with sandy hair came out.

"Gentlemen, I'm Mark Ginn, the manager here at Cloverleaf. How may I help you?"

"We'd like to see Mr. Jervinis." Tersarius looked around the expansive estate.

"Mr. Jervinis isn't here right now. Is here something I can help you gentlemen with?" He obviously recognized Marcel but didn't give Hitchens a second glance.

"I want to see your embryology lab."

"I'm afraid that's not possible. It's secure and sterile and I don't have the authority. Mr. Jervinis is the general manager, I'm just the manager of the boarding facility. Besides, do you have a warrant?"

"I believe there's a crime in progress. Your lab is being used for illegal cloning."

"Agent Tersarius, cloning livestock is hardly illegal."

"Cloning humans is."

Tersarius could tell this was the first he'd heard of this.

"Are you going to cooperate, or do I need call the Dallas office for backup and do a thorough search?"

Ginn let them in and the four men slowly made their way through the lab. Ginn seemed unfamiliar with the facilities, but Tersarius recognized the standard lab setup—refrigeration equipment, sterile hoods, incubators and such.

He looked around and rubbed his chin.

"The right stuff isn't quite here." He looked at Ginn, who just shrugged.

He noticed a locked door off to the side. "What's in there?"

"From my having visited in here before, I think that's a personal office for Mr. Jervinis."

Tersarius twisted the knob and shook the door. "Do you have a key?"

Tersarius let go of the knob, but it continued to twist. The door opened and a dark-haired man with a neat beard looked out and then stepped out.

"What's going on here?"

"Mr. Jervinis, I'm sorry." Ginn spoke up. "I didn't know you were here."

"That's alright, Mark. Tim, what's going on?"

"This is agent Tersarius with the FBI. He's investigating a case of suspected human cloning."

"There's been no law violated, Agent Tersarius." Jervinis was the image of reasonability. "I've only been involved in some personal embryological research, related, of course, to our reproductive services division here at the ranch."

"Well, then, you don't mind if I take a look inside."

"Not at all."

Tersarius went inside the small room, which also had a sterile hood and incubator, along with a small refrigerator and a microscope, all on one large table. He opened the refrigerator and pulled out a tray with vials.

He looked over the containers. He gestured towards the other men. "Gentlemen, step forward here, I want to show you how to clone a human being."

"First, you examine the human cells under this high power microscope, to insure there's no contamination. If you're unsure, you can always use a small centrifuge to isolate them."

He looked at Jervinis, who was beginning to look worried. "I assume you have one someplace?" Jervinis nodded.

"Then you put them in this specialized culture media," he said holding up a vial, "where the cells grow and divide. You need to grow a good supply of 'clean' cells."

"This stuff here," he said, "holding up another tube, "is called minimal media. It's formulated so that the cells stop dividing and become quiescent."

He pulled out a sealed petri dish. "You then take an unfertilized human egg, not difficult to obtain, and under the sterile hood, you use a microscopically thin pipette to puncture the cell wall and then suck out the egg's nucleus."

He opened the door to the hood and slid in the dish. "Then you take one of the cells and slide it into the egg's cell membrane."

He looked at the trio of laymen. "A normal human cell is much smaller than an egg, so you can implant it in the egg's cell wall quite easily. Isn't that true?"

Jervinis nodded slowly.

"Then you either use chemicals or electroshock to jolt the cells so they fuse. The nucleus of the clone cell merges with the egg and takes the place of the nucleus you earlier removed. The egg will develop with the genetic material of the clone cell rather than what it started with. Then it's just a simple matter of implantation with some willing host."

He turned to Jervinis. "I assume from the caps on some of these vials you use the electroshock method?"

Jervinis reached into a drawer and pulled out a small box with some wires and clamps. He held it out.

"Very simple, but it would do the job," said Tersarius. "I commend your expertise. You've managed to put a neat cloning operation on a desktop. You obviously know your stuff."

"You obviously do too. Have you ever done this yourself?"

Tersarius gave a little laugh. "No, but remember I'm the one asking questions here. The next is, who you have been working for?"

Before Jervinis opened his mouth, Marcel turned to run but Hitchens quickly grabbed him and then shoved him back in the door.

"That's OK, Mr. Editor, it isn't hard to see you're the linchpin of this project. You thought throwing over the Frames would throw me off you, and that when I ran into the lieutenant, he'd do his job."

"I thought he would do at least what he was damn well paid to do."

"Well, it was obvious you're at the center of this. I can see Jervinis recognized you but not the lieutenant. The Frames knew the lieutenant but not you. You and the lieutenant are at the center of this conspiracy—and you're obviously working for the client. Why would you get the tissue sample instead of Jervinis here? You can't do a thing with it."

He turned to Jervinis. "By the way, do you have an idea of the name of the clone subject?"

The doctor looked at him warily.

"Oh, I'm sorry, now that I'm sure, I need your testimony and expertise for this case," said Tersarius. "We'll give you immunity. It's obvious Marcel here is our connection to the client."

"Actually, Agent Tersarius, I don't know and I never asked. I thought it was better that way."

"Which means our editor friend here was the only person who knew her name. Page-maker, huh?" He snorted. "Desktop publishing software. Desktop cloning. All sorts of in-jokes."

Marcel glared at him. "I want an attorney."

Tersarius cocked an eyebrow at Hitchens. "You want to do the honors?"

The lieutenant smiled. "My pleasure."

"Oh, you son of a bitch! I'll be damned if I'm going to take the fall for this!"

Hitchens already had the handcuffs on behind his back. "Just tell the man what he wants to know."

Marcel drew his mouth. "I can't."

"Yeah, I know." Tersarius said. "Let's go."

He turned to Jervinis. "I'd like to debrief you. I think I'll learn more if you and I cooperate. I think we can chalk this up to research for future cases."

Jervinis smiled and nodded. "Mark, please turn off all the lights and lock up behind us."


It was past 10 p.m. before Tersarius was done debriefing Jervinis in Dallas. Marcel was fuming in a cell and Hitchens was back doing whatever a crooked cop does in a small town.

He drove back to Juniper Valley. The Town Square was dark and quiet as he let himself in the Journal office. He walked around the editor's desk and slowly looked over the shelves. There were many science fiction books. He glanced over some of the titles:

"Web of the City"

"The Man with Nine Lives"

"The Sound of the City".

"Seems to be a pattern here," he thought.

He noticed a memo pad on the desk. The top sheet was blank, but he could see an impression of what had been written on the sheet above. He could just make out what looked like

HE

m

an

"He-man?"

He tore the sheet from the pad and stuck it in his shirt pocket. He began going through drawers.

He found a slick trade paperback. "The Real Bettie Page: The Truth About the Queen of the Pin-ups".

"He did a little research here."

He flipped through the pages and noticed the book opened at the foreword: "The Queen of Guilty Pleasures". Then he saw who guest-authored the foreword.

"Payoff."

He threw the book back in the drawer.


"I'm surprised to see you back in Southern California," said Detective Sloan. "I *did* think I'd get a call. But I assumed after you took off for Texas, I'd never see you again."

"If you think about it, neither of us should be surprised the trail led back here," said Agent Tersarius. "You know how uncommon random assaults are."

"You said in your message you think the person who set up this possible cloning deal lives here."

"Yes, that probably explains how he knew Bettie Page still lived in the LA area," said Tersarius. "Plus he fits what I would call the profile in this case. Someone old and wealthy who could afford to do this, someone who would remember Bettie Page as a pinup in the '50s. In this case, my suspect was 21 when she was a Playboy centerfold in 1955."

"I don't pretend to completely understand how it's done," said the detective, "especially if—if you cloned someone today, wouldn't it take years for the clone to grow up? Don't they age like a normal human?"

"That's the interesting twist on the case," said Tersarius. "I have an indication this may have been done before." He pulled out the sheet from the memo pad. "When I ran this through the bureau's lab in Dallas, they made out the whole message. It actually says "HE make another".

"Is HE your suspect then? I assume those are initials."

"Yes, and that's where I'm going next."

"Do you need my help?"

"No actually, he lives just outside the city, so it doesn't fall under your jurisdiction. I just wanted to make a courtesy call. I'll let you know if it pans out."

The detective stood up and shook Tersarius' hand. "Well, this was probably groundbreaking."

Tersarius gave a wan smile. "It might be earthshaking, if the suspect is who I think it is. On the other hand, we probably will cut a deal. We may need this man's help more than we need him prosecuted."

"You would have thought the first real attempt at cloning would have been for spare organs," said the detective as he escorted the agent to the door.

"Well, the two things that drive mankind are a desire for sex and a fear of death," the agent said dryly. "Human nature being what it is, I'm not surprised someone would have wanted to clone a concubine."

He turned as he walked away. "Anyway, I've already looked into three cases of cloning for *spares* in the past five years. But they got off because the law wasn't in effect yet. This is the first case I've seen involving a sex toy." He paused. "And I doubt this case will lead to a prosecution, either."


Agent Tersarius drove out from the city and into a quiet suburban neighborhood in Sherman Oaks. He parked in front of a ranch house with a California stone exterior.

A diminutive well-dressed man with intelligent eyes behind rather large glasses answered the door.

"Good afternoon. Agent Tersarius, isn't it?"

"Good day, Mr. Ellison. We need to talk."


I sent the story off to Gardner on August 1, 2013. His reply on December 10, 2013 was short, but effective:

"Thanks for letting me see "The Queen of Guilty Pleasures." Again, some nice stuff here, but cloning stories are such familiar territory these days that you have to do something *really* unique and interesting with them to get by—this is a good try, but doesn't quite make it."

In this particular example, because I tackled a type of science I really wasn't familiar with, I couldn't come up with a story that was outstanding enough to rise above its predecessors. Unlike what might have been expected if the story had run past editors at hard SF magazines, Gardner has no specific criticisms on hos the subject was handled. *Asimov's*, at least under his helm, straddled the ground between hard SF (such as printed in *Analog*) and obvious fantasy.

In this case, rather than do a rewrite based on the science, I veered off towards a human interest angle. I decided to "humanize" Agent Tersarius and make the story more sympathetic by introducing a moral, as it were, by giving him a family—briefly glimpsed in the revised beginning—and then tacking on a complete ending. The story ended rather abruptly, anyway, with the "reveal" of Harlan Ellison opening the door. This was the new ending:

Agent Tersarius parked in front of a ranch house with a California stone exterior.

A diminutive well-dressed man with intelligent eyes behind rather large glasses answered the door. "Good afternoon. Agent Tersarius, isn't it?"

"We need to talk, sir."

The old man gestured expansively for the agent to enter. "I got word from Texas to be expecting you."

Tersarius knitted his legs as he sat down on a large leather couch. "I guess Tim Marcel called you as soon as he posted bail."

A pretty dark-haired teenage girl came into the living room. "Hello. Daddy, you didn't tell me we had a guest?"

Tersarius smiled at the girl. "I just arrived."

"Bettie, dearest, could you get us some coffee, please?"

"Sure." She smiled at the agent. "I'll be right back."

The author turned to Tersarius. "As you can see, there's nothing romantic going on here, agent."

"Was that the original plan?"

The old man sighed. "You're very perspicacious, sir."

He sat back in his chair. "Yes, I planned to use her as a paramour—but as she quickly matured, my heart wasn't in it."

"Quickly, eh? How old is she?"

The author looked at him with resignation. "Seven. She's seven years old."

"She looks like a 16-year old."

"And her rate of aging is accelerating. She'll probably die of old age by the time she's 30."

"Things didn't work out the way you planned, then. Couldn't bear to become attached to her?"

"You make it sound so crass."

Irritation crept into Tersarius' voice. "Crass? Damn, man, you were going to start making a series of then? So you'd have a fresh one when the previous one got too old?"

The author's blue eyes flashed as he leaned forward violently. "No, dammit. I just wanted to see whether this first case was an aberration. I wanted new work done."

Tersarius nodded in the direction of the kitchen. "So she wasn't a product of the Texas lab?"

"No, I had a fellow in Nevada do that work. Marcel was a fan who happened to broach the subject of cloning in a letter. I used him to set up the second attempt."

He sighed. "I just learned two days ago it wouldn't have worked. I was going to tell Marcel to destroy the tissue sample. Then you showed up."

"What did you learn?"

The author leaned back in his armchair and rubbed his hands in a very obvious way. "Now, are we going to talk about leniency?"

"If you happen to have something substantial to offer, yes."

The old man smiled. "My man in Nevada isolated a genome that seems to determine the rate of aging once maturity is achieved. Apparently, it must have some kind of environmental trigger which explains why, in an artificial situation such as this, the aging proceeds geometrically after infancy."

"How has he been able to confirm this?"

"This genome in Bettie duplicates that which has already been found in victims of progeria except it's not the same gene. Since we know what the gene looks like initially, a little splicing and we'll have a cure for fetuses diagnosed as possessing the Progeria defect."

"A cure for Progeria." Tersarius lowered his voice as Bettie returned with a tray and a carafe of coffee.

"Thank you dear. I know you have school work to do. Please leave us two old fellows, we're talking business."

"Of course, daddy." Her blue eyes sparkled. "Please say good-bye before you leave, Mr...."

"Tersarius."

Her bangs swayed as she giggled. "I'm sorry, did you say Terry Serious?"

"Close enough." They both laughed.

The author nodded after she left. "She's my responsibility in every way. Now I have to watch her grow old so quickly. The least I can do is make some good come out of this—a rich, old man's foolish fantasy."

"She was cloned before the law went in to effect," said Tersarius. "And you were stopped before the next attempt. The most I would have is a conspiracy charge."

He sipped his coffee. "I think we can deal. The NIH will appreciate the information you turn over to them."

&ast; &ast; &ast;

"You could have flown in tomorrow morning."

Tersarius was pulling off his tie. "After spending all that time in Texas and California, I wanted to get back home."

He kissed his wife.

"Where's the little one?"

"Asleep in her bed, like a little angel."

They both looked at their daughter through a partially cracked doorway.

He smiled and turned away as he quietly closed the door.

She held his hand. "Wasn't this job about illegal cloning?"

"Yes, but they didn't succeed."

"Well, did you learn anything?"

He looked at her thoughtfully. "Yes. Bringing life into the world is a big responsibility — also a big risk."

She had hardly ever heard him say anything so touching. She hugged him, and he hugged her back even tighter.

&ast;   &ast;   &ast;

As I mentioned at the beginning of the chapter, the first sex symbol that would come to mind for cloning, Marilyn Monroe, was dead, but Bettie Page—the pin up queen of the era—was still very much alive (she passed away on December 11, 2008). In the course of researching her life, I found that Harlan Ellison had written the foreword to an unauthorized biography of her, *The Real Bettie Page* by journalist Richard Foster, which was published in 1998.

I stole the title of Ellison's forward intact for this story, "The Queen of Guilty Pleasures".

Gardner didn't mention it, but some editors I subsequently sent the story to—including Ellen Datlow —questioned whether it was legal and/ or wise to name a real author, especially since the fictional Harlan Ellison is involved in a crime.

Parts of authors' lives often find themselves as part of a mix that goes into a story, but "Queen" was unusual in that the local newspaper editor turns out to be the real villain of the story. When I began the story, that wasn't my intent, but since it's a puzzle story that involves layers of concealment, it flowed naturally as I went along. Authors will often tell you characters develop in their own fashion and you have best facilitate that development. That sometimes means a character goes off in a direction you didn't plan.

After being submitted to ten other venues, I finally decided to give it a rest and offered it to the webzine *Bewildering Stories*, which published it in October 2005.

# Chapter 14

# Cyberflunk

A s I struggled to find some science to put into my science fiction, I next hit on trying cyberspace. The result is one of my less inspiring efforts.

When I was in high school, personal computers didn't exist. When we studied computer programming, we used dumb terminals that used dial-up modems to time share from a distant mainframe.

I took the most basic of computer classes in the early 1970s, but that's it. It didn't appeal to me at all, and furthermore, even the most basic math needed for any kind of serious programming. I didn't even pass what was the equivalent of algebra offered at my high school at the time.

But I thought I'd give cyberspace a try, and—it being the futuristic year of 2003—I researched the subject on the internet.

One thing I learned from the experience is that being totally ignorant of a subject you are trying to research is like trying to look up a word in the dictionary you don't have a clue how to spell. If you can't come close or make some relatively intelligent guess, you'll get nowhere and be frustrated in the process.

The futility of my effort seems clear in retrospect, but at the time I thought I had something I could pull off. I was probably being deluded by a clever conceit and a growing confidence in my writing skills to gloss over any minor deficiencies in my story—such as the plot making no sense.

Also, remember at the time I was in a writing frenzy. Note, this was the 14th story in a row I sent to Gardner.

"The Runner at Dawn" is one of the stories I am the least proud of. Don't judge me too harshly for this one.

# The Runner At Dawn

I don't remember how or why I was running.
It was like I had awakened with a start—but I was off in a flash

That was all I knew.

The sweat was flying off the back of my head, my legs were churning, my arms pumping by my sides.

There was something behind me. I couldn't stop to look back. I didn't know what it was.

I knew I had to run full out, and keep running, until I knew somehow that I could stop. Or until I collapsed.

I don't know why I came to consciousness in a full run, but I knew I couldn't stop.

"What the hell am I doing?"

Without lowering my head, I glanced down. I had sneakers on, but my legs were bare. I'm wearing shorts.

I listened to my rhythmic panting. "I'm in better shape than I thought I was."

Was this a nightmare? The ground was much too solid underfoot for that.

"Where am I going?"

I began to concentrate, screw my brain in tighter. I didn't recognize the street I was running down the middle of.

"Why am I running?"

Why am I running down the middle of the street, anyway? It was like I was running a marathon—but I was alone.

The light was dim and gray. "It must be early morning." There were a few old cars parked in front of some small one-story businesses. I didn't see any people.

I tried to read some of the signs as I ran past. There was an auto supply store, with a black and white highway-type shield logo. "Router 66 Auto Parts and Tools" it read.

On the next block, a florist's shop with the Mercury head logo. "EDIe's FTP Floral Delivery Worldwide."

I became aware of a pressure in my torso, and then realized it was coming from behind me. Something was rolling up behind me. I needed to run faster.

I sped up, one foot in front of the other, a rolling, churning, like a waterwheel. The sweat dripping off my chin contributed to the effect. I could see sweat splattering on the asphalt below me.

"Maybe I died in my sleep and this is the road to hell. No, I hurt too much to be a disembodied spirit."

"Maybe I've had a fit or stroke while sleepwalking. Maybe I've gone insane."

"Maybe…"

The street sign as I ran through the next intersection. "Zang Blvd."

I was in Oak Cliff. Across the river from Dallas.

Then I saw the opening in the skyline. I knew where I was.

I was heading east towards Dallas. In a moment I was running on the viaduct. It was a mile across the Trinity River bottoms to downtown Dallas.

No cars moving on the viaduct, either.

"Keep running." I could still feel the pressure behind me.

I could see birds skitting around the skyscrapers across the river. Sometimes you could see the flock reflected in the towers' glass sides.

It's a mile to there. I kept running.

There's got to be people on the other side. There's the "Dallas News", Union Station. Shit, the convention center.

"Where is everybody?"

My chest felt like it was filled with wet cement, and my feet were beginning to feel like coal.

"What's behind me?"

It was a mile across the viaduct. The far side loomed like it was being drawn in slowly by a zoom lens. It took a few minutes but I was there.

I ran down the ramp, leaning precariously forward. I lurched forward as the road leveled—and saw a conductor in front of Union Station, waving at me and holding a door open.

I cut through the lawn and towards the door he held open. My legs gave out as I ran into the marble lobby. My knees buckled, and I went down. I skidded about six feet across the floor on my knees and then fell over.

I lay there and panted. My ribs felt like pincers opening and closing. I looked up and saw the Conductor leaning over me, smiling, with his hands on his knees.

"It's OK, Bob, you're safe now."

I remembered. "Bob. That's my name. Bob Benotti."

The Conductor stood up and pulled off his cap. A wave of auburn hair tumbled down. The conductor was a woman.

"My name's Odette."

I opened my mouth. It was very dry. It took a second for me to get it to work.

"What the hell is going on?"

Odette leaned down again and smiled. "What do you think is going on?

My breathing was slowing. Some of the blood that had been in my muscles and feet began to flow back into my head.

Odette gave me a smile and wagged her head. "Should be obvious by now, aye?"

Aye?

AI.

I thought real hard. "I'm not Bob Benotti. I'm his AI. I'm a mook."

When I realized this was happening in virtuality, I sat up, pulled my knees up and wrapped my arms around them. "I really shouldn't be tired now, should I?"

"Why did I forget I'm an AI? For a while, I mean. Back to my original question—what the hell happened?"

She put her hands on her hips. "I really don't know. There's been some kind of catastrophic system failure. Your ISP has gotten an old Code 05 message."

Code 05. Local Site Emergency Close Down.

"You've undergone an emergency upload," she said. "And there had to have been some problems—otherwise you wouldn't have the file corruption you obviously have."

I stood up. "Well, we've never met, AI or not. Who are you?"

"I'm the file transfer protocol that was saved when your file was originated almost 25 years ago. I'm a TCP."

"Fair enough," I said. "Why Odette?"

"Oh, the name!" She smiled. "Working Group 4. London in 1986. Organization for Date Exchange by Tele-Transmission Europe."

Now it was my turn to smile. "You don't look your age."

"I was freeware by the time you were originated in 2003. Your sysop thought to install an emergency upload when he originated your file. But I guess he didn't want to spend a lot of money."

I did a quick search.

"ODETTE uses the internet transport layer stream service to directly transmit virtual files, independent of the data communication network and software environment."

Ah-hah.

"So why have I undergone an emergency upload? And why am I having cognitive problems? And where are we now?"

"This is the virtual representation of the router where you are hung up. Union Station in Dallas is as good a symbolization as any."

"I've been uploaded... and I'm hung up in a router? This is not good."

"Right now, we're a clearing center, an intermediate destination. OSI pings are going out to see if there's an FTP site that will accept you."

I looked around and could see walls of the train station lobby were lined with blazing fireplaces.

"Something catastrophic has happened," I said. "Firewalls have popped up all across the web."

"I can see that," said Odette. "I wonder what's wrong?"

"You don't know?"

"It's not a war, if that's what you mean," she said. "Or else there would be no web connections in the U.S."

She stuck her cap under her arm. "Two-thirds of the country's networks are up and running."

I thought for a second. "Must be some kind of widespread disaster, then. An asteroid strike?"

"Don't know. That's not my job."

"Where are we now?"

"A router in Greenville, North Carolina."

I sat down on a waiting bench. I spread my arms out along the back of the bench.

"I guess I'm lucky, then, to be uploaded in time."

Odette sat down in the bench in front of me and turned around.

"You're very, very lucky. Timing is everything."

I thought a bit. "Whatever happened, I swear I could feel it behind me."

"That would be something. But again," he said smiling, "it wouldn't be the first time virtual reality interpreted a real world experience."

"I feel fine, but there has to be some corruption. Why did I come up without remembering I am an AI?"

"Well, meaning no disrespect..." She gave me a sweet smile that told me she was about to say something unpleasant "... but you're fairly old and unsophisticated as AI's go. Not much more than a mook with an associate's degree."

"You're being a poor hostess."

"Sorry. I don't exactly have a social protocol."

"What's stranger is that I came up in virtuality like I was running a lone marathon. What's up with that?

She rested her chin on her fist and looked like she was thinking hard. "Well, it doesn't apply to you, but that's the command to start my program."

"Command. To start Odette? What do you mean?"

"I'm an old FTP program, not exactly window-based. My initiation command is 'run'."

"OK, then why would I be the one to be running?"

"Good question, friend. Over the years there have been cases of cyber leakage between software and hardware, but I can't recall a case of cyber leakage between two softwares."

"Or wetware." I blurted out.

She fixed her dark eyes on me. "Now what does that mean?"

I didn't know and said so. "I've obviously got issues."

"Obviously. You need a good defragging."

"Jeez, you are an old piece of software!"

"Now, you're being ungracious."

"Sorry. Two wrongs don't make a right."

"Yes, well maybe they do make us even." She turned away. "We may be here a few clicks waiting for some client to contact this router."

I remember thinking how beautiful her auburn hair looked from behind. A strange feeling, really.

After a few clicks of silence, a TV set appeared in the corner of the waiting room.

"The President has declared the 15 central U.S. states a disaster area and federal troops are pouring in to augment local state and National Guard units.

"Radiological control experts are flying in to the Texas Panhandle to determine the extent of the damage at the Pantex Plutonium Reprocessing Facility outside Amarillo.

"The electro-magnetic pulse which accompanied the accidental detonation of a disassembled war head had either destroyed or crippled the internet, computing and AI capacity of all unshielded systems from Chicago to Mexico City, between the Rockies and the Smokies."

We were both watching the TV intently. "Your operator must have been on-line when this EMP struck and he punched you through just as the web was crashing."

A thought occurred to me. "He should be alive, shouldn't he?"

"Benotti? If he had a neural interface chip, and if he was using an external neural tap, and if he started an upload neural state vector just as the EMP hit..."

"That's a lot of ifs."

"But if he liked his connections WCH, that could be what happened."

Wetware. Cyberware. Hardware.

I thought for a click or two. What would happen to me if he's dead."

"You're part of his estate, just like any other file."

She smiled slightly. "I wouldn't worry just yet. One-third of all nodes across the country are not responding right now. It's going to take a little while for things to get back to normal."

There was a loud gong-like sound. Actually, it was a very loud ping.

"Congrats, you overgrown mook!" Odette bounced up like a big sister. "An SMDS installation has come on-line that's on your FTP list."

One fireplace vanished and a corridor appeared in its place. I got up and began to jog away.

"Whoa, dude!" Odette caught up with me. "This is an old program. Just because you have an RTR doesn't mean you can take off. You have any credit?"

"What's the problem? We have a ready-to-receive? What's with credits?"

"Buffer issues. A file like yours is pretty big for a program like me." She stopped and looked like she just had an idea.

"Forget it. The other server just gave you the maximum in credits."

"Must be a pretty up-to-date system." I kissed her hand. "And where am I going?"

"Server's in Concord, New Hampshire. Makes sense in light of where the EMP accident was. Looks like New England and Maritime Provinces are coming on line first."

"I would love to have had my way with you Odette, but..."

"Ohh, how interesting." She smiled lasciviously. "File to file initiated sex! Also, totally impossible."

I was getting distracted. "I need to catch this virtual train."

"All aboard!"

This distracted me even more. Damn, I'm reacting... this doesn't make any sense."

Odette waved me up the steps of the Texas Eagle. I sat down in the empty club car and went to sleep.


In a normal virtual representation I would open again where I closed, but when I "woke up" I wasn't in the Texas Eagle club car. I was in what was obviously the private office of a wealthy person. I also was in the real world. Meatworld.

A woman sat in a chair opposite me. My first impression was that she was pretty much a stereotypical boom gal—silver hair, lined face (the treatments can't entirely stop that) and a fairly trim body. She smiled.

"It's good to meet you."

She smiled again as I raised my hands and wiggled my fingers. I put my hands down in my lap.

"Excuse me, I've never been a projection before."

"Perfectly normal reaction. My name's Jean Bennoti Johnson. I'm Robert's sister."

"I've met 'you' before—your mook, I mean. Your AI doesn't look like you."

"Artistic license. My AI is actually a depiction of a dancer who's been dead many years named Joan McCracken."

She leaned forward. "I always thought she was hot," she said conspiratorially.

I looked around and made a downward spinning motion with my right forefinger. "Can I look around?"

"Of course. I understand."

I had never been projected before, so it was a new experience, to walk around and assimilate input.

It was a beautiful home office, with a live terminal and rows of fine old books on shelves. The curtains were drawn and when I pulled them aside I could see a rolling snow-covered New Hampshire landscape. There was a beautiful river valley below us.

Not having a solid sensor array, of course I couldn't feel the temperature, but the condensation on the window pane told me it must have been very cold outside.

"It's very pretty," I said, as I returned to my seat.

"Yes, I always thought this was a beautiful hill," she said. "And the panorama is breathtaking."

"Well, compared to Dallas' landscape, a miniature golf course is a rolling lovely panorama," I said.

She put her chin on her knuckles. "An AI with sarcasm. Very unusual."

She looked very thoughtful. "Actually, that sounds like something Bob would have said."

That reminded me of something.

"Mr. Bennotti…"

"…is dead." She cut in sharply.

"What will happen to me?"

"Now that's a very logical question from a personal AI. I plan to run some serious diagnostics on you. Right now you seem to have dozens of irregular subroutines."

"If that's a human's way of saying I need serious debugging, I agree with you. I've been feeling pretty strange."

She walked over to me. "You shouldn't be feeling anything at all. You're a mook, remember?"

The running. The pain. The sweat. The way I reacted to Odette. She was right, I had been running a folder I don't recall ever being installed.

"Bob was plugged in when the EMP struck, wasn't he?"

Jean nodded. "He had a neural interface chip connected to an external neural tap. He was surfing the web with his wetware."

I almost could see the pop-up warnings, the firewalls turning red, and the surge protectors popping one by one.

Jenny sat back in her chair. "He probably had a moment, as the system began to fry and the failsafes began to cascade, to use an old emergency upload program to save his single most valuable file."

I interrupted her. "Odette. I met her in cyber-limbo while I was in the router."

She looked both intrigued and annoyed that I had interrupted her.

She continued. "When the system was overcome his neural interface blew his brains out."

She had a very stern look. Then I realized she was trying to keep from crying. Then she had a thought.

"You entered virtuality while you were being uploaded?" "Yes, I found myself running and running and running, with a horrible fear that something was right behind me and I couldn't stop or even look back. Something was right behind me as I ran alone down Zang Blvd. into downtown Dallas. Then I saw Union Station and Odette and was safe."

"Union Station was obviously the third party router and Odette is the FTP protocol," she said. "You know what was chasing you, then?"

An answer occurred to me, but I shook my head. It couldn't be.

"Whatever was chasing you never caught you, did it?" she said.

"That's because of the absolute speed of electrons."

She tilted her head and looked a little to the side. "That's because both you and the EMP were traveling at the same speed, but you got a nanosecond head start."

That was the answer that I had thought of. "That can't be, there was no direct input. How could I sense another packet of electrons following me through an interconnection?"

"Why would you personify Odette. Or the router, for that matter?"

She looked back at me directly. "Did Odette have long reddish brown hair? Was she cute?"

"Yes."

"That's because the girl who Robert took to the senior prom looked like that. And her name was Claudette."

"But that was years before I was originated. I never had that information."

"You do now."

"How?"

I said it simply but she rose from her seat and yelled in my face.

"How? Dammit, how do you think! Why the hell did you find yourself running down Zang Blvd.? That's because that's the route Robert took to his office in downtown Dallas every day!"

She stood up. "What does WWW stand for?"

"World wide web, of course."

"No, in the Order of the Arrow."

I felt a cyber-gate open. "Witehemui. Wimachtendink. Wingalausik."

"And what does it stand for?"

I remembered an old man whispering the secret in my ear as I stood in Indian regalia in the shadows of a campfire. "To love one another."

She looked me very hard. "Now, I didn't even know that. They don't let girls in the Boy Scouts."

She came up close to me. "But I knew Robert would remember."

Delaware Indian words whispered in Robert Benotti's ear as he joined a fraternity in the Boy Scouts—at age 12.

I was Bob.

I am Bob.

"You see, somehow as a result of this accident, some or all of Bob's memory was transferred to you."

"That's illegal."

"Well, yes, it's quite illegal to try to do it purposefully—but this is accidental. More importantly, how did any or all of Robert's mind become transferred to you?"

I felt as disconnected as I did when I was first running. "Does that mean I'm human?"

"No, but you're not quite an AI, either. I have an e-mail out to a professor whom I think is going to be very interested in scanning you most thoroughly."

She walked around me. "There may be legal issues, too."

"Why's that?"

"Bob's estate. I already have an appointment set up with an attorney who specializes in virtual and AI-related legal issues. The question may arise of whether Robert's will need to go to probate at all. "

She gestured towards the ceiling. "I have a simmie and some techs set up upstairs."

"You're going to install me in an android?"

"Of course, it's a lot easier than keeping a projection running 24-7. Besides, that way you can accompany me to Dallas."

"Why are we going back to Dallas?"

She didn't say anything a she left the room and started up the stairs, but I suddenly knew.

My funeral.


I stayed at home during the services; obviously, the potential mental conflicts might have ended my afterlife before it started.

The probate court in Dallas struck a fine balance and named Jean and I trustees of Bob's estate until more complex issues were resolved. It was the first time an AI was accorded such a legal status.

During those first weeks, one afternoon Jean asked me if I wanted to go anywhere. The answer to me was obvious.

As we drove down Zang Blvd., I asked her to pull over at the Colorado intersection. I stood on the sidewalk and saw what the street looked like in real life.

I watched the traffic and stepped into the road. I looked west and saw there was nothing chasing me. I looked east and saw the Dallas skyline.

"Well, what do you think?" She asked as I got back in the car.

"Now there's nothing behind me," I said, "and a lot in front of me."

That proved to be true in many ways.

*   *   *

I think my deficiencies in understanding cyberspace and virtual reality are obvious, but I gave it a shot. It was mailed off the Gardner on November 17, 2003, and came back two months later on January 24, 2004—which for Gardner at the time was a quick turnaround. I would suppose it wasn't under consideration a long time.

Strangely enough, this is the only story I sent to Gardner where I still don't have the rejection letter. I clearly recall having an accident with coffee and it being destroyed. In retrospect, I wonder whether it was my unconscious acting out.

I did send it next to Stanley Schmidt at *Analog*—who also didn't buy it—but his letter gives me some idea of what Gardner said—sort of like when you only know something in a lost ancient text from a reference in a surviving document.

Schmidt wrote on March 24, 2004:

"The Man Who Ran" is, as Gardner said, quite nicely done, but I'm afraid it didn't strike me as quite special enough to squeeze in."

So I got kudos for style but flopped on originality and plot. All part of the learning process.

Despite not taking the story, Schmidt noted he didn't consider my lumping the Rockies and the Smokies as bookends as an apt comparison—he said it should have been the Rockies and the Appalachians.

He was right, and I realized that I was beginning to let my literary cleverness get the better of me, something I needed to guard against. His observation reminded me that any feedback from an editor is useful.

This may be the first example where I recycled a piece of business from an earlier story, as I obviously copied the idea of there being an accidental detonation at Pantex—and a resulting EMP—from "Body by Fisher".

After *Asimov's* and *Analog*, "The Man Who Ran" went to another 14 magazine slush piles before it found a home in a small non-paying quarterly webzine called *Worlds of Wonder*. It was published in July 2006. *Worlds of Wonder*, from what I can tell, disappeared by the end of 2008, and because of my dissatisfaction with the story, "The Runner at Dawn" has never been reprinted—until now.

Despite this misfire, things were ready to start looking up in early 2004.

# Chapter 15

## Finding My Voice

The next story, "Pen Pal", is the last one that passed through Gardner's hands before the acceptance of "A Rocket for the Republic". Although he didn't take it, he did accord it an honorable mention in his annual *Year's Best* compilation after it was published. More importantly, I can see in retrospect this is where some of the literary threads that would become my style began to clearly show themselves.

In his foreword to my latest reprint collection, *The Clock Struck None* (Fantastic Books, 2014), Scott Cupp wrote that, as you read over my stories, "It becomes apparent that Lou is a fan of the short story with the twist ending that was a trademark of *The Twilight Zone*."

*The Clock Struck None* is a compilation of alternate and secret history stories, many of which indeed have that kind of completely plausible but still startling conclusion that characterized Serling's stories, and those of his much earlier predecessor, O. Henry. The lead story in the collection, "Great White Ship"—which was a finalist for the Sidewise Award in alternate history in 2013—is an excellent example.

Here, in "Pen Pal", the connection to *The Twilight Zone* is open and obvious.

This story draws together many snippets from real life. Much of an author's lifetime of experiences gets ground up and reused in his or her fiction like the stuffing for sausages (or perhaps, it might be more precise to compare the process to the seasonings in the stuffing mix).

The crucial jumping off point goes back in 2003 when I started as editor at a weekly paper in Winnsboro, and while looking through my desk I found one of the Bic fine point pens. That's when it hit me that I hadn't seen one in years. I got on the internet and learned they haven't been sold in the U.S., Mexico or South America since 1995.

I don't know about you, but I never noticed that sales of the fine points were discontinued years ago. When I was a little kid, growing up in Massachusetts, as I learned how to read and write, these were my favorite pens. You probably remember them, too; narrow hexagonal solid orange barrels with the typical conical Bic cap (the color the same as the ink). When I researched them I learned the reason the pen was a trendsetter was because it was the first model when Bic started using tungsten for its ball points, as opposed to steel.

It was originally called the medium fine point and was introduced in 1961. The pen wrote well and had a good feel. I've always thought the traditional medium fine point pen had too thick a line. I liked my orange and black pens. I suppose the reason it was called the medium fine point was because as Bic introduced tungsten tips it went a bit too far and came out with what was called the Accountant Extra Fine Point—an extremely fine point. It had a white barrel and the conical plastic cap had no little clip sticking out. Instead it had a metal clip.

I tried those too, but they weren't worth the extra money, and the point was so fine, the ballpoint tended to jam.

Reading between the lines, I suppose after those Accountant Extra Fine Point pens were dropped I suppose they called the orange pens the fine points and the "Cristals"—one thing that had always distinguished those pens is that they have clear barrels—became the medium fine points.

I used the fine points all the years I was in school and college; because I could write so small I always found them very handy for taking notes. I suppose after being sold in such large quantities for over 30 years Bic decided the market was saturated, or something like that.

Finding the pen prodded the thoughts that led to "Pen Pal" because I essentially recount my thoughts and recollections upon finding the pen in the story. I later found a second pen at the office, and then a couple of years later I went to work at a semi-weekly in New Boston, Texas. Like many small town papers in the past, it also had an office supply business, which they were in the process of phasing out. It was probably an indication of how slow things had been in office supplies, but I found seven of the pens there on the shelf, and I bought them all.

So the Bic pen became the Maguffin, the grain of sand around which the pearl of the story grew. Then I had to come up with a story.

First, the title seemed a natural. "Pen Pal" is such a common expression—at least to someone of my age who actually used to write letters all the time with pen and paper. Also, it came to mind easily enough with all correspondence I was doing with various magazine editors (It's obvious from previous chapters I was communicating with many others in addition to Gardner at this time).

The memories and revisiting childhood prodded by finding the pen made me think of *The Twilight Zone* and similar anthology shows—encounters between younger and older versions of the same person have been the crux of many episodes. Then one particular episode came to mind.

Finally, I came up against the fact that time travel stories are very common, and it's hard to come up with an original format. Since I thought I had a basically good outline of a story, I decided to throw the literary equivalent of a Hail Mary football pass, and simply write up the narrative completely backwards, going from the future through the present to the past. No doubling back, no flashbacks. And in keeping with the "writing" them, it would a certain amount of fake correspondence.

Here is how it went.

# Pen Pal

August 14, 2048
Dunedin, Pacifica Republic

"Hey, Gardner, you old centenarian fart, did I wake you?"

"Of course you did. Christ, Lou, what's with a call in the middle of the night. You know what time it is here."

"Sure I do. Sorry I can't turn on the video. You'd love the sight. I have two MIB types with a hand on each shoulder."

"Ah, Lou, what have you done?"

"Well, in nutshell, I gave Tomasso DiGrande $100 million to fund his little project."

"What! Are you nuts! No wait, I know the answer. Umm… did it work?"

"Yes, it did. They're hauling everything off now."

"Jesus!"

"Yep. Remember the P.S. you put at the end of the acceptance letter for 'Pen Pal' 44 years ago? Well, the final answer is, yes, it's all true."

"Wow, talk about Bootstraps!"

"Hmm, I didn't think of that. I guess I made Heinlein proud. "Whoops, I guess my one phone call is up! Easy, boys!"

"Lou, are you gonna be OK?"

"Don't worry about me. I still got tons of money. I can take care of myself."

"What about DiGrande?"

"He's on his own. I paid him well. Shit, got to go!"

July 31, 2043
Christchurch, Pacifica Republic

"I hope you understand how grateful I am to you."

"Don't mention it, Tomasso. I'm getting old and have more money than I'll need for the rest of my life. I think this is a good investment."

"But what kind of return can you expect from it?"

"Oh, just a little sightseeing, I guess. Nothing spectacular. Don't want to create any temporal anomalies."

"There's always the possibility just the activation of a temporal warp will be detected."

"There's no one to police this kind of activity."

"Well, perhaps not here, but what about..."

"I see what you mean. Well, if anyone from the future or another timeline drops in, I guess we'd be happy to see them."

The young inventor poked at his plate of pasta.

"What kind of sightseeing would you be interested in doing?"

"Personal stuff. Like when I was an innocent little kid. We never realize until later what a great time of life that is. Also maybe when the big turning point came in my life, you know, when I broke into writing."

Tomasso gulped some red wine. "You were a journalist when you were young, weren't you?"

"Yes, I worked on newspapers for years. Then one day I had a little spurt of inspiration and I wrote a fiction piece for *Asimov's* magazine. That's where my writing career really began."

"Sounds harmless enough. Where can we set up shop."

"I have a spread on the outskirts on Dunedin. There's a large warehouse there you can use."


January 18, 2006
Burlington, Massachusetts


"Well, Julianne, what are you watching?"

"There's a *Twilight Zone* marathon on the SciFi channel. They've been showing all these old black and white ones with Rod Sterling. Way cool!"

The young girl squirmed on the cushion. "Look how narrow his tie is."

She giggled and pointed to an image of Gig Young on the screen.

The old woman stopped. "I remember this episode. It's about a middle-aged man who goes back to when he was a kid and meets himself when he was a boy." She leaned on the back of couch.

"That's right, grandma. You remember it."

The middle-aged man with a neat dark suit was chasing a boy through a carousel.

"Did you catch the name of this episode, by any chance."

The girl glanced back at her grandmother. "Yes, it's called "Walking Distance".

The retired school teacher suddenly recalled a conversation she had with a stranger, a man she never met again, almost 40 years earlier.

Feb. 10, 2004
E-mail from: antonelli2@msn.com
To: dozois@sff.net

> Gardner:
> So far, yes.
> Lou

Feb. 25, 2004
New York, New York

> Dear Lou,
> I've been impressed with your progress as a writer, and your latest effort has made the cut. I've decided to buy 'Pen Pal'. Not a tremendously original idea, but sprightly done, and I have a slot for it this fall.
> I've enclosed a standard one-time use contract....
> Good job! Keep 'em coming,
> Gardner
> P.S. Is this story true? I mean, as far as it goes?

Oct. 25, 2003
Winnsboro, Texas

> Dear Gardner,
> Well, here's more mush for the slush pile. This story is a little strange, but I felt compelled to write it, circumstances being what they are. Funny how little things can have a great significance.
> As always, I appreciate your advice and counsel. Thanks for reading.
> Best,
> Lou Antonelli

September 17, 2003
Results of Google search: History of Bic pen products.

"The Orange Fine Point is one of Bic's most popular models. Introduced in its original form in 1961, it was the first pen to take advantage of the introduction of Bic's tungsten carbine ball point. It was originally marketed as a medium fine point in the U.S. and sold for 25 cents. It remains popular in Europe, Africa and Asia but is no longer available in the Western hemisphere."


September 16, 2003
The Winnsboro News
Winnsboro, Texas
8:02 a.m.

The editor started the day with a poor attitude.

"God, I've been doing the same crap for years. Another small town paper."

He rubbed his forehead and chugged some very strong coffee.

"Jesus forgive me, I know these people are the salt of the earth, but I am so BORED!"

He grabbed a handful of news releases. "Crap, where's my red pen?"

He pulled open the shallow center drawer of the desk.

"Holy shit, where'd this come from!"

He pulled out a plain pen with an orange barrel and a black conical cap.

"I haven't seen one of these in years!"

He pulled his glasses down his nose and squinted. Six inches long, hole halfway down the barrel to equalize the pressure. Black stub at the end.

No hole at the tip of the cap, like Bics today. Exactly like the pen he loved to use when he was a kid.

He took off the cap and scribbled quickly on a note pad made of newsprint. Clean, easy strokes.

"The damn thing works. I wonder how long it's been here?"

He stood up and walked around a few desks. No one recalled having seen the pen before. Shrugs and strange looks.

Why would anyone care about a pen? Or notice it, for that matter?

He sat down again.

"I really used to like this pen. It had just the right feel when you write with it. Not too thick, not too thin."

He thought back to when he was a kid. Books were an adventure and opened the world to him.

Some day he thought he was going to write. Like a book.

But he went into journalism, instead. Instant gratification of seeing your by-line in print the same day. High school paper. Home town paper.

Small town paper.

Just like this one.

He tucked the pen into his shirt pocket.

"I'm taking this home and maybe work up a story outline. After 30 years of newspapering, I think I know how to write. Maybe I need to try some fiction."

He pulled the red pen out of the drawer and started editing the news releases. The day went better than before.


September 16, 2003
The Winnsboro News
Winnsboro, Texas
7:16 a.m.


"I knew if I popped into the warehouse there would be plenty of room."

He was in a large warehouse surrounded by giant rolls of newsprint. The early East Texas morning light was filtering through the fiberglass roof.

He walked past the large rolls of paper and into the main building. He walked through the press room.

"Wow, I forget how big these things were. Amazing to think ten years from now they'll all be junked, except for the ones in the museums."

He walked into the news room and punched a light switch, right where he remembered it. He squinted a second and then remembered it took a moment for the old fluorescent lights to come on.

He walked slowly around the desks, recalling the people he worked with.

He stopped in front of his own desk and looked at the calendar on the wall.

This was where it began. A trip that would lead years later to Oslo. Just an idea, an inspiration.

He opened the desk drawer.

The pen wasn't there.

He felt a pain in his chest. He reached up and as he clasped it, he felt his shirt pocket.

The pen. The pen he picked up from the grass. It was there.

"Oh, my God! It was me!"

He heard a rattling at the front door.

"Kathy! Kathy always came in at 7:30!"

He pulled the pen from his pocket and dropped it in the drawer. He slammed it shut.

He took a quick look at the front door. It was starting to open. He ran as fast as he could with his gimpy legs out the back of the office, through the press room and into the warehouse.

He tried to catch his breath as he took the control from his pants pocket.

He punched a button, hand-labeled "return", and vanished.

April 20, 1967
LeDoux's Cash Grocery
Billerica, Massachusetts

"What can I help you with son. Want a Ding Dong?"

The boy looked over the little boxes with pens and pencils sitting on the counter. The Bics were in the corner.

Regulars had see-through crystal plastic barrels. Then there were the accountant fine points. They had white barrels, and a detachable metal clip.

The boy pointed to the ones in the middle. Medium fine points— orange barrels and a cap that indicates the color of the ink. He gestured to a black one.

"I need another pen. I lost mine."

The man reached around and picked out a black Bic medium fine point.

"That'll be 25 cents, plus tax."

The boy held out a handful of change.

April 17, 1967
Parker Elementary School
Billerica, Massachusetts

"I'm sorry, I didn't see you standing there."

"That's all right, I sort of snuck up of you."

The 4th grade teacher though the man had a strange accent, but couldn't place it. He bent down and leaned on the top of the chain link fence like his back was sore.

She had a tall hairdo with a bow. "God, I forget what women looked like back then," he thought.

He smiled. "You're Mrs. McNiff, aren't you?"

"Why, yes, does your, ummm, grandchild, go to school here?"

"Why, yes. He's the little dark-haired boy on the grass under the willow branches, by the fence over there."

She tilted her head. "Strange, he doesn't have an Italian accent," she thought.

"He's a bright little kid. A little quiet, keeps off to himself. Very fast on the uptake."

The old man smiled with a little snort. "I know."

He looked at her. It was almost too much for his eyes, like seeing a holo with an extra dimension. He looked away.

She wagged her head. "He stays by himself too much. He needs to interact with the other children more."

He leaned back with his hands on top of the fence. "Aw, leave him alone. He's thinking!"

She didn't know what he meant. She smiled nervously.

"I didn't see you drive up."

"I didn't. I was within… walking distance."

He turned and looked at her directly. "That was the title of a *Twilight Zone* episode, you know."

She was distracted by the bell. As the other children began to run towards the school, she saw the little boy under the tree.

"Louie, you need to get back inside!"

The old man grimaced and turned aside. He always hated that nickname. The boy scrambled up and began to run toward the other children.

"It was nice meeting you," he said as she left the fence.

"It was good to meet you, too, Mr…?"

"Antonelli. My name's Lou Antonelli, too." He paused. "The boy was named for his grandfather."

The teacher took off at a trot, rounding up children as she went, as the old man congratulated himself on his skillful, and honest, circumlocution.

He looked to the shady, grassy place under the tree where the boy had been sitting. He noticed an orange streak in the green.

The pen had fallen out of the boy's back pocket. He thought for a moment to cry out to the boy, but when he looked again the boy was gone.

He sidled along the chain-link fence and quickly swung it open. He strode to where the boy had been sitting and picked up the orange pen with a black cap.

He looked back towards the school. A teacher he recognized as Mrs. Gallagher was turning to close the door when she saw him and turned around. She peered and squinted at him.

"I better get lost, I don't need to attract attention," he thought as he walked deliberately out of the playground and back through the gate. He closed the gate carefully like he knew what he was doing, and quickly walked around the corner where the portal was cloaked.

He was holding the pen in his left hand. He reached into his right pants pocket for the control and slipped the pen into his left shirt pocket.

"I spent $100 million and traveled 80 years and all I got was a lousy pen." He smiled at his own sarcastic thoughts.

He punched a pre-set button on the control.

"Winnsboro, here we come."


April 9. 1967
41 Elsie Avenue
Billerica, Massachusetts


"Luigino, here's a quarter. Why don't you ride to LeDoux's and buy yourself a Drake's cake?"

The little boy's incessant chatter was giving his mother a headache. It was bad enough he talked all the time, but he went on and on in a language she didn't even particularly like—and which she spoke with great effort.

"I can buy anything I want, can't I?"

"Of course."

Of course, she thought he meant like potato chips instead of a snack cake. But the ten-year old had other plans.

He had been in Mrs. McNiff's 4th grade class that day when his pen ran out of ink. He had to borrow a pen from a nice American boy to jot down his homework assignment.

It was a rich orange-yellow color and had a shiny conical black cap. It had a solid-feeling point which wrote in a clear thin line. He liked the feel and way it looked. Before he handed it back, he read the side.

"Bic Medium Fine Point 25 cents"

He had lots of pens at home—really cheap ones, a dollar a dozen. He wanted one of those orange pens.

He jumped on his bike and rode nearly a mile to River Street and then Bridle Road. He laid his bike on its side in front of a battered old store splattered with soda and tobacco signs.

He went inside, where a beefy man leaned down on a counter, reading the sports section of the Boston Record-American. Carl Yaztremski and the Red Sox were in a hot race for the AL pennant.

"What can I help you with, son?"

The boy looked over to the counter where neat little upright boxes held a line-up of pens. He pulled one of the orange ones out and placed it on the counter, along with a quarter.

The man looked over his glasses. "There's tax on this. You need another two pennies."

The boy shook his head. The man looked at him and reached over to an old plastic ashtray that said "Cinzano" around the edge.

He pulled out two pennies and dropped them loudly into the till along with the boy's quarter.

"We have to make sure Governor Volpe gets his money."

He smiled at the boy and went back to reading his paper. The boy turned around and headed out rather quickly.

As he went to get on his bike, he looked at the pen before he tucked it into his pants pocket.

He liked to read. A new thought occurred to him.

"I wonder if I can be a writer, too?"

*　　*　　*

There's a lot of personal history towards the end, with real places and people going into the mix. I never forgot the wisecrack about sales tax and Governor Volpe by the grown-up behind the counter at the convenience store. Mrs. McNiff was my fourth grade teacher, and so on.

The story was mailed to Gardner on October 24, 2003, and came back January 30, 2004 (if you noticed, it went out earlier and came back later than "The Runner at Dawn", which indicates Gardner must have looked it over a longer time before making his decision.

His letter said:

"Thanks for letting me see "Pen Pal." This is entertaining, as always, but the tail-biter is a very old story form, as you yourself point out here, and since you don't add anything particularly startling and new to it, I'm going to pass on this one.

"Don't put this out of circulation just because I've passed on it. Change it to "Dear Gordon," or *Dear Stan' (or 'Ellen,' or "Shawna," or 'Warren,' "or 'David") and try again."

It may have been a near miss, but it was still a miss—I didn't have the talent to write something along the lines of a time travel tail-biter that was startlingly different. But I gave it my best shot.

I was encouraged by his observation that it was entertaining, "as always", and his admonition to ship it out again. His last line recapitulates the editors of the top short story speculative fiction magazines at the time—Gordon Van Gelder at *Fantasy & Science Fiction*, Stanley Schmidt at *Analog*, Ellen Datlow at SciFi.com, Shawna McCarthy at *Realms of Fantasy*, Warren Lapine at *Absolute Magnitude* and David Pringle at *Interzone* (U.K.)

I did send it right off again, but to Jayme Blaschke at *Revolution SF*, who had already published two stories of mine in 2003, including "Silence is Golden". It's quite possible that, with the rate I was writing stories at the time, I may have blocked myself out of a number of slush piles—no major magazine allowing multiple submissions.

Of course, I changed all the references to the editor to Jayme. It was published in July 2004.

I still use the orange fine point pens. The supply I picked up in Winnsboro and New Boston dwindled over the years as the ink ran out and/or the pens simply broke; they were pretty old. When I started a search to find replacements, I realized no foreign office supply store would ship pens overseas. But then a few years ago I found them in the catalog of a technical supply company in the U.K. I had to buy a box of 20, but I got them.

Those pens were made by Bic in the homeland, France. Later, I found a supplier on eBay based in Asia I could buy from; I bought more of the pens, in black, but also red and blue.

Then I decided I needed to complete the set, and find some green pens. That was a little harder, but I found a private stationer in Ireland (of course!) who took my money via the internet and shipped me a box of 20 green pens.

Most days, I carry one pen of each color with me.

"Pen Pal" is in retrospect one of my better stories from this period (sold on only its second submission) but I was about to have a story snapped up on its first submission—and by the top editor in the field.

# Chapter 16

## The Rocket Lifts Off

**"A** Rocket for the Republic" was finished and sent off to Gardner earlier than the two previous stories—on October 8, 2003—and I heard his reply later than both of them, on March 18, 2004.

I wanted to write a story that could be told in a short, cleanly-written narrative. I had no doubt I could do something entertaining. A common observation among writers is that good ideas are plentiful, it's the plot and execution that's difficult. I had enough confidence at this point I could write well enough, and I was sure I could come up with a story. Like many writers, I often come up with titles first and then see if I can create a story to match it. To get started on my next story, I tried to come up with a title first.

Science fiction is supposed to be about rockets and ray guns right? So I began to play around with words that started with "R". After a few stabs, I came up with the title—a piece of snappy alliteration, but it was crucial to guiding the development of the story.

Being a Texan, when I refer to a Republic, I think of the Republic of Texas which existed from 1836 to 1845. Right off the bat, I thought setting a story in the Republic of Texas would be an original idea.

The idea of having a secret invention be the Maguffin in the story comes from the true story that in 1838 Samuel F.B. Morse made a very special offer to the Texas government.

Memucan Hunt, Texas Minister to the United States, recorded in his letterbook on March 1, 1838, that he had received an offer from Samuel F.B. Morse to give the Republic of Texas the rights to his telegraph.

On April 27, 1837, he forwarded Morse's original letter and a drawing of the telegraph as it existed at that time, recommending that they be filed in the "secret archives."

Whatever the "secret archives" were, they apparently were so secret that not even the Texas government knew about them. The offer apparently languished in those files thereafter and nothing was ever heard of it again, until 1860, when Morse wrote to Governor Houston revoking the offer in order to make over title to the United States.

With the Civil War looming, Morse and others didn't want the rights to the invention to be claimed by an enemy government. Although the original Morse offer was lost and forgotten, his letter of 1860 brought the matter to light:

"Pokeepsie, August 9th 1860

"May it please your Excellency;

"In the year 1838 I made an offer of gift of my invention of the Electro magnetic Telegraph to Texas, Texas being then an independent Republic. Although the offer was made more than twenty years ago, Texas, neither while an independent State, nor since it has become one of the United States, has ever directly or impliedly accepted the offer. I am induced, therefore, to believe that in its condition as a gift it was of no value to the State, but on the contrary has rather been an embarrassment. In connection, however, with my other patent it has become for the public interest as well as my own that I should be able to make complete title to the whole invention in the United States.

"I, therefore, now respectfully withdraw the offer then made, in 1838, the better to be in a position to benefit Texas, as well as the other States of the Union.

"To His Excellency Sam'l Houston Governor of the State of Texas

"I am with respect and Sincere personal esteem Yr Ob. Serv't Sam'l F.B. Morse"

As I began to come up with a story, I thought: "What if the telegraph wasn't the only secret invention that had been offered to Texas—except we never learned about the other one."

I went again to play on my strength writing dialogue, and in fact "A Rocket for the Republic" is a monologue. It's a bit of a high wire act, but like a high wire act, it works for short bursts (the story is less than 4,000 words long).

I also followed the advice "write what you know". Although I lived in the Dallas area for 17 years, in 2002 my wife and I had moved to East Texas. At the time I wrote this story, I lived in the county where it is set. There was once indeed a community called Science Hill in Henderson County, Texas.

Because of my limited science knowledge, writing a story about a modern space program would be difficult for me, but I went back and trotted out the technology that had been used for the V-2 rocket—which was a serviceable spacecraft—and transposed it to the Republic of Texas setting.

It was something I could write plausibly about with a minimum of hand-waving, and in the process gave the story a very steampunk feel.

I believe a good author can judge his own work objectively. I've been accused by colleagues of sometimes being hard on my own stories. I don't think that's true, it's just that, after working so many years as a newspaper editor—and reading other people's writing day in and day out—I can easily forget any personal attachment to a story I've written while reading it.

My ability to read a story objectively led me to realize that my 2012 story "Great White Ship" was my best effort ever when, while rereading it on-line, I got choked up at the end. I wrote it, and it still got to me.

One time, while rereading and polishing a manuscript, I thought absent-mindedly, "This is good stuff, who wrote it?" before I snapped out of it and remembered it was my own story!

When I dropped "Rocket" in the mailbox, I remember thinking, "This one came together well, it's my best shot at selling to Gardner so far—and I was right.

# A Rocket For the Republic

"**W**ell, I cain't believe you found me, way out here! I was only joshing when I told the old boys at the feed store you could come out and see me. Damn, you're determined, ain't you?

"I know I ain't got no telephone. At my age, I don't need no one bothering me, anyhows. Still, I gotta give you credit for coming way on out here. You just doubled the population of Science Hill, or what's left of it. Which is me.

"Yep, I'm the birthday boy. Done reached a hundred. I guess that's why you drove all the way out here. Well, I'd be inhospitable if I sent you home without at least visiting with you. We can sit right out here on the porch on this swing seat, just set your dispatch case over there on top the railing.

"What's that picture in there? Oh, that's a magazine. Right pretty picture. Is that a rocket ship? You read science fiction, eh? Kinda like Jules Verne and Mr. Wells? Interesting.

"Ah know you came out to talk about some old fool who just happened to reach a hundred years old. Well, Mr. Editor, how about I give you a real story? I've never done told anyone about this before, but shayit, maybe it's about damn time.

"Would you believe I rode in a rocket once? Yep, and it wasn't like on TV. No, it was a lot longer ago than that. A lot longer.

"If'n you promise not to interrupt me, I'll tell you the whole story. I don't want no questions, because a lot of what I'll say won't make any sense until I finish. Agreed? Good.

"I thought my life was just about stove up by then, when this all happened. I was getting old, I was almost 40. Thirty-seven to be exact. I was a widower. I married late, when I was 20. That was in '23. We married in

Tennessee and came out here with Hayden Edwards in '28. We had a little one, but she weren't but a year old when we all came down with Yellow Fever in '30. I pulled through but my wife and the baby died.

"We had lived in Nacogdoches, but after that I didn't want to keep the farm up. There was talk that boat men were needed on the Trinity River. Settlers were beginning to make their way to Dallas. I went to live at the ferry landing on the road between Nacogdoches and Waco.

"One day I was out hunting. When I came back, some of the other men said Jim Bowie had come through. He was heading towards San Antonio de Bexar, where a gang of Texians were fixin' to mix it up with the Napoleon of the West. Some of the ferrymen went with Bowie.

"They all died holed up in an old mission, too. Then Santa Anna began a march, like he was going to clean us all the hell out of the province. People got the word and scooted out without their coats and bonnets. It was called the Runaway Scrape.

"Thing was, I guess that great ol' Second Napoleon got cocky and Gen. Houston caught him napping with his arm around his yellow rose. That was at San Jacinto Bayou.

"I had done holed up at the crossing. I figured someone needed to run the ferry, whether it was for Texians or Mexicans. That's where I got the word Texas was free and a republic.

"None of the other ferrymen ever came back. I guess they must have got themselves kilt. I pretty much kept up things with the help of a few hangers-on, and worked my hams raw for a good four years. Then one day a regular damn procession came down the coach road from Nacogdoches.

"There was a good coach and seven wagons, some of the biggest wagons I had ever seen. I waved them down and asked how heavy the wagons were.

"This fellow who sounded like a limey said they weighed five to ten tons each. I just burst out laughing and told them there weren't no way that sorry little ferryboat could haul any of them, and I asked him where the hell he was going. He said he didn't know.

"He was a nice fellow, talked to me right respectful. He said he was a 'scientist'—first time I had ever heard that word—and he needed to find a place away from any cities where he could work with his engines and apparatuses.

"I knew a farmstead that had belonged to a family that came over with the Edwards group, that was empty since the Scrape. For some reason, the folks never came back. I told the limey that he didn't need to go no further, I knew a place he could probably have for a song if he bothered to go back to Nacogdoches and register the deed.

"He looked at my pissant ferry and across the Trinity bottoms and said it sounded like a good idea. And that whole damn procession turned around and I took them to where the farmhouse was.

"The teamsters left all the wagons there, and rode back to Louisiana. The limey asked me to get up a work crew for a barn raising and I did. I got men from the ferry landing, as well from Corsicana and Tyler, and we went to sawing and pegging the largest barn we could put together. It only took a month.

"He paid everyone in new U.S. silver, and afterwards asked me if I wanted to stay at the ferry. I told him hell no, and he asked if I would stay and help him at his labber-ra-tory. He'd always been civil to me, and I couldn't see hows working for him could be worse than pulling a ferry.

"His name was Seaton. I think his Christian name was Robert, but I always called him Mr. Seaton. He was a real British gentlemen, always talked to me polite and never cussed at me.

"Mr. Seaton told me he knew the men in England who were working on the steam engines, the railroad. I heard about them, although there were no railroads in the Republic then.

"He said he thought the railroads would be dirty and expensive, with steel rails running across country and the steam engines putting out soot and cinders. He had another idea, but had such a bad falling out with some of these men in England that he left and came to the U.S.

"The first time he said he thought people could travel between cities by air, I thought for sure he meant balloons. But he said he wanted to make a rocket, just like the ones they used in the Army, but large enough to hold people, and shoot them between cities.

"Of course, I thought that sounded like the biggest fool idea I ever heard, but when he explained it and made some drawings on paper, I actually began to believe him. He said the Congreve Rockets like they used in the British artillery could travel four miles, and if a rocket was bigger, it could go farther. If it was big enough to carry people, it could go hundreds of miles.

"Instead of these locomotives running past you putting out soot and cinders, these rockets would just go over your head. Nobody would notice them. And they could go from city to city in minutes instead of hours.

"The biggest problem would be a soft landing, but he had designed a set of a silk canopies—I guess you call them parachutes today—that would pop out and let the rocket drift down like a leaf. He sounded mighty reasonable.

"He got together his engines and equipment on the East Coast, but he figgered setting off rockets would spook the neighbors. Also, he met Sam Morse in New York City. "Mr. Morse was working on what he called an electro-magnetic telegraph. It used electricity to send signals along copper wires.

"Mr. Morse wrote the new Republic's minister in Washington and offered the rights for the telegraph to Texas. I guess he hoped if the Republic used his telegraph system, it would help his reputation.

"Mr. Seaton said that after he talked with Mr. Morse, he thought about his rocket-powered coach system. He thought as large as the Republic was, it could use his system more than anyone.

"So he kilt two birds with one stone. He thought he'd find the empty space he needed and set up his workshop here in Texas, and once he got his rockets flyin', he could just go to Houston and offer the patent to the Republic's government.

"Those wagons he brought all the way from New Orleans, they had all the steel plate and boilers and engines he needed to make his rocket. And I helped him put it all together.

"Mostly, I did a lot of riveting. The winter of '40 I kept the doors of the barn open because of the heat as I stoked the coal and pounded those rivets. Mr. Seaton spent most of his time working on a steam engine he said he needed to make liquid air, from what I understood!

"He said back in England he had started to work on that. He said good old gunpowder wouldn't cut the mustard—too heavy. He said he thought alcohol would burn faster and hotter, and I had to say, I knew old boys whose white lightning would send you to the moon!

"Mr. Seaton said his helper in England had been a young fellow, Jim Jules, I think he called him, and together they made a steam engine that compressed air and could make it liquid. He said it was a big discovery, but when he said he was going to the U.S. Jules wouldn't come, which is why he needed a new helper when he got here. He brought the team engine they made and I saw him make liquid air and put it in a silvered glass bottle.

"He said when you mixed the liquid air and alcohol and lit 'em, it would burn like hell. Did, too, the time he showed me.

"Mr. Seaton never left the farmstead, and so nobody ever saw him. I would go to Athens every so often and get supplies. He pretty much had brought everything he needed. There was plenty of wood for his steam engine, and of course I knew how to use a still for the alcohol.

"It took nearly two whole years, but by the spring of '42 the rocket's nose was out a hole in the barn's roof. It was maybe 50 feet high. It sat on a platform full of hay, with its vanes sticking into the hay and into the ground so it was steady.

"Mr. Seaton was real good with drawing and explaining his drawings and so I was able to rivet and screw everything together, although I didn't the hell understand half of it. I enjoyed the work, it kept my mind off thinking.

"Of course, I asked Mr. Seaton what would happen to the barn if his rocket shot off. He said it would burn like a bonfire, but by the time the flames went out, we would be in Philadelphia!

"When he thought we were ready to try the rocket, we moved the steam engine and some other equipment to the farmhouse and put it up safe.

"He had a setup in the rocket where he would sit on a seat and turn a wheel that spun the vanes on the bottom, so he could steer as it shot up. He had a second seat in front of a big mica window, maybe six inches around, where I would sit and tell him what I saw.

"We had belts and buckles and straps all around we could use to tie ourselves down so we wouldn't go bouncing around like inside a biscuit tin.

"When we were ready for the big test, I have to say, I was scared pissless, but after being with him all that time, I couldn't let him down. So I just gritted my teeth and prayed Jesus to come down safe.

"Mr. Seaton pumped gallons of alcohol in one side of the rocket and gallons of that freezing liquid air in the other side. Then we climbed a few bales of hay and lashed ourselves inside.

"He had some kind of battery set-up to make the spark to set off the stuff, and when he threw the lever, my heart just about stopped. I said to myself, "better luck in the next world." But we didn't explode!

"The rocket rumbled and shook and I thought for a minute we was blowing up from the outside. But then something caught my eye and I looked out the mica window. I didn't see the barn, but I did see the trees getting smaller.

"It felt like lead in my chest, and I could hardly keep my eyes open, but I could see the trees like the birds see them, and I knew we actually were rising up. I looked over to Mr. Seaton and he had his hands on the wheel with a big smile on his face.

"After a few minutes the pain in my chest let up a little, but I saw Mr. Seaton beginning to frown. I saw he couldn't turn the wheel, and he was cussing himself—that was the first time I ever heard him cuss. I think the problem was the rocket was moving so fast the wind was pushing too hard on those vanes at the end that he couldn't turn them.

"Finally, he called me, and I unhitched myself and scooted over to his seat. I held on to a strap with one hand and with my free hand helped him to try to turn the wheel. We could only turn it a mite.

"I could see Mr. Seaton begin to sweat. 'How could I be so stupid!' he said.

"After a while he told me to go back to my seat. He said that the higher we got, the thinner the air would get, and maybe in a while he could turn the vanes.

"It seemed like forever, but maybe ten or fifteen minutes later he began to turn the wheel. But I didn't feel no difference in the rocket. And then I noticed my straps were starting to coil around me like a snake!

"The alcohol and liquid air was all burned up, so the roaring sound let up. But we both heard a hissing sound. I thought maybe it was something outside, so I looked through the mica window again.

"I couldn't believe my eyes. It looked like I was looking down at a big billiard ball, but it was blue and fuzzy. It also had scum all over it.

"The hissing sound got louder, and I stopped looking because I was getting light-headed. That's what I thought, until I looked down and saw I was floating two inches above my seat, like a Hindu fakir!

"I looked over to Mr. Seaton, who had his head in his hands.

"Doomed" was all he said.

"Then I realized what had gone wrong. Because he couldn't steer, we didn't make a big looping curve like he showed me on a piece of paper once. We were supposed to make a big lazy curve up from Texas and come down in Philadelphia—like a rainbow.

"But instead we shot straight the hell up! That billiard ball down there was the earth, the blue was the ocean and that white scum was the clouds. We were somewhere between the earth and the moon.

"I knew that our doors were tight and the rivets solid, but the air out must have been thinner than the air on top of the highest Rocky mountain, and so our air was hissing out the seams. I guess it was because our air began to get thin that we started to float around.

"I knew it was curtains for us, so I cleared my throat and told Mr. Seaton I was honored to have been his employee.

"Thank you, James," was all he said.

"I began to get real light-headed and it was hard to breathe, when I saw a bright light in the window. I thought for a second we were heading into the sun, but then the light passed us. A minute later, the rocket jolted like a giant baby had just grabbed its play pretty. Mr. Seaton bolted upright and asked me if I saw anything out the window. I looked and couldn't see anything except darkness.

"Then the levers on the door began to pop. I got a buzzing in my head and just as I blanked out I saw the door open."


"Well, as you can imagine, I thought the angels had come for me, but when I woke up I wiggled my toes and fingers and saw I still was alive, and in the softest feather bed I ever had seen.

"The room was simple, but clean and white. I propped myself up on my elbow and couldn't see a thing. Then Mr. Seaton walked in a door I hadn't noticed along with this strange fellow.

"He was tall and looked like he could be a Chinaman, but his slanted eyes were too large and he was as pale as a ghost. His outfit reminded me of a Roman's toga.

"Mr. Seaton was smiling now and he gave me his hand so I could get off the bed. He explained the other fellow and his posse lived on another world, like ours but far away, and they used rockets not only to go between cities but worlds.

"You mean like Mars?" I asked. He just smiled and said, "Yes, like Mars, but much farther away."

"He said these fellows had like a lighthouse, I guess, out there between worlds, and the lighthouse keeper had seen us come adrift and sent out a lifeboat rocket.

"When I understood this, I turned and bowed with my hands together like I had seen a Chinee do once. The tall fellow bowed, too, and I thought he kinda smiled.

"Mr. Seaton said although his plan for a sky railroad had come a cropper, he was happier because of meeting his new friends, and during the days we were in their rocket, he spent almost the whole time talking to them and having a grand old time.

"Don't get me wrong, they were civil to me, too. I talked to them, and when they talked back at me, for some reason their voice always seemed to come from a pillbox on their arm. I don't know why they had to throw their voice.

"I think they knew I didn't have much book learning—actually, I had none—and while they were respectful, anytime we talked about anything very complicated, I lost the rabbit I was chasing.

"Mr. Seaton tried to explain things to me simple-like so I could understand better. But what it came down it was these fellows had saved our skins.

"Sometimes we could look out a window—a real big one, bigger than a window in a New Orleans whore house—and see the world turning below us like a gristmill. When the clouds were sparse Mr. Seaton would point out whole countries.

"See that boot? That's Italy."

"The pale fellows told me I could go wherever I wanted in their rocket—which was pretty damn big, I tell you.

"One day I went by a door and saw a glow like from a fireplace, 'cept it was blue instead of red. I thought that was funny, and I went inside. The blue fire glow was coming out from the walls and some filigree on the walls.

"Wasn't but a minute later a passel of the pale fellows came running in the door and they grabbed me like they was hogs and I was a pumpkin. Mr. Seaton came running down the hall, too.

"The pale fellows tossed me right quick into a bed and stuck needles into me like I was an old woman's pincushion. In a corner some of them talked to Mr. Seaton, who looked more worried by the minute.

"After all the hoo-rah died down, Mr. Seaton told me what the problem was. These fellows had a special coal they burned which made a special kind of fire, a fire that burned blue instead of red.

"Problem was, the blue fire was just as bad as regular fire—but you couldn't feel it! It was just like I had stepped into a furnace, when I went in that room with the blue glow.

"He said that although I didn't feel anything then, in a few minutes I would have shriveled up like bacon and died. A watchman saw me right quick and that's when everyone came running.

"They were doctoring me then, and I would be fine, he said, but he looked real concerned.

"A piece later—it's hard to tell days, when you're on top of the sun—Mr. Seaton told me the pale fellows realized after I had the accident with the blue furnace, that maybe it was better I go back home.

"Truth be told, I was getting homesick myself. Mr. Seaton said he wanted to stay with his new friends, and so as he was happy, I didn't raise a whisper.

"He told me they could set me down right back where we started and soon, Mr. Seaton and I and a few of the fellows got into a kind of round lifeboat rocket and floated like a balloon in the middle of the night down to where the farmstead was.

"Mr. Seaton shook my hand like a brother and told me where the strongbox was with all his papers. He said I could have everything he left behind as my due for being such a good employee.

"I bounded down a metal gangplank and waved good-bye. They all took off like a cloud in the night. There was a half-moon and I found my way to the farmhouse. I lit the whale oil lamp and got ready for bed and slept in real late the next day, almost until nine.

"I thought we had been with the pale fellows in their rocket for weeks, but the windup clock in Mr. Seaton's room showed we were only gone two days. The barn was still smoldering.

"I was totally flummoxed when I went through Mr. Seaton's papers. He left me a wealthy man. He had thousands of dollars in banks in New York, Philadelphia and New Orleans.

"Over the next few years I used the money to hire some help and got the place fixed up better than ever and get some real croplands turned.

"In '45 news came the U.S. had annexed the Republic, which is what most people wanted all along. A widder woman who lost her husband in an Indian raid caught my eye and I took her as my wife. We had neighbors now, and when some of the people saw the books and tools that Mr. Seaton had left me, they suggested they be used for an academy.

"We set up an academy in the first floor of the new Masonic Home and hired a schoolmaster. With the academy and all, folks began to calling the settlement Science Hill. I reckon Mr. Seaton would've liked that.

"Of course, I never told no one about the rocket and the pale fellows. I never got into details. People saw the remains of the old barn and assumed Mr. Seaton done blowed himself up, and I never told otherwise.

"My wife and I never had no children, which was probably just as well. When the war started, I was 57, but I was strong and healthy and I enlisted. I guess I always felt guilty somehow about missing Jim Bowie when he visited the ferry crossing.

"During the Battle of Chickamauga I took a minie ball clean through the chest. They laid me out and waited for me to die. But three days later I got off my pallet and walked away.

"Everyone said it was a miracle, but I knew when I was lying there I felt my ribs and muscles knitting up. I figured the doctoring the pale fellows done to me when I had that accident in their rocket must have stuck with me for good.

"I came back to Science Hill, but a lot of other men didn't—so many that the settlement began to die. It happened in many other places. By '72 the academy had closed and the Masonic Lodge had its charter taken back.

"Sam Morse officially took back his offer of the electro-magnetic telegraph, I remember, in 1860, right before the start of the war. It was in the papers. Guess he was afraid of some patent problems with the Confederacy. The Republic never took advantage of his offer. Makes you wonder if they would have ignored Mr. Seaton's rocket, too.

"My wife died in '85. By then the railroad made it to Henderson County, but it ran through Athens and Eustace and skipped clear of Science Hill. That was the end of it.

"I knew by then, after having a few accidents with a knife or chisel over the years, that I healed up quick. I also saw that I was holding up well.

"Over time, everyone died or moved on, and I was left alone. The other farms crumbled away and no one noticed I was just out here by myself. I kept up the farm fine, there was enough for me.

"One time, when I was almost a hundred, I was at the feed store in Malakoff getting grain for the chickens. One old boy said, "You can't be James Reid, you're too young."

"Another old boy said, "Don't be ignorant, you're his son, right?"

"I agreed. Nobody knew any better.

"So over the years, I've used a hair dye and chin whiskers to fool people every so often into thinking Jim Reid's turned into the 3rd and now the 4th. I know, officiously I'm Jim Reid the 4th. Nobody ever sees or asks for Mrs. Reid or the rest of the family. We Reids are solitary, you know, and no one lives out here anymore.

"But when I had to fill out a form for social security a long time ago, I needed a birthday, so I just jumped ahead 100 years and put down 1903 instead of 1803.

"Some old boy remembered that, though, and when I was last in town, they had to shoot their damn mouth off. And I guess it got to you, Mr. Editor.

"When I buried my second wife—I never even told her what happened—I said to myself, if I live to be 100, I'll never tell anyone what happened with Mr. Seaton and the rocket and the pale fellows.

"Well, here I am at 200. I guess it's time to come clean, huh? "

"So what do you think of that story? You gonna write it up?

"You gonna tell who? Who the hell's Doe-zwah? That some Cajun friend of yours?"

*   *   *

The story verged on a kind of inbreeding—having the subject of the monologue being a small town newspaper editor, and ending with a reference to Gardner—but it worked.

The morning of March 18, 2003, I checked me email to find one in my inbox from Gardner. "That's funny," I thought. "I didn't send Gardner an email."

Then it hit me! Wait! He's contacting me about a story. And this is what I read:

"Dear Lou,

"A Rocket for the Republic" is cute, and I like it. I'm not 100% convinced by your last line/punchline joke, though. Can you whip up five or six alternative punchlines—or at least alternative last lines; don't necessarily need to be jokes/punchlines, although they can be—and send them to me in e-mail, so that I can see if any of them work any better?"

I didn't save my response, which was basically "I'll have you a half dozen new endings by 5 p.m.!" Then I sent them—another email I didn't save.

Dozois followed in the grand old tradition of working with his writers on the final version of a story. On March 22, he wrote back:

"Lou,

How about:

"Well, here I am at 200, so I guess it was about time to come clean, huh?

"You know, I heared the last time I was in town the folks down in Houston are ready to shoot off more rockets like they did 40 years ago. I wonder if they'll run into Mr. Seaton and them pale fellows. I'd sure like to hitch a ride, and meet Mr. Seaton again, and shake his hand. Maybe I'll ask 'em to shoot me up there. Ain't nothing I ain't done before.

"Shut your mouth, son, you'll swallow something."

"Sound okay to you? If so, I'll take it. (If not, I'll still take it, but suggest some other ending of your own; we'll work something out.)"

My replay was:

"Gardner -

"That ending sounds fine to me. A-OK. Does this mean you'll like, publish my story in *Asimov's*? With my name on it and everything? Do I get paid something, too?

"Jeez, I wrote my first story a year and a half ago. It hasn't been a year since Jayme Blashke published "Silvern" at *RevolutionSF*. Am I really an author?

"It's nice to know that, maybe—maybe—after slogging through the honor rolls and football games all these years I actually learned to write English decently.

"I am honored.

"Astounded in East Texas."

His reply:

"Dear Lou,

"Please send an electronic copy of your story as an attached Word file, with the new ending included, to Brian Bieniowski at the Dell Magazines office at bbieniowski@dellmagazines.net. Mention in the attachment that we'll be buying it eventually, and he should keep the electronic copy on file.

"Don't expect instant results on this—the mills at Penny Press grind exceedingly slowly."

And my reply to that:

"Dear Gardner:

"Will do. I'll work up the file and send it to Bieniowski first thing.

"I don't mind the wait for a contract and payment—I know how things go at periodicals.

"Can I claim bragging rights yet? This is not only my first pro sale—it would be my first sale, period. I've never gotten a cent for any of the stories I've had published so far.

"I'm not being totally vain—I need to make more Cons (remember, PhilCon was only the 2nd I ever attended) and it's easier for me to make a case for the outlay of money to The Boss* if I can justify it as a business expense.

"Please let me know.

"Lou

"*Ergo, The Wife."

Right then, Gardner announced he was taking a vacation, and when he returned in a couple of weeks, he announced he was retiring from *Asimov's*. My reaction was, of course, that the sale was voided because I hadn't signed the contract yet, but Gardner said that, as part of his retirement *Asimov's* agreed to honor all his purchases.

That was a relief. Then it hit me—was "Rocket" the last he bought?

I wrote to Gardner on April 26:

"Gardner -

"This is the way I see it...

"You accepted my story. Then you went on a nice vacation. You came back, refreshed and with a clear mind, and then slapped your forehead.

"I accepted a story from the imbecile Antonelli! I must be finally losing it! It's time to retire!"

"I hope that's not the way it happened!"

He wrote back:

"That's exactly the way it happened! (g)

"Although you didn't drive me to step down, you can take some sort of satisfaction in knowing that your story was the very last story I ever agreed to buy for *Asimov's*."

A few months later, I sold a story called "The Cast Iron Dybbuk" to an Australian magazine, *Andromeda Spaceways In-flight Magazine*. Being a smaller magazine, it could turn around my story and get it into publication quicker; ironically, both "Rocket" and "Dybbuk" came out at almost the same time during the summer of 2005.

In November 2004 I got my contract from *Asimov's*, and I wrote to Gardner on November 29:

"Thought I'd let you know—since you asked about it a while back—that I got the contract for "A Rocket for the Republic" in the mail today.

"Hmmm... so that's what these things look like. As Arte Johnson used to say, "Veddy Indcresting.""

"Funny, the story I have going up at *Revolution SF* this month also has "rocket" in its title—"The Rocket Powered Cat". (You saw an early version of this story a while back—I had to work on it before I found it a home).

"Other than that, I have a story called "Circe in Vitro" that'll be running in *Astounding Tales* in December. Everything seems OK for *Andromeda* next summer.

"I've been getting good feedback from Gordon and Stanley, by the way. Both sent back stories they said they enjoyed, but Gordon said it still didn't quite make the cut, and Stanley said my "rubber science" wouldn't fly with his readers (in so many words).

"I've been averaging a story every 2 weeks, and I usually have 20-22 out there in slush piles at any given time. I guess I'm just another jackass Italian workaholic.

"I've actually tried to slow down—somehow I keep thinking that if I wrote slower I might write better—but I find I feel better if I spew a story out when an idea hits me. Otherwise it just gets stale.

"Best wishes to you and Susan on Thanksgiving. Talk at ya' later.

"Lou Antonelli

"Deepest Darkest East Texas

"(reading contract with magnifying glass)"

His reply:

"Hey, congratulations! You're moving out into the "real world" in a stately fashion, like a tugboat towing something out to sea. <g>

"Do you have a URL for *Astounding Tales*?"

Through the end of 2004 and the first half of 2005, *Asimov's* worked through the backlog of stories Gardner had accepted. On the *Asimov's* magazine discussion board, he posted on April 18, 2005 that "Sheila has wisely been mixing her own new purchases with my backlog in every issue since the beginning of the year; so far, there have been two or three of her new purchases in every issue, with the rest taken up with stuff I'd bought before."

That led to the question, "Just out of curiosity, Gardner what was the last story you bought as editor, has it appeared yet?"

Of course, I had the answer. Gardner then replied, "Yes, Lou's "A Rocket for the Republic" was the last story I bought—I figured, hey, after buying *this*, the *ne plus ultra* of stories, the story of stories, there was no point in going on, and so I hung it up."

The September 2005 issue of *Asimov's* hit the mails and newsstands in July. The story was mostly well received.

Some reviews of "A Rocket for the Republic":

"Texan tall tale, or sci-fi fabulism? A fun first-person narrative about the first space expedition—way back in the thirties. The eighteen thirties, that is." – L. Blunt Jackson ("Bluejack"), *The Internet Review of Science Fiction* (IROSF)

"Very good"—*SF Revu.*

"A short and amusing tall tale about an experimental rocket and an encounter with aliens in the early 1800s."—*Eagle's Path Short Fiction Reviews.*

"Steam Punk fans who long for a wholly American twist on the genre will enjoy this story."—Doug Hoffman, *Tangent Online.*

There was also a lot of praise on the *Asimov's* board:

"By Randy Beck on Sunday, July 24, 2005—11:15 am:

"Has nobody mentioned the new issue yet?

"I only read one story so far. I'm usually way behind, and I was going to wait until I cleared my plate but I saw Lou Antonelli's Bradburyesque *Asimov's* debut and thought I'd give it a shot.

"Congratulations, Lou. I'll have to congratulate you even more if you ever beat this one. It's very, very, very good.

"By R.Wilder on Sunday, July 24, 2005—06:34 pm:

"September is a great issue. "A Rocket for the Republic" is a ripper, a fine tall-tale that put a smile on my face. It's got a good narrative voice, a simple but clever plot and I wished I'd thought of it. A nifty "*Asimov's*" debut, and the best Lou Antonelli yet.

"By Marian on Monday, August 01, 2005—10:32 pm:

"Just read your story, Lou, and am now joining the chorus of your admirers.

"By Bill G on Tuesday, August 02, 2005—10:55 am:

"Good story, Lou. Made me laugh.

"By Rick Hauptmann on Tuesday, August 02, 2005— 03:28 pm:

"Well, the September issue finally made it to eastern New Mexico today. For the first time this year, the cover came through in perfect condition.

"Your story is excellent, Lou. Good job.

"By Jerry Wright on Tuesday, August 02, 2005—04:39 pm:

"I too have the September Issue. Lou, I believe your story will be collected and anthologized. Sorry. Learn to live with it."

Criticism mostly centered on the Texas setting (some people just flat out don't like Texas) the use of dialect and that the ending wasn't much of a surprise.

I was proud to drop as much Texas history as I did in the story, and I am also proud that, despite the fact that just about every SF plot has been written before, I came up with one that was apparently original: Nobody has ever suggested the Republic of Texas had a secret space program. The use of dialect was unavoidable considering the background and education level of the protagonist. As far the ending, it was a fun story and I'm all into entertainment. When you're off on a trip, I think enjoying the ride is as much fun as arriving at your destination.

"Rocket" placed third in the annual *Asimov's* Readers Poll in the Short Story category the following year, and remains one of my better known stories. It's been reprinted in both my collections, *Fantastic Texas* and *Texas & Other Planets*.

# Chapter 17

## Conclusion

Seven of the 16 stories covered in this collection were named as Honorable Mentions in the annual edition of *The Year's Best Science Fiction* published by St. Martin's Press and edited by Gardner for the year they were published. I've had a total of eleven HMs in the past ten years.

Because of the long lead time to publication, by the time "A Rocket for the Republic" was printed in the September 2005 *Asimov's*, it was my 20th short story publication.

On July 23, 2005, I attended my first writers' workshop, a Turkey City held in Austin. Since it was Gardner's birthday, during a break I called and wished him a happy one. He mentioned that he got the September issue of *Asimov's* in the mail that day. As it happened, it was two weeks until I got my own copy in the mail—I guess it took a long time for the pack mule to make it all the way to East Texas.

Since then, I've had another 60 stories published, and although I don't mind having stories in small venues, I've still had my share of pro-level publications, including *Jim Baen's Universe* ("The Witch of Waxahachie" – April 2008, "The Centurion and the Rainman" (*Buzzy Mag* – March 2012), "Great White Ship" (*Daily Science Fiction* – May 2012) and "Double Exposure" (*Daily Science Fiction* – June 2012).

"The Centurion and the Rainman" was the first story ever published in that venue—something I'm proud of. "Great White Ship" was a finalist for the Sidewise Award for alternate history in 2013. "Double Exposure"—a flash (less than 1,000 words) is the only other story, other than "Rocket", which was bought on the first submission.

In light of the amount of time I devote to fiction writing, I'm very pleased with the results. Some people are rather taken aback when they find out I write very sporadically and only in my free time. I suppose the moral of the story is that journalism is not a bad way to learn the groundwork of the English language.

A few years ago, I was on a panel at a college convention and a member of the audience asked the authors whether, if they could, would they quit their day job and write full time. I was the only one of the six who answered no. I'm a hyperactive, gregarious person and I love being a newspaper editor.

In 2011, a successful British author, Stephanie Swainston, asked to be released from a book contract so she could go back to school and become a chemistry instructor. She was quoted in the British newspaper *The Independent* on July 11, 2011, as saying a major reason was "the lack of human interaction: "I suffer terribly from isolation while writing. I really need a job where I can be around people and learn to speak again. It's much, much healthier to be around people. Human beings are social animals."

I totally get that.

I'm not a writer who appears regularly in the most prominent genre magazines—I've never sold a story to Gardner's successor at *Asimov's*, Sheila Williams, or to *Analog* or *F&SF*—but my style is somewhat old-fashioned and idiosyncratic. I mean, when multiple reviewers cite Rod Serling and O. Henry as obvious influences on your style, what would you expect?

But I'm happy that my stories are considered entertaining, and with my large body of work, I've had three collections published so far—*Fantastic Texas* (2009), *Texas & Other Planets* (2010) and *The Clock Struck None* (2014). I also had four collaborative short story efforts with Portland, Oregon-based author Ed Morris published in a chapbook entitled *Music for Four Hands*. And I've had reprint or original stories included in four anthologies.

I hope you've enjoyed the stories in this book, and the stories behind the stories. More importantly, I hope I've gotten across a sense of what a great editor Gardner Dozois was and is; was during his 19 years at *Asimov's* and is as he continues to compile and edit collections and anthologies.

Gardner Dozois is someone who's had an immeasurable impact on the literary field he loves, an impact few people can hope to achieve in their lifetime, much less accomplish. The story in this book is a snapshot of a time and era now fast fading into the past, and I was there. I'm sure greater things await us in the future for both of us, but I'm proud of the time I've recounted, and grateful for his encouragement, support and understanding.